1

A
GARDEN
of
THIEVES

Tarde venientibus orsa

II

For those who come late,
only the bones

ILLUSTRATOR

AUTHOR

A GARDEN

of

THIEVES

VOLUME 1

by
Dean Unger

Village Lane Press
Lake Cowichan, BC
2017

Third VLP Printing, March. 27, 2018,
after a signed/limited edition of 200.

The traditional Kingfisher on the front cover was designed and painted by Cree / Gitsxan artist, Trevor Husband. Trevor's studio is located in the Cowichan Valley: www.trevorhusbandnativeart.com

Published by Village Lane Press
Editing & Design by Dean Unger
Printed in Canada by Printorium Bookworks,
Island Blue Print Co.,
Victoria
British Columbia

Please note that, aside from certain specific politician's who assisted with, and/or manufactured the Texada Island land scandal, characters in this book are purely fictional. Any likeness within the story to any specific person, or place, is unintended.

This book is affectionately dedicated to my
grandmother, Evelyn Bennett; to Shanon, Carah, Selena
and Lance; to my mother and my father, and to my
family and friends at large.
You know who you are.

A special thank-you to my daughter, Selena,
for coming up with the title for this book; to
daughter, Carah, for helping
to improve the cover design with her
insightful suggestions; to my mother for her
proof-reading assistance; to Linda Metcalf,
for all of her brilliant and insightful
suggestions which, together, ensured the best
possible outcome.

Thank you, also, to the First People of the region in
which the book takes place, the Tla'amin Nation,
who have figured large at various times in my life, in
my mind, and my career.
Thank you to the staff at the BC Provincial Museum
Archives, the Victoria Times Colonist Newspaper
Archives, The Powell River Museum, the Kelowna
Museum Archives , and the Vernon Museum. And,
finally, my heartfelt appreciation to the many people
who've shared their story during the course of my
research over the last twenty years.

———

TABLE OF CONTENTS

CONTENTS CONTINUED...

AUTHOR'S NOTE

PROVIDENCE

I will suggest that we all have our secret corners, where the seeds of our careless sowings are kept in darkness, where they can cast no shadow. We pull the cloak of time cleverly and carefully around ourselves, only to have it parted unexpectedly, by event or circumstance. The cloak is fast pulled round again, to conceal, but concealing a weakness does not remove it: it will appear again when we are least prepared.

The intent with which a thing is acquired is, in some way, the measure of its merit.

There is a pretext for what will follow here. That is, much of what is written is historical fact. Some details, like the amorous and vitriolic Amor De Cosmos - our corrupt Provincial Premier through the mid-Victorian era, are more or less specifically correct. Other facets of the story are accurate clips that are true to the cultural mores and beliefs at the time. It is essentially a view from thirty-thousand feet, but blown out into a vivid, moving tale with accurate descent, down into the lives of those whose fates unknowingly weave and unravel the tale before our eyes.

A Garden of Thieves, is an historical novel that reveals, by inference and by fact, the circumstances behind the Texada land scandal, and the social and political structures that were in place during late colonial British Columbia, that facilitated the calculated transfer of all land in the Province of British Columbia, from the collective First Nations, to the Crown. The form that the land policy eventually took, ultimately resulted in the smothering of First Nations culture – not one culture viewed collectively, but many individual Nations, that were each unique unto itself.

Presently, there are 198 distinct First Nations in the province of British Columbia, each with their own unique traditions and history. There are more than 30 First Nation languages, and close to 60 dialects spoken in the province.

Many did not survive integration, and have disappeared in the mists of history.

The struggles the Natives endured over the last two centuries, as a direct result of this poorly executed interference, is an outgrowth, an evolution, of the circumstances they were presented with. From the time of European arrival here, and well beyond, for the First Nations, there was no context for understanding the white man's rule of law. It was forced upon them.

Much of the bigotry that ultimately became entrenched in "white" culture, resulted from impatience and a lack of understanding, that, no matter what measures were enacted, the Natives just didn't seem to get it. In searching the historical record, it's not much wonder.

The Sliammon Treaty Society website, in a well-researched chronology of events that occurred this side of European arrival, relates that the year 1838 marked the beginning of the fur trade for the Tla'amin people. The "Beaver", a Hudson's Bay Company steamer, encountered Tla'amin Natives at the North end of Texada Island, where trades were made of muskets for furs piled to the same height.

In 1872, Dr. Israel Powell was named 'Indian Commissioner/Superintendent' to the Tla'amin people, and later, after stripping their traditional land from them in a fashion contrary to treaty laws and regulations – most notably, Lot 450 - he was named

Dominion Inspector of Indian Agents, along with the title of visiting Superintendent & Commissioner for all of BC, an office he held until 1889.

Powell River and Powell Lake were both later named after him.

Lot 450 pertains, in part, to a 15,000 acre illegally purchased timber lease issued to R.P. Rithet. a close associate of Dr. Powell. This allocation was inclusive of land south from Grief Point, and extended north to Sliammon. This lease encompassed three permanently occupied villages and many seasonal village sites, despite that they were, in theory, legally protected from sale or claim. It should also be noted here, that Commissioner, Gilbert M. Sproat, was initially among the fair-minded in the Government, and went to great effort helping the Sliammon, Klahoose and Homalco Nations, in attempts to iron out the land question. However, it seems while one hand was giving, one was on the take: he was at the helm of the Land Commissions office when it all went down.

Also of note here, was the fact that, at the same time this was going on, land was granted to white settlers free of charge up until 1879.

The Treaty Society website also points out that most of Sproat's apparent advocacy efforts fell upon deaf ears, because of the economic interest in the area. He eventually resigned in protest after a concerted and organized effort to discredit him for being "too generous with land allotments". This lynch effort was led by I.W. Powell, and supported by Joseph Trutch.

The Tla'amin themselves were stripped of their traditional names and given legal Christian names, to make it less confusing in attempts to identify and register them to the Canada Census. While all this was happening, new place names were given throughout Sliammon territory by anyone who happened by, with no First Nations consultation. Not surprisingly, many of these places already had recognized names from the Tla'amin people.

In 1920, Tla'amin children, between the ages of five and fifteen years old, were apprehended from their families en masse by Indian Agents and the North West Mounted Police, and sent to Catholic Residential schools; the last one of these, St. Mary's, in Mission

12

finally closed in 1984.

Even until 1960, there was a "Whites off reserve /Natives back on reserve by dusk" curfew still in effect. Natives still had limited seating in restaurants, pubs and the movie theatre in Powell River without proof of enfranchisement. This segregation occurred in every form of public transportation and service including steamships, trains and buses.

Despite extensive exposure to the realities of integration here in BC, and across Canada, I was shocked, during my research, to discover an entry in British Columbia Provincial Police records, housed in the BC Provincial Museum, in Victoria, that up to the late nineteenth century, there were still hangings for "Indians practicing sorcery". It is also recorded that, in 1892, Father Chirouse – the Godhead for the church in Sliammon, was sentenced to one year for "whipping an Indian" (a scene incorporated, for posterity, but via "symbolic" players, into A Garden of Thieves); and, in 1894, a notation was made regarding a Mr. Hollingsworth's and his purchase of "Sarah Cliff, a half-breed Indian girl." These Provincial Police archives, are testament to the minutae and specific details of First Nations life, during and after integration; they do far more than any running narrative, to pin-point how insidious the dismantling of First Nations culture was.

History is but a looking glass to the much larger picture. I am reminded, here, of Alan Watts, who writes, "The five colours will blind a man's sight. The eye's sensitivity to colour is impaired by the fixed idea that there are just five true colours. There is an infinite continuity of shading, and breaking it down into divisions with names distracts the attention from its subtlety."

We are capable of endearing ourselves to only one at any given time. As with truth and its many shades of meaning. But, to suddenly see the meaning of a life, or the far-flung effects of an event in history, from the infinite possibilities of meaning; to realize that there is a story that, if known, would have changed the course of things... What then? And then, one day, whether intentionally or by accident, a light is switched on and the room is lit up, and in the telling of it, it's light spreads well beyond the room to other places and other worlds.

What follows is no apology for the original intent behind the colonization of BC, nor the manner in which it came to pass. Neither does the spirit of intent, here, support the brazen bigotry at the heart of what ultimately became the legal document behind the massive acquisition. It is merely a story written true to the facts of the matter. A Garden of Thieves, is the culmination of twenty-four years of research, interviewing, discussing and digging.

To do the subject proper justice would entail a book in itself. As such, I include, here, only a cursory overview of the main points and conditions that existed at the time land claims policies were enacted, to offer important and accurate context to the story.

Although there *were* well intentioned men in the mix, in the end, the questionable and nefarious intent of others won out.

Edward Bulwer-Lytton, the Secretary of State to the Colonies, and Governor James Douglas himself, could be said to have had Christian morals at heart in devising the system of subjugation, but, when the Crown later replaced Douglas with Joseph Trutch, all bets were off. This man was an outright bigot who refused to recognize the legitimacy of land claims decisions made by his predecessor.

In an excerpt from the *The Indian Land Question 1846 - 1857*, a book of documents published in 1857, William A.G. Young, the first Colonial Secretary, brazenly insists, after Douglas was ceremoniously removed from office, that all reserves should be reduced as soon as may be practicable. "The Indians have no right to any land beyond what may be necessary for their actual requirements, and all beyond this should be excluded from the boundaries of the reserves. They can have no claim whatever to any compensation for any of the land so excluded, for they really have never actually possessed it, although, perhaps, they may have been led to view such land as a portion of their reserve, through Mr. McColl (Royal Engineer for the Crown) so loosely 'reserving such large tracts of land, out of which, at some future day, the various Indian Reserves would have to be accurately defined.

From the moment Joseph Trutch took over operations from

Douglas, it seems he was of the same mind as Young, for he began a systematic dismantling of all that had been done to that point. When Trutch was finished, he had effectually reduced Douglas' initial reserves by 92%.

In 2007, the history magazine, The Beaver, assembled a list of the "Worst Canadians" as of that year. Trutch made the list.

Earlier in the game, during the pre-Trutch administration, Edward Bulwer-Lytton, after whom the town of Lytton, BC, was named, showed a more or less humane approach, citing the tenets and principles of an enlightened motive, for a humane demeanour in the approach to playing the role of steward to the First Nations.

In a letter to Governor James Douglas, Bulwer-Lytton writes, "The feelings of this country would be strongly opposed to the adoption of any arbitrary or oppressive measures towards them (the Indians)..." And later on, "I commit it to you, in the full persuasion that you will pay every regard to the interests of the Natives which an enlightened humanity can suggest..." He continues, "proofs are unhappily still too frequent of the neglect which Indians experience when the white man obtains possession of their country, and their claims to consideration are forgotten at the moment when equity most demands that the hand of the protector should be extended to help them."

In his statement he was careful to assert that, as the requirements of colonization pressed upon lands occupied by members of "that race", liberality and justice should be adopted "in compensating them for the surrender of the territory, which they have been taught to regard as their own."

Even with all his influence in the Mother Land, in facing Trutch, and the sentiments he upheld, Bulwer-Lytton, found he was fighting an uphill battle. He was already a famous author when offered the post of Secretary of State to the Colonies. He had achieved fame with books published early in his career: *Zanoni*, a translation of an encoded Rosicrucian parable; *The Last Days of Pompeii*; *The Power of the Coming Race* – a book that became the inspiration behind what is now known as the Hollow Earth Theory, and, by 1828, he had risen to critical acclaim with the publication of Pelham. Among the many distinctions in his life, it seems he had an enigmatic effect on those around him, and did much by way of subtle influence and suggestion, to inspire Bram Stoker, in his later writing of the infamous, *Dracula*. Bulwer-Lytton also penned the quotes: "beneath the rule of men entirely great, the pen is mightier than the sword", and "pursuit of the almighty dollar", in the book, *The Power of the Coming Race*.

In bringing his full influence to bear upon the situation, and to drive the point home, Bulwer-Lytton summarizes, in his critique of Reverend Herbert Beaver, a fanatical priest stationed at the Columbia Headquarters, that, respective of ones position and the influence they hope to effect, one must, "live a life of beneficent activity, devoted to the support of principles, rather than of forms; he must shun discord, avoid uncharitable feelings, temper zeal with discretion, [and] illustrate precept by example".

These same principles were his own, and were brought to bear in his relations with the First Nations of British Columbia.

In laying out reserves, he left the choice of the land, and the size of the land to the Indians. Surveyors were instructed to meet their wishes and "to include in each reserve the permanent Village sites, the fishing stations, and Burial grounds, cultivated land and all the favorite resorts of the Tribes, and, in short, to include every piece of ground to which they had acquired an equitable title through continuous occupation, tillage, or other investment of their labour.

Meanwhile, here in BC, as his total land policy evolved, Governor James Douglas, grew certain that the time would arrive when the First Nations people might aspire to a higher rank in the social scale. He held great hope they would lay claim to a better condition. Douglas permitted the Indians to acquire property by direct purchase from government officers or through pre-emption. He went on to assert that this should be done "on precisely the same terms and considerations in all respects, as other classes of Her Majesty's subjects."

However, despite Douglas' assurances that the Native Indian tribes were to be protected in all their interests to the utmost extent of the Government's present means, subsequent events proved the contrary.

16

For the time being, under Douglas' rule, the first payouts, for a handful of initial land claims, went to a handful of First Nations communities, and the ball was officially in motion. To offer an idea of the economies of scale that were in play, in another excerpt from the *Indian Land Issues* document, the language included in the original land claims contract confirms amounts paid to the first handful of Nations to sign. The Teechamitsa Tribe handed over "the whole of the lands situate and lying between Esquimalt Harbour and Point Albert, including the latter, on the Straits of Juan de Fuca, and extending backwards from thence to the range of mountains on the Saanich Arm, about ten miles distant." They received, as payment, twenty-seven pounds, ten shillings sterling. The document was signed at Fort Victoria, on 29th of April, 1850.

The Swengwhung Tribe, of Victoria Peninsula, South, of Coloeitz, were paid seventy-five pounds sterling for what was deemed to be their land. The Ka-ky-aan Tribe, of Metchosin, forty-three pounds. The Chewhaytsum, of Sooke, were paid forty-five pounds sterling. The Queac'Kar, of Fort Rupert, were paid sixty-three.

What was, in 1850, twenty-seven pounds, ten shillings, is approximately $4000USD, or roughly $5000CDN, by today's standards. All other agreements that followed are in the same vein, though prices paid vary according to the land acquired.

In 1920, seventy years later, according to statistics Canada, the average weekly budget of an average household was somewhere in the neighbourhood of $21.00CDN. When calculated for the rate of inflation, the average sum paid to the Natives for their land would not quite be enough to purchase a single home in metropolitan Vancouver in the 1920s.

As further example, for context: In 1827, when Governor James Douglas had threatened to quit his fur trading post at Fort Vancouver, his salary was raised from sixty pounds sterling, to one hundred pounds sterling annually - roughly four times the lowest amounts paid to First Nations, for what was loosely determined to be their land.

This, the land, was their heritage, their right by posterity and possession. To say there was no context against with which to measure the decisions made at the time, is debatable: the British had been Colonizing territory across the globe for centuries. At its root, after careful consideration of the facts, it seems that, ultimately, basic human greed, voracity, and covetousness was responsible for what came after.

All in all, Governor Douglas left his administration, and the colony, in strong stead. Roads had been built, mining districts opened, the Fraser River had become the colony's main thoroughfare, the American threat via the Finian Raids was silenced, and the road opened for future prosperity.

He should also be commended for his empowerment of woman-kind in an era where paternalism was prominent, to put it lightly.

Meanwhile, just before things went south with respect to responsible integration policy, F.W. Chesson, Secretary to the Aborigines Protection Society, who could foresee the early results of Trutch's interference, wrote an impassioned plea to Bulwer-Lytton: "from all the sources of information open to us, [it is clear] that unless wise and vigorous measures be adopted by the representatives of the British Government in that Colony, the present danger of a collision between the settlers and the natives will soon ripen into a deadly war of races, which could not fail to terminate, as similar wars have done on the American continent, in the extermination of the red man."

Chesson cites the reckless inhumanity of gold diggers in America, where it had already been proven that miners took an exceedingly dim view towards the unfortunate Indians. A story in the New York Times, confirmed that it is the custom of miners, generally, "to shoot an Indian, as he would a dog; and it is considered a very good joke to shoot at one at long shot, to see him jump as the fatal bullet pierces his heart."

Trutch himself is said to have uttered similar sentiments at times.

"But there is another aspect of the question which is of equal importance," Chesson continues. "The Indians, being a strikingly acute and intelligent race of men, are keenly sensitive in regard to their own rights as the aborigines of the country. There can be no doubt that it is essential to the preservation of peace in British Columbia that the natives should not only be protected against wanton

18

outrages on the part of the white population, but that the English Government should be prepared to deal with their claims in a broad spirit of justice and liberality. The recognition of native rights has latter been a prominent feature in the aboriginal policy of both England and the United States. Whenever this principle has been honestly acted upon, peace and amity have characterized the relations of the two races, but whenever a contrary policy has been carried out, wars of extermination have taken place; and great suffering and loss, both of life and property, have been sustained both by the settler and by the Indian."

While this was all going on, the newspapers of the time seemed, for the most part, to be run by fiery editors with a will to power and influence, or, at the very least, the benefit of financial opportunism: John Robson, editor of the British Columbian, and, Amor De Cosmos, of the British Colonist newspaper. Incidentally, both editors accused and inferred that Douglas was despotic, a charge that may have had tremendous influence upon what was, for Douglas, the final outcome.

It seemed every effort was made against Imperial/Federal intrusion, and if there weren't obvious infractions, with little effort something could be found to gripe about. In reading early copies of De Cosmos British Colonist – which would later become the Victoria Times Colonist - the paper is rife with unsubstantiated claims against the nefarious doings and intentions of the Federal Government, who would, at any cost, undermine Colonial independence, as well as glowing endorsements from questionable names, if not anonymous contributors.

Under the weight of constant pressure, the British Royals eventually divested Governor Douglas of his office, with both the Colonial administration, and the Crown appointments being extinguished at the same time. But they tempered their toxin with honey – the loss of position came with the honour of being elevated to second rank in the Order of the Bath.

In comparison, the ideal editor these days must possess a modicum of judgement, be self-possessed, and perceive and enact the best interests of the population which he/she serves.

At the hands of both editors, Douglas was saddled with the blame for establishing what was disaffectionately called a "family-company compact" – that underlying his stratagem in establishing the colony, he brought along a tendency toward protectionism that was seen to benefit the few rather than the many. But the self-same spirit that existed within the family-company compact, was also rampant in the newly formed representative government of the Colony, with De Cosmos now preparing to take on a larger role within the Colonial Government. He used his influence with the British Colonist to hide his intention beneath the guise of beneficence, or outright sturdy, yet, concealed self-interest.

De Cosmos effectually pounded a first of indignation with the one hand, while, with the other, he had quietly posited Mr. Henry Bevan into the Land Commissions Office as Land Commissioner, responsible for issuing – and rejecting – land grants. He used his newspaper as the voice of dissension, to cement temporary favour among the voting colonists.

A new generation had moved in and were now in place to harvest their share of the wealth from the new colony, for the most part at the expense of the First Nations. De Cosmos, along with Trutch, was an outspoken voice against land concessions to First Nations, citing that the practice was a hindrance to economic growth and prosperity. And he would carry on as though none of it existed, seeming to make up his own rules and policies as he went.

All-in-all, the stage was set for the one of the largest land scandals in Canadian history.

From the very start, it was my intention to try, in my research, to nail down the seeds that lay at the very heart of the legacy of hurt we have enacted in Canada through this brand of colonization – the affect and effect of the need to impose the British rule of law upon newly acquired territories, and whomever or whatever might presently exist there; not just here on the coast, but throughout the prairies too.

The long and short of it is that the historical record conclusively damns De Cosmos for his efficacious greed, and self-serving intent, at the expense of First Nations, under his protection. The cost of this approach also came at the expense of the thousands of settlers who'd come here to make an honest living. De Cosmos, with his gregarious yet affronting and often aggressive style, earned him some powerful enemies in positions of influence. In pouring through court transcripts for the case, and in reading the coverage of D.W. Higgins, the new editor of the British Colonist, now renamed the Times Colonist, the notion crept into my periphery that, perhaps it was not too grand a step to imagine that his exile from the Colonial Government - and popular swimming holes there-of, might have been orchestrated, at least in part.

In the end, whatever the case, in later years De Cosmos went mad...

Meanwhile, the stage had already been set, and with their legislation they tore through people's lives, their cultures, their very existence, in many cases clawing back land that had already been given.

For a long time it was said that the Coast Salish never lived on Texada. Though the hunting and fishing there was very good, their belief that the island rose one day from the ocean in a great cataclysm dissuaded them from keeping a village site there. They believed that, as surely as it had risen from the sea, one day it would return: it was well known that an edgy spirit could be fickle, so it stood to reason that, one day, the spirit that had caused this to happen could well suffer a tantrum, and send it back to the bottom of the sea. To live on the island would, of course, be foolish.

In any case, for the purpose of the story, it seemed germane – logical even – to create a Salish Village on the Island. Though overt reference to the fact was, in my experience, limited, if non-existent, there were whisperings here and there, that it might be true; a silent golden thread to follow.

Then, one day, I sat down with the brother of a former Tla'-amin chief - twin brother, actually, and he told me an interesting story. One day, years ago, he and a friend had been cutting up a large windfall at Shelter Point. Inside, smack dab in the centre of the tree, was a cast iron cannon ball... Short of a few drunk sailors blowing off steam with some target practice, or a mutiny of some kind, there were few reasons, during the age of European arrival, to want or need to fire a cannon ball shoreward. One does not need to let the imagination wander too far. And you'd probably be correct. In actual fact, in 2013, Aquilla Archaeology submitted an impact assessment for Shelter Point, to the Powell River Regional District. The extensive report succinctly, and with perfect grace, revealed to council that there *was,* after all, a Coast Salish Village there on Texada. A big one. It is, the report suggests, potentially one of the largest Georgian Period Salish settlements found here on the lower BC coast.

Here, I reserve comment, as I fear I may come off a little reproachful. Instead, I assent to a statement by Jennifer Manuel, who writes in her recent book, The Heaviness of Things That Float - an historical fiction based here in BC, that after coming to terms with a contradiction among stories of arrival (the First Nations perspective) that tangle with the stories of first contact (European perspective), *"Stories of contact" is a phrase that sounds as feathery and constructive as God's touch upon Adam's fingertip, when in fact these stories have been violent and corrosive. Weeds choking plants of sustenance... I know nothing about contact. I know only about arrival, and the dangers of presuming too much."*

When I close my eyes, I can easily see that cannon ball laying there, still, and slightly glistening in the dying sun. Upon its pitted surface was re-written the entire history of Texada Island. And there is, in all likelihood, much more to the story than was believed.

...The prospect of mortality, regardless of intellectual readiness, supposedly, to accept it, shakes one to the core.

I am also reminded here, of a magazine article – National Geographic, if I remember correctly - I read recently about a cave in

Kvaslund, in the northern reaches of Norway, where there are crude but entirely discernible carvings in the stone walls, showing that whomever had etched them into the rock had apparently discovered a lucrative method of hunting reindeer. In the cave-wall narrative, two men in a simple boat had reasoned that, being familiar with the behaviour of migrating reindeer, the deer were at their slowest and most vulnerable when they were crossing a body of water: river, lake, flood plain – where they could easily overtake and dispatch the animal. Their unmistakable intent was to, doubtless, preserve the invaluable information of their conquest. It was a simple matter of life or death. This leap of intellect could help ensure they would not go hungry. The carvings are also a symbol of something much greater. They are, in effect, a primary truth, an object that would communicate to those who would come after; an object to be interpreted.

The explosion from the cannonball found nested there inside that tree shatters the silence of ages. It marks a truth also to be interpreted. And it was, at one in the same, a new voice that the Coast Salish had not yet heard; but, too, it was an old voice, they had no need to hear the like of, to know the truth of it.

In the telling of it, I will offer up no defence for the blooms and blossoms borne from the minds of average men, with a hunger they cannot feed, or an itch that they cannot scratch. For what follows is a story of exceptional opportunity, and of unimaginable greed and corruption that slithered to the very core of the young government of the time. It reveals how, with even just a quarter turn south, forthright and militant ingenuity becomes opportunism that is moderately - even mildly - tainted with reasoning that's somewhere south of wrong.

But, it's also a story of the ambition of excellent men and women, trying to make a home in the pioneer west, more specifically, on the Island of Texada, in the mineral rush city of Vananda, British Columbia c.1880. Some of these were born to it. Some of them worked skin to bone earning their place. But life in many of BC's early Company Towns was not always easy, and not always for the reasons you'd be inclined to think. There were unspoken rules of conduct. In the end, no matter how honourable a person was, her fate was sometimes, owing to the fates and poor choices, decided by a small gathering– a so-called peer-group – some of them friends, all of them directly in line and in keeping with the values of the time, or so they aspired to suppose. These, then, by their estimation, would tell decisively whether said individual was perhaps getting it "not quite right" and that they would almost assuredly have to pay for it in some fashion. If that fashion were to be Public, that would probably be fine. In the 1880's that could mean anything from a closed shop to profoundly altering ones general sense of well-being – as well as the ability to even perceive such a gift.

These were the makeshift laws, and often groundless regulations, created and enforced to the betterment of the Company bottom line.

Vananda was a pioneer western town to be sure, but, as with there are two kinds of people in the world, there were the hard-working pilgrims come to lay their claim, and there was the landed gentry – also mostly well-intentioned, but yet, few among their host that equate most assuredly to a *rot* at the centre of it: a poison, a den of thieves harboured in a Garden of Eden, their doctrine started and inspired of entrenched Impirical ideals and created by the greed and the hatred within mankind – one for another, one race against another, regardless of colour or creed, and fuelled by an inner rage to eliminate the competitor.

And with the flood of the Old Country blood, Empiricism – mostly British – was rampant. No matter how much the early colonists tried to stamp out the virulent scourge, new blood, fresh from Britain, was always springing anew from the sides of steam ships passing at ports of call up and down the wild coast of British Columbia.

We didn't know how truly hard it was for them... The Natives. Not at first anyway. *Ethno-relations* was a moniker devised to imply there was some brand of Democracy at play in the heart of the new ideal. The Brits and the English would do their best to introduce the notion of commercialism and the rules underpinning the concept of land ownership.

At first, and for a long time, there was little understanding of material ownership among First Nations, nor concerning what was expected of them, understandably.

24

Eventually, the intellectual bridges were more or less built, and things fell into a rhythm of debatable merit. The whites grew despondent, began to cast aspersions, and were inclined to make judgements. Often, disenfranchised First Nations – the Haida, the Salish, the Nootka – and many others, would wind up on the doorstep of the legislature in Victoria, with no-where to go and not a clue how to fit in, or where to go for help. There they would remain, until the BC Provincial Police were harried by the public, who claimed to be speaking in the interest of public welfare, into doing something rash. The First Nations families that had come there for direction and understanding, were often forcibly driven from the city: Their culture and their land were being systematically dismantled, and what was left unmolested was eroding, from the inside out, in the shadow of grief.

The generations of First Nations that lived it, or witnessed it, are all past now. Most *felt* the wrong of it through and through. But it had been going on too long by then. And it was set to go off like a scatter-bomb.

The seeds were planted sometime in the fog of history. European vessels were plying the intricate and haunted shorelines and deeper forests for a good two hundred years and more. It was during this time that the dissent were spawned – largely beyond notice. And it went on this way for years. At first it seemed as though all were friendly, and that overall, spirits were optimistic in nature and orientation. Then, in 1872, the Canadian Pacific Railway hired surveyor Sandford Fleming to forge a route of passage through the Rocky Mountains, and onward through the coast mountain range. Fleming had, for some time, been conducting his work here in British Columbia. He had become accustomed – skilled in some respects – with the local language, customs and beliefs of the resident First Nations that he encountered.

As time went on he became increasingly vexed. He was the first to sense that something was not quite right. For his part, until things were properly managed and running smoothly, he would not accept gifts, nor assume to navigate unaided within the culture of a foreign land. He would make every effort to seek council before acting in situations, or speaking out on topics he was not properly versed upon.

With his new-found resolve in order, he would advise the Dominion Government of the powder keg he felt was near the breaking point. In his reports he reasoned, the Dominion would have had plenty of time to exact corrective measures as a system to enact land transactions in a responsible way. George Monro Grant, who accompanied Sandford on this epic voyage, wrote *Ocean to Ocean*, a sweeping account of the voyage and the challenges met and perceived along the way. One can't help but suffer the impression, after reading the book, that its publication contained safeguards against any lack of forthright measures on behalf of both the Government and the Canadian Pacific Railway to properly and diplomatically stem the problem. It seems that, like Bulwer-Lytton and Chesson, both Fleming and Grant were unimpressed, to say the least, at the direction things had taken. Further, this was more or less the same spirit with which, eight years earlier in 1864, Alfred Waddington concluded that the Chilcotin Massacre resulted from a breach of fundamental trust (this was during the smallpox plagues that ravaged BC First Nations, due to infected blankets being distributed among them).

The subtle fear that was pinching at Fleming's neck and nipping hard at his heel, keeping him from sleep, was the pervasive and powerful unrest that he sensed among the Indians. He predicted that if the situation was left unchecked, it would threaten to arrest efforts to develop the western forts of the Hudson's Bay Company into legitimate, fortified centres of trade and commerce. As Fleming saw it, the government seemed content to let the Indian Nations who willingly, and with much anticipation, entered into negotiations with foreign sailors for possession of all manner of trinkets, and to barter away boundless tracts of The Great Spirit's Green Earth without a firm understanding of what this meant.

'The problem', he inflected, 'will try when the Salish Brave is made to understand that I desire to purchase a plot of his – of the land – from him, and that I need to have his cooperation, his implicit understanding, and his permission that I would then "own" the land in question. It would be mine. And all the encumbrances and advantages therewith.'

What would come to pass was just as he had imagined. It was not at all possible, within a legally definable framework, to take, or to have, or to own any of "these things". Here, and among the vast majority of the First Nations spread along the BC Coast, the concept of ownership, as was understood in the Old Country, did not exist. This detail seems to have been largely overlooked, save for what was eventually written in Grant's book.

Though some could sense it, none really forsook all the complex inter-relationships that scattered implications over miles and through time. The damage and the horror and inhumanity that would come to pass, in order to force a political *force majeure* with a pedigree of Old Country influence - men in positions of power and spheres of influence – was a rule of law upon a land that cooperated more than bullied, that compromised rather that crushed.

The men and women that formed this Pedigree were outside of the status quo, beyond the reach of the people who came here to make a hard-won home and an honest living. Settlers did not have family stipends to support them. They did not have parental or incidental trusts sheltering their every decision. They too, were rugged to the bone. And they were patient and wont to help, often quite at their own expense. These were pioneering folk, creating homesteads on land hard-won from the ocean of forest. And they were bloody tough as nails. By their own rite, they would come to live and die on and of the land. They would slave – and later, work – in the mines, in the forests and on the sea. All were afflicted by some form of subjugation that, although different in rule and application, was by its nature, subjugation none-the-less.

All, despite creed and caste, could feel the bitter chill of this new religion that blew in from coastward and invaded the New World, like a steady, blinding sea-mist, sliding in perfect silence, building slowly, gliding over the surface of the ocean, swallowing ships like creeping death. It was a vile slick, pulled irresistibly toward its potential: to inflict maximum damage: Shrapnel and corruption were consistent and far-flung. Its influence crept and consumed, like a dirty shimmer of warm putrid air hanging above the remains of the last inversion... Waiting for change.

Again and again the record skips and we find ourselves in familiar territory. It is here that we *must* do something. We must reach out and offer gold where before we had only watched.

Truth and light - profound and singular - and immutable by their very nature – stream through the fabric of Time, seeking to reveal. This – what began as a faint mist, scarcely surviving - had thickened and grown, and spread and evolved, now, into the host, and the self-appointed architect.

The seed was planted after I'd inherited my grandmother's journals.

I was seventeen and lost, and it was an unexpected boon. I was at a crossroads at a crucial time in my life. A wrong turn here and it could well have been the last decision I ever made. It was as if she wilfully reached out and somehow arranged for this to be dropped in the dust at my feet: I vividly recall picking up the thick manilla envelope, and trying to blow the dust from it. I pulled out a few among the papers within and sat upon whatever came nearest to hand.

The piece on top was sparsely arranged. This, I imagined, was for effect - a scrivener to give the words an extra dimension, as if they weren't doing enough already.

There it was, "Veritas and Antinomy", the first piece I would read, and would breathe life into a friendship, of sorts, a mentorship, and a potent source of inspiration and family pride. The title, I discovered later on, was written in Latin. She was a fan of Voltaire. Veritas: A fundamental and inevitable truth; and, Antinomy: a fundamental and, apparently, unresolvable conflict, a perfect contradiction of terms: beauty and evil; freedom and slavery; It was just like a hit of adrenaline to fertilize the writer that lay hidden, dormant, sleeping away a long mindless night. There, in the basement at my grandfather's house, the very first flames flicked at my heels to grab a quill and scribe. This sound revelation was rooted in my very core, but there was a time that I let it slip from view. I was too busy in the music world to see.

The long and the short of it is, that what I was haunted by, was her voice – her spirit. It was alive there on those pages.

There is a photograph of my Grandmother on my writing desk: a black and white portrait, taken in her newly starched nurses uniform, just after she graduated nursing school in 1947. I keep it there to remind me what I'm here for.

She looks upon me now, as I write this letter, imagining – nay, knowing – this *is* her voice.

To My Dearest Grandson,

How should one start this? I'm in unfamiliar territory now. Fingers feeling for purchase. Do I call you Mr. Unger? - Absolutely not! Formalities are for fools. Time wasters. Truly. And if you took a step back for a moment and viewed it objectively you'd see what an ass you were being for your efforts. No. I know you well enough. Though all these years have passed, it took but one look into those eyes when you were a small child, a newborn.

I could not for the life of me figure how God, in all her wisdom and empathy, would require me to endure such torture, yet feel such bliss.

I held you whenever I had the chance. Whenever I could, when my strength was level, and I could sit up and use the wall behind us – the foundation - and the bed upon which we sat would be the cockpit.

I gazed into your eyes, and I tried with every last synapse, cell and connection, to experience an entire life with you in those very few moments of time. And you stared up at me with those eyes. I will never forget it. They were the colour of a melting glacier on a sunny day, in the bluest turquoise-blue ocean, and yet, bordered by grey. I was amazed to see you staring right back at me. Right into my soul. You were so young. Yet, there you were, gazing at me wizened and alert, as though you had lived before, and so you knew all about it. It was as though you knew my thoughts... As though you thoroughly understood that I had something to give you. Something important. Something that couldn't wait, but would have to for lack of a better plan.

I wrote this letter to you on your first birthday. You were actually six months old, but, for the sake of posterity we agreed, what few of us mattered, that it would be acceptable if we jumped ahead by six months and celebrated a birthday party. It was the last time I held you in my arms.

I wanted nothing more from this life but to have a conversation with you once you had become a young man, to tell you what you would need to know about the past; about what happened. But of course this was not to be. I knew it was unreasonable and silly of me to ask God for one last favour. She'd been so pleasant and ambivalent over the years. Noninvasive. Non-judgemental.

I woke up from a deep sleep later that night knowing that I had to write to you. I had to pen a letter that would find you at just the right moment, when you were old enough to understand. I was initially annoyed at my own obtuseness at not realizing the obvious solution: I was a writer. Write!

With the best of intentions, I started what was to be a letter. I soon discovered, however, that God had gazed upon me that night with an ambiguous smile, and credited me just enough time to finish my correspondence in good form, before I was called too. What came was more a full-on manuscript than a familiar missive.

So there it is. We will simply, then, by this very

communication, collapse time upon itself and sit here side by side for as long as we have. After all of this, if your philosophical mind tools to other climes, I shouldn't hold it against. Mind you, ask the questions of life while you can still do something about it.

Whether my Ashes are spread ceremoniously on the Ocean, or dumped into the fire with the spent cigarettes matters not to me... Some would accuse me of being romantic. But I suppose, for the sake of political types – and writers looking for superlative and droll finis - one should stick to what seems a more appropriate send off, like being dusted on rose bushes, or painted on waves or some such.

...For now, why don't you stay a while. For this is the story that those eyes of yours beseeched of me that early-September day, long ago.

I do not mean to sound bitter. In fact, I am not bitter. My time for the joys and the storms of life has come and gone. This *part of the play is for you! Therefore, I say, Fortis in arduis: take courage, and be strong in your difficulties.*

Love & Light,
Your Grandmother,
Evelyn Bennett

I can say with resolve, that my heart, my soul, can once again bear the burden of truth. So, in Quixotic fashion, I turn, with pen in hand, and with this mighty sword will break these impetuous chains that threaten to sink me.

From the beginning then....

PROLOGUE

Alae iacta aest

Щ

The die has been cast

"Quit fussin' with the ropes," she said, wading toward him through the tall grass. "The horses aren't goin' nowhere tied to the wagon like that."

He let the ropes fall limp from his hands. She walked toward him gliding gently through the grass. She looked like a lonely ghost drifting through the field; the bold moon in the midnight sky caught and held her dress and her flowing blonde hair.

"My God. You look a vision walkin' up there ahead a me like 'at. An angel! ...How far'd you say it was?" he asked.

"Leave the damn horses!" She hissed, as she took his face into her hands and kissed him deeply.

He'd never been kissed that way, the way she kissed him now. He was a prisoner to it.

She took the ropes from his hands and slipped her fingers into his, pulling him away from the wagon.

He allowed himself to be led. He was mesmerized. With each step the thin white fabric traced the contour of her perfect legs as her dress flowed over the grass and caught on small branches in the field. It narrowed at her waist and outlined her elegant form with a perfection rarely seen, he thought.

She was indeed a Goddess. Any man would want her. Many men did, in fact. And now, here he was, alone with her out in the middle of nowhere. Given the chance, he was certain most would take it; that she was married mattered not.

When she'd first looked at him from across the beer parlour, he was sure she must be after someone else. Then Charlie Rose jammed his elbow into his ribs and said he'd seen her looking, too.

She had come to the table with a bottle of whisky in her hand and invited herself to sit. From the start she'd commanded the conversation, her silken laughter cutting the room and swirling to the rafters with the cigar smoke.

After a few drinks, her eyes narrowed seductively and she slid from her chair onto his lap. His conscience was screaming, but the whisky she'd kept in front of him made him forget why it wasn't a damn good idea to throw one into her, just like she'd asked for. It had been years - a lifetime, it seemed, since he'd had the affections of a lady...

She said she knew a spot where no one would bother them.

No one would find out.

In the wagon, with a little fresh air to clear his mind, the voice in his head started again. Then she'd started in kissing his neck and his hands and whatever else she could get at without too much trouble.

Damn it! No one would ever find out.

She'd gotten a little ahead of him. He tried to keep up, picking his way through the silver-lit forest and ducking branches as he went.

"I've seen old ladies make better time than you. You sound all outa' breath back there."

"There'll be plenty left for you. Don't worry," he panted.

"I'm not worried."

Just up ahead, the silhouette of a small miner's cabin appeared through the branches. "Zat where yer takin' us? You sure err's no one inside?"

"You worry too much old man." She pulled him around the corner of the cabin, where a covered porch still managed to hang above the doorway. Some of the railing had fallen away, but the timbers still looked strong... Well-packed.

She let go of his hand and balanced her way up the half-fallen steps before ducking into the cabin.

A lantern flickered to life inside.

He stepped inside the door. The mantle she had placed upon the weathered lap-board table threw long shadows around the room.

His stomach tightened. His nerves threatened again to unwind, the voice of reason wading through his whiskey-soaked mind, seeking purchase.

"Come in and shut the door," she cooed. "It's much warmer in here, don't you think?"

The floorboards creaked under his weight. Tattered curtains barely covered the small window by the table. There was another window above and to the left of a cold and rusted pot bellied stove that squatted in the corner.

She pulled the strap of her dress down and, glancing coyly over her shoulder, retreated to a small room at the back of the cabin. "Take your clothes off," she said, her voice now silky and alluring.

Once in the room, he stared at the single bed pushed up against the wall. He pulled the suspenders off his shoulders and unbuttoned his shirt.

"Should I build a fire first?" He asked, as something tumbled from his pocket onto the toe of his boot and clattered to the floorboards.

It was his pocket watch.

"Everything alright in there?" she called.

"Just waitin' for you to show your pretty face again."

He reached down and picked up the watch by the chain. He let it dangle from his fingers. He read the inscription, "J.W.P. From the Guild." He thought to tuck it back into his pocket, but saw a nail sticking out of a post in the wall, just beside the table. He admired it's movement for a moment before hanging it from the nail. Seeing it there made him feel more at home.

I need to slow this down a little, he thought to himself. *Soak it in. Why the rush?*

"Why don't you be a gentleman and put that lantern out; give a lady some respect?" With her back to him, she let her dress fall away. She looked like a Greek goddess carved in the purest, smoothest

34

alabaster – what they had seen in school books. He gasped at the sight of her slender waist.

"Alright now, wait for me on the bed," she cooed.

Most of the room was dark with the lantern out, but the moonlight fell in through the window and cast a strip of light across the blanket there.

"Man it would feel good to rest my head. I haven't slept in days." The old bed springs creaked loudly as he sat down on the mattress.

Then there was the precious sight of her body, her delicate feet padding across the floor toward him. She stood over him. He could smell the sweetness of her skin, that he would soon taste.

She reached down for his hand and pressed it against her warm stomach and slid it gently up to her breast. She drew his hand up to her mouth and licked the tip of his finger. With her tongue, she traced his strong fingers, his hands, sending... almost violent ripples of pleasure through his body. She was different. She was aggressive – not like the other woman he'd been with. She had natural inclinations to sex. She exuded it – the way she talked, the way she moved... And now she was here in front of him. Right now he would give anything to be with her.

She descended with him into the wash of moonlight and her glorious body was laid out before him.

His heart was pounding, his head swimming with disbelief. His eyes welled up and, despite himself, a tear rolled down his cheek. Oddly, for a moment, he thought he saw a look of fear, or maybe regret, sweep over her angelic face. Then it was gone. *Just the shadows*, he thought. *What did it matter?* Being out here in the woods, in the old trapper's cabin with her seemed inevitable.

He was next to her, and their bodies came together. With the moon looking over them, and the night breeze whispering its secrets through the ancient cedars, it was as close to perfect he'd ever seen.

Then, from somewhere in the dark, he heard it.

The voice of caution tugged at him again.

She pulled his lips to hers, and he was again drunk with passion.

Another sound caught his attention as it broke through the delicate skin of this night. It was the unmistakable sound of a boot thudding on the broken porch steps; the deep thud of heavy footfall breaking across the floorboards.

Coming quickly.

She pulled his face down kissing him deeply with her warm lips, her hands sliding down his back, so delicate, so.... perfect. She moaned, and that moan strummed a chord that rang through his whole body, and nothing... absolutely nothing, could break its resonance. He closed his eyes and let her take him...

On the floor, down beside the bed, a black boot stepped into the moonlight. Thick fingers grabbed his hair and wrenched his head back. Before he knew what was happening he was pulled to his feet by a man – an enormous man, with the strength to crush. He felt the cool air against his skin. He knew that, in this moment, he would have to fight for his life. His doom had come.

He lunged at his attacker, but the advantage of surprise did not belong to him.

He made a clumsy dash for the door.

A boot stuck between his feet and he slammed to the floor.

There was a stinging blow, something cold and hard across his forehead.

Now a boot on the back of his neck and the cold floor pressed into his face.

It was clear to him that he was helpless, not only to defend himself, but to protect the girl who brought him here... *The girl! Where was she?*

He swooned, and in his pain could think only of the time he was in the schoolyard as a small boy, and another boy, standing at the top steps, dropped a large rock onto his head. It was the same brand of pain.

A loud crack echoed through the room.

His mind tried to follow it, to make sense of it, but then he could not be sure whether the "crack" was coming from outside or inside his head.

Realization spread slowly through him. His body was shutting down. It was a warm, wet feeling, creeping slowly from his heart outward. There was a distant gong chiming, and there was ringing and then dark clouds scudding across a vast and distant reddening sky...

The voice in his head, which had moments ago warned him to take action, to save his life, was now telling him that the opportunity to take measures had gone. In fact, the voice now was little more than a whisper, that these were the last moments of his life.

"I'm dying." He thought he spoke the words aloud, but no sound came. He wanted to say goodbye to his mother.

His senses began to flicker, and, like a long row of candles, snuffed out, one by one

The girl!

His gaze drifted, dream-like, to the bed where, only moments before, he lay in blissful rapture; where she still lay bathed in moonlight... And the last thing he saw, was the moonlight glinting from her teeth... and her beautiful smile.

All of this... and still she smiles.

Ω

WHAT
THE
TIDE BRINGS

----

*Nescis quid serus
vesper vehat*

$\triangle$

You know not what night-fall may bring.

Vananda, British Columbia, September 1, 1889

The Kingfisher clutched a thin branch on a newly fallen tree, its head cocked to watch an unsuspecting dragon fly hover over a furrow of blackberry flowers streaming in the breeze.

Eve Walker brought the bird slowly into her camera lens. Behind the bird and the flowers, the branches of the newly fallen giant Cedar stirred against a brightening red and silver-blue sky in the east. The last feeble bursts were all that remained of the newest storm - already the second this season. Eve's father had promised that when a storm at this time of year brought this kind of fury, it was usually a harbinger of a long, hard winter - wet and not merely blustery, but with tempest.

The word "tempest" fluttered through her mind. It was a word that nestled well in the vocabulary of her stepmother - a devout Scottish-

38

protestant dowager, whose father had spent her entire youth blasting hellfire and brimstone, self-deprecation and inherent guilt. It was all hers by birthright.

The snap of the shutter sent the bird streaming to the tide line, where it rested atop a massive rock. She let the camera fall, and watched as the Kingfisher staged its indignant protest. Something flashed in the sun and her gaze was drawn to the waves lapping the shore at the base of the larger rock, upon which the Kingfisher continued to scold her for her impropriety. The gentle waves coasted in and threw themselves ashore at the last possible moment, washed around the rock and broke easily there. Indeed, something lay there in a heap. Something unnatural.

Eve hesitated a moment before she picked her way along the rocks to inspect what it was the night tide had brought. She remembered as a child running the beaches at Gillies Bay, after a storm surge, to see what had been left behind. Sometimes there were large glass floats sticking half out of the sand, that her father told her had come all the way from China. Once there was a corked bottle that still had some mysterious liquid in it, and you could almost hear the grievous shouts of the careless sailor who had dropped it by accident over the side of his ship.

She would lay in bed late at night, during the vicious winter storms that came without fail, and imagine that the ocean was alive; a mostly restless soul that, when angry, or perturbed, would throw itself as high as it could against the shoreline, and snatch whatever it could from the land and sweep it out to sea. She would close her eyes and imagine the helpless objects that would have been so violently snatched and compelled by the giant waves in a brutal one-sided negotiation. Sometimes, before she drifted off, she would even see those distant shores, where these play-things would be discarded when the sea grew bored and was on its restless way again, to search for something new.

She took a few steps closer, the camera held in ready should the situation deserve documentation. Then she stopped dead in her tracks. Her mind reeled. She riffled through a list of reasonable possibilities, even though she had already come to terms with what lay before her.

She stumbled backward and momentarily lost her footing on the seaweed covered stones.

She grasped the boulder, to stop herself falling, even as her eyes locked onto the dead man's listless stare.

"*Trial by fire it is then*," she said under her breath. With that, she willed herself to step closer, sending the irate Kingfisher away once again. She crouched down and placed one hand on a small patch of sand for balance. It seemed as though it were simply a man lying there awkwardly on his side in the water, gazing and confounded at a barnacle-covered rock that lay defiantly near his head, as if "it" was somehow profoundly different from the others. He stared blindly along the earth, as stoic and still as a rock resting there among other rocks, as time drew its lazy hand over the earth.

Though she might be mistaken.

Yes. Now she was certain: there were faint signs of regret... How it must have been to die in such a way. She railed against the notion that somehow death was so... *unkind...* that those pale, cloudy eyes still might see.

Cruel fate indeed.

At last she looked away from the pathetic scene before her. She stared, unseeing, at the dawning late-summer sky, and the tree line behind it, and at the many branches breaching the beach-head, scooping outward from the massive trunks, and trying for the sun.

For a moment, with the wind in the trees, and the waves washing ashore - just for a moment - she could feel the man's spirit drifting nearby: '*Now what am I to do?*' he'd say, looking down upon his body, thinking it a useless, hollow shell.

Though properly humbled in the presence of death, she could not overlook that *this* was news. She stepped back and prepared to snap a photograph.

It was at that moment voices rang through the trees.

Children... Schoolchildren, coming down the path, to the beach!

Of course! And the sun had already broken over the mountains. People would come walking their dogs. Children – the older kids – would stroll by on their way to school; the Hamiltons and the Campbells and the Riordans would walk to the end of Kimball Road, where the dirt path led to the ocean and then split left and right, in due course, following the shore-line for miles in either direction.

Eve spotted Tess Whitcomb-Riley just as she appeared at the trail mouth and stepped carefully from the ledge down onto the rocks. Behind her came her entire class of young school children – the first and second grades - followed by a young teacher's aid whose name she could never recall. Eve was quick to close the distance, waving her arms and signalling that Tess should hold back, that she should keep the school children away.

"Evelyn Rose Walker . You're a sight for sore eyes," Tess smiled and quickly looked down again to watch her footing on the seaweed-covered rocks. She started toward Eve, her students popping through the trees and swarming onto the beach around her - dozens of children, alive with the promise of unbridled imagination.

"Take the children back to the trail!" Eve yelled. Tess slowed her gait, her smile fading as she saw the look of gravity on Eve's face.

"What is it?" she said, craning to get a better look.

Then the blood drained suddenly from Tess's face as her eyes found what Eve strained to conceal. For a moment it seemed all she could do was stare.

Eve caught one of the boys as he tried to pass, but it was too late.
A young girl nearby stopped in her tracks and screamed. The other children gathered around, alert now to the danger, but straining to see nonetheless.

Now, the younger children started to cry as they turned blindly away, stumbling back to the safety of the trail.

A young girl slipped on the rocks and fell to her hands and knees.

The image had already begun to sear their tender young minds.

Tess picked the girl from the rocks and pressed her bloody, barnacle-scraped hands into her dress. What, for the students, had only moments before been a refreshing morning walk had fast become a nightmare.

"Back to the trail. Quickly! Children! Quickly!" Tess scrambled, clutching at her dress to keep it from underfoot, while her mind searched for what she would offer when the parents asked the inevitable questions. "Please!" She called again, her voice panicked, "Come away from here. Now!"

"Miss Riley!" Eve snapped. "Send Cyril to get Constable Gentry and... Miss Riley!" She snapped again, trying to get Tess' attention while attempting to avert disaster to the greatest degree possible.

Tess took the oldest boy by the shoulders. "Take the children back to the school. Get them settled before the parents arrive."

She followed behind the sorrowful group until the children had all left the beach, and could no longer see the body. Then she returned to Eve's side.

"Who is he?" Tess said, inching closer, as if daring herself to come closer than she ought. It was clear from the look on her face she could only see the horror of what presented itself, not thinking that in those last moments, on the hinge between life and dying, that there must be some kind of peace.

"I don't recognize him. I don't believe he's from here," she assured herself. "Horrible to die that way."

Eve set her camera safely on the rocks and crouched beside the body. With her fingers she carefully lifted the seam of his pocket and thrust two fingers inside, working her hand into the soaked denim, searching for a billfold or scrap of paper – anything that might offer a clue to who he was.

"My God Eve! What are you doing?" Tess gasped.

"We need to find out who he is."

"What's this 'We?' There is no 'We', Eve! Leave it to Bobby. You've got no business."

The first pocket was empty. Eve stepped over him and crouched again, searching.

"Eve, I'm serious -"

At that moment, Constable Bob Gentry appeared alongside Charlie Morgan, who hopped awkwardly down onto the beach.

"Jesus H," Gentry gasped, grabbing Charlie's arm to stop himself slipping on the rocks.

"What are you doing Evelyn?" Gentry snarled.

"Trying to find out who he is, Bobby."

"Constable Gentry!" Bobby reminded, preferring, as he did, to be called by his earned title. "I *need* you to step away from the body and let us do our job."

"Settle, Bobby. We're too familiar, you and I, for you to pass that firm bullshit off on me. You're taking this officer of the law thing too far."

"You're taking this newspaper writer -"

"Journalist," Eve cut in.

"...writer thing a little too far, now step away from the damn corpse 'fore I -"

"Constable Gentry," Charlie chimed, interrupting the contrite conversation between Gentry and Eve. Charlie was, by now, kneeling over the dead man. He had propped the corpse on its side and set about inspecting the torso. "I think... Ya, I'm pretty sure there's..." he continued, as he slipped his entire hand inside the dead man's shirt, taking measures to ensure it wouldn't fall open. "Ya this here is -"

"...going to have to wait until we get him back to the House of Law." Gentry interrupted again, this time almost yelling over-top of Charlie Morgan, who now looked confused.

"We can look him over for evidence, and for any sign of what he'd run up against, once we're beyond reach of prying eyes. I suspect he's off one of the halibut boats coming down from fishing in the North country.

"Did any of the kids see this?"

Tess nodded.

"Then I suggest you get on back to the school and see to their needs 'fore their parents catch notice of what you've led their children into," Gentry said, not breaking his stare with Eve. "Meantime. I thank you both for your help."

"Is that what you call doing your job?" Eve said as she scooped her camera up from the rocks and followed Tess to the trail.

"Wait a minute," Bob said, eyeing the contraption hanging from the leather strap in Eve's hand.

"What's that?"

"It's a photographic camera," Eve said, "We'll be running photographs with the paper - first to do so on the coast here - possibly in the entire west of the continent. I came down here with a mind to catching the water at sunrise. That's when I found him," she said, glancing again at the corpse.

"You mind your business now, Eve. Things are done a certain way and it's best not to interfere where you've no business interferin'. . I'm sure the last thing the afflicted family will want is camera pictures of his body in the paper."

Tess grabbed Eve by her arm, "C'mon Evie. Nothing good can come of being here now."

As they turned to leave, Eve lifted the camera and snapped a photograph of both Gentry and Charlie Morgan standing over the corpse. Gentry turned and gaped at Eve in apparent disbelief. He walked briskly toward her, picking up momentum as he went. "If Corporal Sutherland says there's a story for the paper," Gentry hollered, "he will work it out with Reynolds, same ways he always does. If Reynolds wants you to write the story, that's his own bad judgement. Now I don't mean to speak with a rough edge to a lady, but seriously, Eve, 'til then you need to back off." And with that, he grabbed her by the shoulders, as if to set her on her way down the trail, further from the body, further from the truth.

Without thinking, Eve brought her elbows up sharply and deflected Gentry's grip. Her sudden reaction startled him backward onto his heels. This quickly became a problem, largely because his standard force-issue work-duty boot had a heel and sole that were custom made for timber and mud. None of these features were any good on seaweed-covered beach rock.

Bobby glared at Eve for the shortest of moments before his boots came out from under him altogether, and with resolute force.

Ω

STORM SURGE

Ad augusta par augusta

To high places by narrow roads

"I was mortified that Quentin would show up to bail me out."

Tess looked sheepishly at Eve.

"Oh, I see. He already knows then."

"Quentin sends his regards. He paid the fine -"

"Damn it. What do you mean he paid the fine. I thought you were going to handle it?"

"I was on my way to see Cletis, and I wound up shoulder to shoulder with Mr. Reynolds. There was no way out of it."

"What happened to us finding my way out of it – to show some initiative and ingenuity?"

Tess winced, "He already knew, Eve."

"Thought I'd be showing him the ropes – at least for the first little while. I swear he's omnipresent... I bet he's trying to prove something: that he can bring his way of doing things here, instead of trying to fit in."

"That's absolutely not going to work here, is it?"

Eve cocked her brow at Tess.

"I'm agreeing with you because I know that's what's expected. Overall, though, I don't have the slightest notion what you're on about."

"Damn right it's not going to work. This here is a different beast. These are loggers, and fishermen and miners... In a tight-knit community no less."

"Again, I feel I must agree... I don't think the same rules apply."

Eve stared blandly in reply. "Thanks. A lot."

"I'm on my way to the school," Tess said. "Mr. Reynolds is waiting for you at the Paper."

"It's Quentin, Tess. Flesh and blood like any other man. It"s not like he's the Pope. And I'm sure he's lacking in virtue, too... *New York, my ass.*" The last bit she added under her breath.

Eve watched Tess hurry toward the school house. She pressed her eyes closed for a moment and shook her head in disbelief. There was nothing to do but wade into it. She continued on toward the inevitable collision with Reynolds.

She walked the boardwalk through town, lost in thought and largely oblivious to all before her: a man leading a horse by the reigns; a young boy crying as his father leads him into the barber for his first hair cut; two ladies coming out of the confectionery with small white bags in their hands. These small things - bonbons and horses and haircuts – none of it mattered. These people were oblivious, and were all the better for not knowing. For the moment, Eve envied them their simple innocence. She had imagined starting small, undertaking the minutiae of the trade - until she grew in competence and skill. She imagined Quentin would let her stew for a while, then pull her back from the roiling pool at the last possible moment. All the same, she had a job to do. She stopped to rest a moment and collect her thoughts. She leaned against the corner of the outfitters shop and kicked the toe of her boot against a timber, to knock mud loose from her heel that may or may not have been there to begin with. Across the street, and three shops down, she could see the front door of the newspaper office where Reynolds was likely already hard at work.

She folded her arms and closed her eyes, letting the sun warm her face. Her momentary reprise was shortly interrupted by a hushed conversation taking place nearby. Standing near the hotel entrance, two well-dressed women were engaged in a whispered conversation. As if on cue, they both turned to cast stiff and disapproving stares from beneath the brims of their preposterous hats. Eve fixed their gaze and spat on the boardwalk. Both hats jostled as the women turned on their heels in disgust and tromped to the hotel door and disappeared.

"Mindless tramps," Eve said under her breath, setting out to vanquish the last few feet to the office.

She set her hand to the door of the Coast Miner newspaper, and paused for a moment to deepen her resolve.

Inside the office she took her coat off and hung it neatly on the rack behind the door. Quentin peered over his glasses at a test sheet he had just run through a hand press. She couldn't be sure he wasn't watching her for signs of weak constitution.

"I found a body this morning."

"Quentin looked up suddenly at Eve. "A dead body?"

"That would be the clinical diagnosis." Eve drew a chair from across the floor and placed it front of Quentin's desk.

"My stepmother would have a bird if she found out."

"You mean if she found out you're working here?"

" No, I mean about the dead body. Obviously."

"You might also have meant to refer to the fact that you are now a convict. Please..." he availed her, a look of exasperation painting his face. "Look. Do you wish to work in the papers or not? I think it's time you bore some britches and seized life by the balls, Evelyn," He said with a smirk dawning inexplicably at the corners of his mouth.

"What could possibly be funny to you right now?" Eve bristled.

"Oh it's nothing. Just couldn't help considering all the implication and religious furor over the notion of Eve grabbing life by Adam's apples..."

Eve shook her head. "Really now! Maybe we should just set our minds to discovering how witty we can be, and let the problems sort themselves out."

"Problems will come and go, Evelyn. I have become weather-beaten over the years and grown a thick skin. You, on the other hand - now we'll get the true measure of you. This, your body, is not *just* a story, it's an investment. The outcome will likely affect numerous lives – both innocent and guilty alike. And we'd better do a damn good job of it."

"And don't allow people to get under your finger nails," Quentin continued, nodding at the two ladies who were once again standing outside the Hotel across the road. "...Or Gentry and Hudson – or any other man who opts for that brand of disgrace. Once people see that you are doing this come hell or high water, they'll get on-board. Those that don't, have got something to hide. And God help 'em if they do have something to hide, because you'll dig that up too... These folks here, I suspect strongly, want to play in the big city yard. That's all well and good, but there'll be some hard lessons along the way... The world is watching, Evelyn."

"You mean New York is watching. Isn't that what you mean?"

"It's like I said: The world is watching, Evelyn."

"It's Eve, if you please."

Eve drew a blank stare from Quentin.

"Any case, New York *is* the world. Time has taken care to weed out those who are loose with their words, and looser with their commitments... to say nothing of honour and integrity."

"And this is your dream? To save us all from collapsing back into the dark ages; to take up with the Indians and issue our paper in limited runs, hand-printed on Birch bark?

Quentin chuckled. "No, Evelyn. We – you and I – are going to bring this city forward, and help her to maintain the footing she currently holds over centres to the south: San Francisco, Seattle, Victoria. We do that with progressive, accurate, fair-minded journalism, for a level playing field, to weed out the plans of anyone who might try to hack our agency off at the knees."

"I have another question."

"Did you wish to put up your hand?"

Eve grimaced. "There are people - ...I mean, I've already received... threats... Well, more like strongly worded dis-encouragements. If I had no wind in my sails I might flinch. It seems there's no place for a woman's wiles in the management of this city. Being of the weaker sex, my womanly notions and discretions are somehow odious."

"So why write me those letters? If I recall correctly you were about ready to take on the paper yourself after the former owner dropped off the map, no? Why the hesitation now? -

"Wait, before you answer that, let me tell you something..." he

48

paused to red-pencil a Type line for removal from the proof that lay on the desk in front of him. "I have been in newspapers for a long while – for a lifetime really. While social evolution here, at this end of the continent, is still in the dark ages, change is coming. And it's coming fast, Evelyn."

"It's Eve."

"Do you think that yours was the only proposal, the only humble request for gainful employment, Evelyn? ...Alas, you are mistaken. There were many hundreds – mostly from within the journalism stables, spread across the country – in America, that is. Yours, however, was the only query – more than a query – it was an impeachment – from a woman. It was a demand, yet couched in elegant language, properly seeded with diplomacy, and a hard-hitting challenge: '*doubtless there are several hundreds of men whom I could choose to bring with me from out East; perhaps a handful more here, that possessed the required skills to at least get by.*' I believe were your words. But it was in *your* letter, Evelyn Walker, that I could sense a real passion for the profession. Most left me feeling nonplussed: that they could win me by dropping a smattering of important names, or by eliciting cool and aloof codex' that were sparsely populated with examples of largely uneducated vitriol.

"Evelyn, Eve... I do not know if, at the end of the day, you will have your success. I only know that, at least in one of the letters I did receive from you when I was in New York, I caught a glimmer of something worthwhile. I am going to do my very best to bring whatever it is within you, to flower.

"If there are those who want to maintain status quo here, they will have to simply be content with their lot, as befits the lazy-minded. More accurately, it is the uneducated and the lazy. And, for the record, I would gladly take "uneducated" on any proposal, rather than both lazy *and* uneducated. Any jack-ass with a schoolhouse education can waltz to the doorstep of the Institution of Journalism – even look the part, but often their expectation is that the journalism racket will be an easy meal-ticket. After all, we can all write, right? Or so their lackadaisical trumpet blast sounds.

"No. It takes a great deal more than that," Quentin continued. "In fact, in you, I have my own deep-seated hopes. But this is talk for another time."

Eve was dumbstruck as the first flash of true inspiration electrified her. Within her breast the seeds of something greater began to take hold. Her gumboots were muddy and she could now think beyond her own wavering self-assurance. She could not help but smile, though she attempted to keep it to herself.

Quentin pushed himself away from his desk and stood, his right hand on his hip and a cup of coffee in his left. After a moment, he thoughtfully placed his cup on the desk and pulled a silver tray, adorned with a small humidor, closer to where he stood. He pinched a cigarette paper from a small canister, and sloughed a small amount of tobacco from the humidor onto the tray. Then, with a practised hand, he dropped a pull of tobacco into the paper and tamped it down. With a flick of his fingers he was left with a perfectly proportioned cigarette. He struck a match and returned his hand to his hip, the coffee being replaced by the lit cigarette.

"It's quite right that you should feel as you do now, Evelyn. The decisions we make today will lay the groundwork for all that will come after. It's as I said – change is already happening... It's happening in the East, that is," he stated pensively, as he walked to the window. He drew from the cigarette, his eyes fixed on some point in the middle distance, not at all seeing the world outside, but was trained fully on the thoughts forming in his mind. "You see, the modes and methods we thought defined, perfectly, the spirit of what we were trying to do are already demanding we be more progressive. Newspapers reflect the concrete, right as rain, but more than that, they are working to define our culture – not by closed mandate – which was the old way, perpetrated by the old guard, but a grand scheme that has eyes and ears for the emerging culture, not just what *is*, but what will be. This is the direction we are headed. If we are to do our part here, we will – and don't mistake me now - we will not *define* culture, we will provide the *voice* of our culture. And from within our emerging culture comes our identity. This is true on all fronts: business, crime, industry, city planning, government policy, and – women's rights. Make no mistake, these will be battles won and lost with great effort. It is a noble effort. One that must not crumble under the scrutiny of protectionism and lazy thinking."

Eve drank in a moment of silence, and was mystified when Quentin turned to her and started in again.

"I will not say I'm sorry that you ran up against the Provincial Constabulary. In fact, these are the battle lines being drawn. And you struck the first blow. Your man, Gentry, judging from his reaction, we'll need to bring to bear upon his demeanour further scrutiny, until we find out where his loyalties truly lie." Quentin strode to his desk and began selecting papers and folders to slip into his attache. "And I have a suspicion that we may be opening Pandora's Box." Quentin stopped what he was doing and his eyes locked onto Eve's. "My advice to you: Be ready! If this is really what you would do, Evelyn, despite all of the adversities, my intention is that, within two years, we will have built a news journal good enough to compete with the best metropolitan rags."

Eve did not confide her growing unease, nor the fear that now slithered in the pit of her stomach. Then, as if he could hear her thoughts, Quentin did his best to salve the flicker of uncertainty that must have flashed across her eyes.

"Time to get down to brass tacks then is it? However did you manage to get yourself thrown into jail, the very first day on the job?... Nix that. I can hazard a guess. The point is, you are already getting under someone's skin. The question is this: Why, outside of misplaced manhood, skewed ideals, and needless bravado, did these fellas take the tack they did."

Eve opened her mouth to respond.

Quentin jumped in again, "There will come a day when they will not mind asking you for your help, if it will help them to do their job."

Eve glared in return.

"Who was it then? Gentry *and* Hardy? Gentry and Morgan? Spare your secrets for them. You and I are on the same team. We work together. Until you get your legs under you and develop your style for dealing with this kind of horse shit, I am your muscle. In fact, I'm your muscle in all things, at least until you decide to acquire a peace-maker, something I encourage out here, especially under the circumstances.

For most men chivalry is sometimes good to fall back on, but it's usually an after-thought."

His eyes fell upon the camera still hanging around her neck.

"Did you manage to capture images? Photographs of the body?"

"I have one: a picture, with Bobby Gentry and his deputy standing over the body. Bobby took exception. That's when things got dicey."

Quentin mashed the cigarette into a purple and green okra-agate ashtray. He paused a moment to sip at his coffee, then swept up his jacket and a notebook.

"Come on. We need to put these clowns in their place." Eve grabbed her own book and fell in behind Quentin.

"They have had their way here, these boys. They've never had to share their dominion. They will soon learn the true power of the press. We are the Fifth Estate, Evelyn. Don't ever forget it...You do know what that is, correct?"

Eve remained silent.

"The newspaper itself," he said, locking the office door behind him, "is the voice of measure and even keel. The bridge between the public – the people – and the decision makers. To ensure equity and fairness and disclosure. That is the Fifth Estate. Though not a weapon in the traditional sense, the agency of journalism acts as another level -"

" - an intermediary between that which is purported to be true by parties with a vested interest," Eve interrupted. "and that which is actually true, as meted out by the facts. The proven facts. The people who... everyone else - who is outside these vested interests must be given the advantage of objective truth."

Quentin nodded intently, a smile playing at his lips. "The force you wield in your pen is sharper than any sword, though you will soon learn," he said, as they made their way to Eve's wagon in the neighbours yard, where Charlie grazed beneath a cherry tree. "the pen is a force none the less. And one to be reckoned with. This, my dear Evelyn, is exactly why I chose this place... Why I chose you."

"Saddle up. I'll explain on the way."

Eve rolled her eyes, but was careful to keep herself in check. The last thing she wanted to do was to throw down land mines, to complicate things between she and Reynolds. It was just... the man could talk. And talk. And then talk some more. He was the living incarnate of a thunderstorm, ready to make noise at the slightest provocation.

She hooked Charlie to the wagon and cautioned a glance at Quentin, to get her bearings. She felt she knew what to expect of this man. But the breadth and depth of his character, and his mind, were proving more than she had guessed. It was starkly evident she actually knew very little of him.

"Make them think. Make them earn every battle," Quentin said. "Then – and this is a bit of acquired wisdom – if necessary, make them think they've won. Even when they haven't. Keep them guessing." Quentin pulled himself up into the wagon. "They'll soon wish they'd never heard of you.

"I learned everything I know from a man named Charlie Giordano: If you need time – buy your time. We all want a safe community. Right? Right! If they'd rather live in the shadowy world of vacuity and moral ineptitude... soon you'll be leading them around like two dogs on one leash. These boys need to earn your respect, Evelyn. And they *damn well* better respect you."

"Clear as winter ice on a fast moving river."

Quentin shot her a glare. "They *need* to respect you. Either you deal with it up front and have it be done and put behind you, or, you wait for it to come to you. Because it sure as hell-fire *will* come to you... Right to your doorstep."

Ω

THE STILLNESS
BEFORE
THE BREATH

Corvis oculum corvi non orvit

‡

*A crow will not take the eye
of another crow*

Constable Charlie Morgan leaned back in his chair, legs spread apart in exaggerated fashion and feet flat on the jailhouse floor. He looked up when Eve walked in, eyed her from head to foot before turning his attentions back to the conversation at hand: "Now, where was I?" he said to Porter Hughes, who had his sidearm lying in pieces on his desk.

"You *are* on the public payroll correct?"
Charlie stopped mid-sentence and stared at Eve.

"Why then, do you make a habit of ignoring the public? I don't think we need to be overly formal do you? Just a handful of questions," Eve said. "I can fill in the blanks."

"Nothin' to be said." Porter piped in.

"It's a small town. People know something's happened. Is it not to your advantage to see that the facts weigh in over conjecture?"

Charlie pushed himself from his chair and came around to the counter.

"I'll let you in on a little secret," he said, his face reddening as he spoke. "You don't come in here swinging if you want us to play. You gotta wait for the pitch."

"I'm a little surprised," Eve said, "You need to pay more attention. I regret being the one to bring you up to speed, but Jonas has been away now... *for almost a full year*!" Eve leaned forward to emphasize her point.

Darcy's mouth twisted into a sneer, "The Lord giveth and the Lord taketh away, Evelyn" he said nodding, smugly. "You're right! Prescott is gone. No-one's seen hide nor hair of him, I'm afraid," he said, nodding slowly at Eve.

Porter Hughes sat back in his chair smirking. "You yourself should maybe oughta' take a page outa' Prescott's notebook. Now there's a man knew how to watch his step."

Eve shook her head.

"If people have to start talking among themselves to find out what happened, it's the police who look bad isn't it?" Eve said.

"You'll want to settle their fears, of that I'm sure."

"I'm tellin' you... you're intereferin' with my ability to do my job's what *I'm* sayin'. Another word and I'll have you arrested for interfering with official police business."

"Just so I'm clear on the matter, are you telling me I can't be here?"

At that moment the door at the back of the station slammed shut and Bob Gentry hobbled down the hall, his boots and wooden crutches thudding heavily on the floorboards. He stopped when he saw the three of them standing there, neither saying a word to the other.

"Evelyn. Have you been looked after?" Gentry enquired curtly.

"*Looked at,* would be more the point."

"Take a seat Charlie," he said pointing to Charlie's desk.

"What can I do you for? No. Wait. I can guess why you're here. And all I can tell you is we've got nothing for you, yet. Red says we're going to be run off our feet over the next bit, so you might just as well put that pen and paper away for a while, til things settle."

"Was he killed by accident? Or…"

"Now you listen here Evelyn Walker, don't go spreadin' stories," Charlie piped in again. "Let us do our job. Gentry just goddam said we'd let you know when there's something to be said. Besides, I know your stepmother don't approve of what you're doin'. How do ya think she'd feel if she hadda' come down here and pull your little behind outta jail again?"

Gentry raised his hand. "I said close the door and have a seat Charlie! There's no sense in kickin' up dust."

"You'd do well to leave my stepmother out of it *Morgan*."
Charlie made toward Eve. She was fast to duck out the door just beyond reach.

"Go on home, now, and stay out a trouble Evelyn Walker."

"Oh, and one more thing," Eve piped up, looking directly at Charlie. "On what grounds was it did you say you were going to arrest me?"

Gentry smouldered at his understudy.

"What happened to 'we'll teach those boys a lesson'," Eve chided.

"I thought you did just fine. I've already gone on record saying it's you they need to sort their issues with…

"Whatever!" Quentin snorted, "There is evidently something – an unseen current - that has them on edge."

"What? You mean outside of the fact they very obviously don't take to what I'm trying to do here?"

Eve took Quentin's silence as a good place to change the subject.
Are you settled at your hotel? Need help with bags?"

"I've arranged for the purchase of a home, actually." After a moment spent searching his pockets, Quentin produced a folded sheet of paper from his billfold.

"It's a dull grey number, Tudor style. Built by an Italian from what I gather. If you're going to buy a house, buy one that's built by the Italians. They take pride in their work. White trim, small fruit orchard, apples, cherry, even a Chinese White Pear I'm told."

Eve looked at him strangely.

"You look unsettled." Quentin said. "...As for my baggage from the hotel, you needn't worry. I've arranged for the rest of it to be brought along after the smoke clears."

"It's not that: the house you mentioned - that's Jonas Prescott's old place."

"Doesn't strike a chord. Should I know him?"

"He ran the newspaper you just bought. Started it in fact."

"Truth be told I didn't have much of a hand on it. The man who arranged the purchase didn't mention it either. Seems fitting though, all things considered."

Quentin folded the paper back into the billfold and slipped it into his pocket. "Where is he now, this Jonas Prescott? Probably prudent to pay him a visit and see just where things are at from his perspective."

A brief moment of silence passed between them.

"No-one's seen him since last Spring." Quentin waited for her to continue.

"Not a complicated story really. One morning the paper didn't show and no-one's seen him since."

"All the same, it doesn't surprise me," Quentin said. "A man can only break the news so long before the news breaks him... How far is it to the house?"

"Not far. It's a twenty minute ride." Quentin dropped his bag into the wagon and walked around front to introduce himself to the horse again. Charlie lifted his head lazily from a worn tuft of grass.

The horse eyed Quentin casually and, after some contemplation, brushed his lips over Quentin's vest, trying for the gold watch chain.

"Not much for food value in that old thing," Quentin chuckled, as he hefted a good pat at Charlie's neck.

"Are there many horses around New York?"

"I had a paddock at Freyland's. Used to race at the amateurs."

"Will you send for your horses eventually?"

"Sold damn near everything I had to come out here. Except Kismet. She's the one I rode out West with the Pony Express. I left her with my niece in Seattle.

Eve untied Charlie's lead and waited for Quentin to get properly seated in the wagon before leading out to the road. She climbed in herself and snapped the reigns, sending the wagon jostling over a patch of rough ground before settling on the worn path.

For a time they rode onward in silence. Eve guessed from the way that Quentin held himself, that he was used to making his own way and not accustomed to taking the passenger's seat. She thought to ask about the letters again. She had gotten off on good terms with the man and didn't want to ruin it. She had always dreamed about moving to one of the big cities, to write for a good paper - a real paper - where the writing was good and meant something. When she'd heard Quentin Reynolds was coming from New York to revive the Coast Miner - in a way, it was as if the city was coming to her.

Eve steered the wagon onto Johnson Road and let Charlie pick his way through the pits and bumps in the untended path to the end of the street. She drew the horse to a stop and pointed at Jonas Prescott's house. From the road, the yard looked empty and overgrown, but the house itself, with its darkened windows and estranged affect, somehow managed, through all of it, to appear stately.

Quentin stepped down from the wagon and straightened his legs.

"It'll take some time to shake the sea out of my legs," he said, turning to consider his new home. Have you entertained any notions about where you think Mr. Prescott may have gotten off to?"

"It's as I've said. One day the paper didn't come. One day led to one week and then on to a month, and then longer still. He left all his belongings just the way he had them. My father figures he wound up in the cracker bin somewhere."

"Indeed," he said lifting his bag from the wagon. "I'd invite you in, but as you can see I'm not ready for guests." Eve watched Quentin walk the path to the porch steps. She reined Charlie into the tall grass and brought the wagon about.

"Hold on there," Quentin called from the veranda, a subtle shade of alarm in his voice. "You'd better come and have a look."

Eve brought Charlie to a stop and drew the lead rope around a fence post.

Quentin looked in through the study window. "What do you make of this?" he said, stepping aside. Eve cupped her hands and peered in through the glass. The room had been entirely ransacked. An oak office chair had been cast aside, the desk drawers were hanging open, some of their contents having spilled onto the floor; papers and books were pulled from the bookshelves and thrown around the room.

Quentin walked the length of the porch and looked through the living room window. "It looks as if the entire dammed house has been turned out..." Then, seized with sudden determination, Quentin charged to the front door and thrust the key into the lock.

Eve followed.

Inside, the air felt close, and what little light made its way into the room, through half-drawn curtains, cast an eerie pall. It was as though the will of the offender might still somehow be lurking there in the shadows, or, at the very least, might have left behind a seething presence of anger - or grief - or whatever it was that had driven them to commit such an act.

"No point you staying on in harm's way," Quentin said.

"You'll need some help cleaning up. I really don't mind," she insisted.

"And I thank you. But I'd rather you go home to your family. Send for the police on your way. I'd appreciate it."

Eve started for the door.

"And Evelyn," Quentin said, "I'll expect to see you at the paper, at seven AM. Bring a sharp pencil," Quentin insisted as he turned his back and charged off into the dark recesses of his new home.

Ω

A Father's Word
Stems the
Hand of Fate

Dum spiro, spero

While I breathe, I hope

"You mind your father today, Eve. No runnin' about?" Catharyn peered sternly at Eve as she stuffed her camisole into a canvas bag.

Eve carried the breakfast tray past her stepmother.

"You ignore your mother now, is that it?" Catharyn said, looking for her reflection in the kitchen window and brushing a wisp of hair from her face.

"I'm not ignoring," Eve said, as she balanced the tray on her arm and knocked softly on the bedroom door.

"*I'm awake,*" her father said quietly.

She went into the room and set the tray down on the bedside table. "Did you get some sleep last night?"

"The warm milk you brought was like rain in the desert," Percy forced a smile.

Eve drew the curtains and pushed the window open for fresh air.

"I'm away now," Catharyn called from the kitchen. "Percy! You mind she takes care a ya fer the day."

"I'll be fine, Cathy. Eve's fine too."

Catharyn muttered under her breath, and slammed the door to

60

ensure her displeasure was duly noted.

Eve arranged the pillows behind her father's head.

"Don't mind her, Eve. You don't have to fuss. You go and do what needs doin," her father said.

She set the breakfast tray on his lap and pulled the chair in close to his bed.

"Did you meet with that newspaper man from stateside yesterday? What'd you say his name was?" Percy said between bites of jellied toast.

Eve smiled at her father and kissed him on the forehead.

"I take it things went well, then?"

"Quentin Reynolds. He asked me to see him today, to come prepared to work."

"That's good, isn't it?"

Evelyn prepared her father's tea.

"What's he like, this editor from the big city? All flash and strut, I'll bet. Can't help himself on account of he knows a whole lot more than us small town folk."

"Eat your breakfast," Eve said, shoving a mouthful at him.

"He's smart," she said, "but he is a bit pretentious." She tore a small piece from the muffin on the tray and popped it into her mouth.

"Met him only once and already he's pretentious?"

"Worldly," Eve corrected herself.

"Not getting off the hook that easy, Eve Walker. Tell me a story."

"Alright. Pretentious. He's from New York, and you can tell it from a mile off. He's got his chin up and his hat pulled down and a walking stick under his arm. He's heard it all, seen it all, and could certainly teach us all a thing or two."

"It's to be expected, I suppose," her father chuckled.

It was quiet for a moment.

Eve stiffened as she watched Percy's face grow pale, then slowly redden.

His breath had escaped him again.

She stripped the breakfast tray away and pulled him forward. She rolled him onto his side and began rubbing his back vigorously. Finally, after what seemed an eternity, he coughed from deep within his lungs. She waited, knowing it would be several moments before he could take air. His face slowly turned purple, his eyes drew wide, yet, all with the patience of a man long afflicted. Eve spoke gently as she rubbed his back and soon there came the high-pitched wheeze that signaled his lungs had finally opened again.

When his coughing subsided she helped him settle back again and brought the warm tea carefully to his lips, to soothe his throat.

"When is he expecting you to see him?" her father gasped.

"Take some rest," she said, laying a gentle hand on her father's arm. "We can talk later." She cooled his face with a damp cloth.

"We can talk now, damn it. I'll not have this sickness come between us." He paused to catch his breath and gulp some tea. He rested then, and took several deep breaths.

"That's a mite better, ...So, as I was sayin', when are you expected to be there?"

"This morning."

"Well you'll sure as deuce not waste the morning sitting here. Off you go."

"It can wait," she said softly, but could see from the spark in her father's eye that she might still go.

"If you expect to be taken seriously you'll see to your commitment." He paused. "You are only as good as your word. If he sees you can't be trusted with keeping time, than nothing will come your way again. Nothing of any worth, to be certain."

"Catharyn expects -"

"If Catharyn expects, then Catharyn can bloody well do," he erupted, a faint rumble resonating in his chest. He took a moment to settle himself before starting in again. "Your life is ahead of you Eve. And I'll not permit you to waste it doting on this sick old man. We all make our way. If your heart of hearts tells you to reach – well then, you better goddam reach. *You* make your *own* way. And don't let anyone tell you different."

Eve leaned in close to kiss his forehead.

Before she left the room, she started a record on the gramophone and laid the copy of *London Illustrated News* Aunt Gracie had mailed from Toronto on his bedside table.

HANNIBAL
IS AT
THE GATES

Abyssus abyssum

&

Hell calls hell

Constable Gentry paused as he placed his hand on the doorknob. Inside, he could hear the fluid drone of Tess's voice as she led the children through what sounded like the alphabet, or a dose of cursory arithmetic. As a matter of course, Sutherland had asked him to pay a visit to the school house. He brought Jim Morris with him. He was to reason with the children, that they should say nothing whatsoever to their parents about what had happened on the beach.   More than a dozen hands shot immediately into the air: What happened at the beach? They simply wanted to know, to hear the story again from an adult, so they might confirm its authenticity, and then charge off in all directions, to re-tell their stories with added vigour, much the way children do. At this point, however, it was patiently explained - again - this time a little louder, and with a less pleasant tone – that until the police had a chance to work things out, the children should keep their bloody mouths shut... Rather, they should keep quiet, as it were.

"Is that why you got the crutches?" asked a young boy at the front. He was small for his age, and his hat was pulled down hard, so his ears stuck out from under.

"Did yooouuu keep your mouth shut, or sum'n'?", came the next question, from another boy with frizzy red hair and freckles.

"We *don't* have *time* to talk about the crutches today, OK kids?" Gentry said through his clenched teeth.

"Why doesn't your legs move much when you walk with them... *crotches?*" A fat kid, dead centre of the front row, sat with his mouth hanging partially open and his lazy eyes half shut, nevertheless, staring impishly as he awaited a response.

"OK. Time to go," Gentry said to Morris under his breath.

They were almost out of the room when the closing door caught one of Gentry's crutches. The slight sent him staggering with stiff, aching legs, painfully forward. The classroom behind him erupted with laughter.

Gentry stood shock-still now, wracked with pain and looking as though he were in a state of catatonia as he departed.

Despite being asked not to talk about what had happened in the school yard during break time, the girls consoled each other about what they had seen. The boys replayed what had happened with proper solemnity, the story building with intensity and heroics with each telling.

By and large, as noon hour waned, there were several children – a dozen perhaps – who made their way home from school for midday meal. As the children sat at their respective tables, in their respective homes, they talked quietly amongst one another, between full mouths, about something terrible that had happened, or would happen, or might happen. It seemed that someone had died, or might die, or almost died, and in doing so - or not doing so - made quite a bloody mess of the beach, in an area usually reserved for frolicking and crab-hunting, no less.

Normally oblivious to much that concerned their children, the mother's ears pricked when it became obvious something deeply unusual was afoot.

The mother of one of the boys told her best friend - in strict confidence – who, in turn, ran to tell her friends at the post office. Conjecture and surmise regarding the dead man's identity, and what it was he must surely have done to meet such an unenviable end, was the favoured topic. Who was he? How far had the ocean carried him?...

What was his name? Where was home? Did he have a wife? Did he have children that were waiting for his letter that, until now, had come every week upon the Sunday, and, now, would never come again? Had he drowned, or was he the victim of some nefarious undertaking?

News of the body on the beach had begun to wend its way like wildfire up and down the island, reaching even the remotest corners 80 miles to the southward.

For Red Sutherland, there was nothing to be done about it.

The fuse was lit.

Ω

A GARDEN
OF
THIEVES

Quis custodiet
ipsos custodes?

ʃ

Who shall watch the watchmen?

The old gardener for the governmental parliament buildings, in the pioneer city of Victoria, BC, took a Snapdragon bloom gently between his thumb and forefinger. He pushed his face in close to inspect the petals, peered beneath the leaves to see that there were no unwanted pests living free of charge on the hard labour of others. They all did their part, most often with proficiency.

He released his gentle hold on the flower and clasped his hands behind his back continuing on his morning inspection.

The day was perfect: bright yellow sun in a pastel-blue summer sky; the salty ocean breeze blowing westward and inland; the pleasant smell of warm soil; bees buzzing importantly; beetles jostling about with their own brand of import... He was glad, indeed, that he had agreed to join his employer from the Hudson's Bay Company office in London, on an adventure of a lifetime, in the new world. Here he would tend Pacific gardens in the westernmost reaches of the Dominion, to his delight.

A Monarch butterfly alighted upon a heritage rose bloom. He

leaned in for a closer look and gentled the butterfly into his hand. At that very moment, the tall, hand-carved oak doors of the parliament exploded outward into the morning, like an overworked steam-donkey that finally let go. The startled gardener stumbled backward and fell to the ground, the butterfly succumbing to its sudden fate and was crushed in his hand.

From inside, delegates, members of the Colonial Government, and esteemed guests, spilled man over man through the doors and down the noble stairs – for their own part fulfilling their lot with perfect grace and stoic air.

Indignant shouts, bellows of rage, and sagacious blasts of provocation shocked the sensibilities of the firmament – awake now, as if from a dead sleep.

Nearby, several crows, likely feeding on a fresh larvae hatch in the roots of the lawn, scattered skyward.

All nature, its seemed, gave wide and sudden berth to the erupting chaos.

As if on cue, once all the men had funnelled out of the building, they began to form a circle around two central combatants. The Premier of British Columbia, Amor De Cosmos, stood rolling up his sleeves and staring dead-eye at his opponent, as though he had all the time in the world. The other slipped out of his waist-coat and handed it carefully to his man, who, in-turn, draped it neatly over his arm before standing aside to await further developments.

The opponent, a Company representative from the Fort in New Westminster, opted to strike first and charged De Cosmos with his head down.

The crowd erupted. Though all were dressed in the best finery money could buy, not a single utterance of civility or good measure, in the name of gentlemanly behaviour, was cast among the seething crowd of beasts.

The man from New West was taller by a hand, and a good two-stone heavier than De Cosmos, but De Cosmos handled the comer with ease, dispatching him with two thunderous straight-arm blows, followed neatly by a crisp and punishing left hook. No sooner had he dished out his judgement upon the first man, than it was that two more came at him as he stood over his vanquished foe.

A concert of well-aimed blows rained down upon these as well, such that De Cosmos did not suffer even the slightest abrasion. He summarily finished the conversation by seizing the man closest him by the lapels and jarring him off his step. He then brought the man's full weight to bear upon his compatriot, such that his compatriot was out cold well before he came to a safe conclusion on the pillowy lawn.

"The rule of law must be honoured! To the Letter!.," De Cosmos bellowed to the crowd, as quiet once again descended over the garden.

"Truth, my good men, is NOT malleable! *Truth* cannot be bent to accommodate the will of man," he paused with a far-away look in his eyes, like a man accustomed to the wide-open spaces of the earth.

"Omission of a single comma can change the very heart of an idea," De Cosmos orated, "*This* is the exclusive point we are discussing here. Mr. Wentworth," he said gesturing to the first man, who was just now coming to his senses, "when this man here called me a 'long-legged Yankee son-of-a-bitch', he might have stopped himself at 'son-of-a-bitch'. My legs are simply not that long.

"Ultimately, the matter will come down to a question of democracy, in the purest sense of the word, to be decided by the collective. So, on the matter of punctuation, and in the novelty of philosophizing on the nature of truth, I am obliged to insist!"

"I'll be damned!" a portly older man sputtered, his jowls shaking with indignation. "Mountains are NOT moved by the absence of or presence of a... It does NOT come down to a bloody mark on a page! Your parables about grammar and the witless fairy tales you write in your so-called "*newspaper*" should be kept in whatever shameful diary you keep. At the end of the day all of your pontificating – Well! He sputtered again, "you are nothing more than a pamphleteer! A grub-street hack."

"Here! Here!" A chorus of agreement went up, while a handful from the De Cosmos faction volleyed in turn.

"Oh, but you are mistaken my good man," De Cosmos continued. "Parliament is the *very* place for it. We have a responsibility. We are the highest achievement of God's good work. *He* has made us Stewards of this place. And we have, in our short-sightedness, dammed ourselves behind a wall of our own making. There is no taking back what has already been given. The matter is settled, for Indian and white man alike."

"Stop your pedagogy and petty maneuverings. It's sly moves, it is. It's like the man said: we all knows yer just positioning for your own bloody paper. Keep your literary fancies out of it eh!?"

"...As I was saying," De Cosmos continued slowly, his eyes closed in mock patience, "we are God's highest ideal, we are the organizing principle by which fate ventures into the unknown. This measure, however it shall come down, should be nixed at the gate... or, as you insist, will prove to be our insurance policy against the unforseen, our measure of foundation, the roots from which will grow the body of our sorority, our society – as any tree will blow in the wind -"

"Enough Goddam preaching. C'mon, let's go back inside. He can't keep flappin' if he ain't got an audience.... Can he?"

"- as a tree is subject to the threat of any storm, our foundation must be strong enough to weather any adversity. On this I *must* insist. The terms of the reserve land settlement have already been ratified. We simply cannot re-negotiate what has already been carefully weighed and measured from all angles. You may think it a clever inspiration to simply and subtly alter the spirit of the document, the very texture and importance that it represents, and then walk among them with one arm around their shoulders and the other carving the air in front of you as you explain how it is that you empathize with their frustration, their failure and humiliation at not... getting it. It must be terribly difficult to understand the language. I know! It can get complicated... And so on. You see?"

"You insist! You insist! If we weren't all suffered to listen to your spouting week after week we might actually accomplish something."

A murmur of agreement rolled among the crowd who were making their way back into the parliament building.

When it seemed that all had been said, and nothing further would come of it, another man stopped and turned around, against the flow of people, and began hollering, "Even if you are the – as you put it – self-appointed steward of God here in this place, I surmise – nay, I daresay it's a concrete guess even - that God does not fuss over periods and commas. The truth is in the idea itself -"

"Well now. How *could* I have been so *utterly* blind. Let's all put our shovels away and hope that God digs us out then, shall we? Let us do nothing and wager our future success on hope of a miracle -" De Cosmos trailed off. He looked down pitifully upon the two men still laid out on the lawn. "Someone get these men to their feet," he said to no-one in particular. "We have much to do if we are to be saved from ourselves." With that, he turned on his heel and disappeared inside, followed closely by his aide.

"Cartright! Draft an ordinate! But do not submit it to the caucus. And call a meeting with council – *our* council," De Cosmos cautioned.

"*Our* council, sir?"

Do you have wax in your ears Cartright? Is it not the simplest of notions? Yes, our council! Call a meeting! Julian, Hill, Wheeler, Wilcox, Spencer and his men. For God's sake, don't forget Terrance – we'll need your brother."

"And what shall I call the... er, policy, as it were."

De Cosmos sneered. "*As it were?* That'll be enough of that spotty Whig slander here..."

De Cosmos continued to stare at Spencer, but his mind was clearly elsewhere.

"The Quiet Title Act," he said, after he'd managed to come back to the moment at hand.

"What?" The young page uttered, falling out of form.

De Cosmos paused a moment to consider the boy in silence before continuing on.

"It! The bill! The Quiet Title Act.*"

"Begging your pardon, sir. But were you not just arguing against it?

"Against what, specifically?"

"Against the, um, Silent Title Act: weren't you fighting *against* it just now?"

"YES! YES! Of course I was arguing against it my dear man. What on earth is the trouble with you Cartright? You seem awfully wrong-headed this morning. Are you unwell? Do you not, after all, have the constitution for what is required of you? It is *The Quiet Title Act*, after all. Not sure where you've gotten the notion that *silence* has aught to do with it."

"Yes sir. Begging your pardon sir. I mean, Yes! Absolutely, I am constituted, well-constituted for it, I'm quite fine, sir...Thank you for asking..." Spencer trailed off. Then he straightened himself. "I was just confirming sir."

"Conforming, Spencer?"

"I believe I said *confirming,* sir."

"You believe it, or you know it to be an irrefutable truth?"

"It is in fact irrefutable, sir," Spencer uttered, now standing at attention, and looking as though he were trying to avoid an imminent court martial.

"Well then. Not a moment to waste. Have the men meet me at my office at 11pm, sharp, this night."

"Until then, sir..." Spencer reached to shake De Cosmos' hand and a sheaf of papers slipped from his fingers, scattering over the heavily waxed granite floor.

De Cosmos left him standing there, a faint smile playing at the corners of his mouth. As he walked down the great hall, he glanced toward a majestic stained glass depiction of Saint Anthony. His mind fell immediately upon his own name. It was a name he had chosen for himself, thought through in fine detail. Amor De Cosmos: love of the universe. It was simple. It was fitting. And, it was... memorable.

I will have what I require, regardless of what these ungrateful fools concern themselves with. I am for the future of this city, of this great empire. I have been chosen.'

Ω

GRIT

Ad nomen vultus sustuht

Ψ

*On hearing her name
she raised her eyes*

A wagon sat blocking the road in front of the Coast Miner office, while two men carried crates of supplies and large sturdy rolls of newsprint inside.

Across the street, three women emerged from the confectionery carrying small white bags. They stopped to watch the men carrying heavy stacked boxes from the print shop to the wagon. The women were joined shortly by the shop merchant.

A man jostled by, his cart led by a single old mare, and stared lazily as one of the men heaved a roll of newsprint over his shoulder and strode back into the shop.

Eve led Charlie down the narrow lane between Quartermanche's and the Coast Miner and emerged at the back of the building, to see another wagon half-loaded with crates and effects she guessed had belonged to Jonas Prescott, the man who'd gone missing. She tied Charlie to the hitching post and slipped past the men coming up the cellar stairs as they struggled with a heavy steamer trunk.

In the office, Quentin stood holding a pen and clipboard and considered Eve sternly over top of his glasses. He pulled a watch from his pocket.

"Despite what you may think, Evelyn, the news happens on its own time. Either you're part of it, or you're not. And if you're not, you might as well pick up your bedroll and kick some dirt on the fire."

Quentin adjusted his glasses.

"You can put your things beside my desk for now and help me unpack this equipment. I expect to have the first issue rolling off the press a week tomorrow. That means you're here at seven o'clock sharp every morning," he said pulling the packing straw from inside one of the crates. "Back home we used to have a saying: if you can see not to trip over the front step, you're probably late."

Eve set her bag beside Quentin's desk and hung her coat on the rack at the front of the shop. "How's Percy this morning?"

"Percy?"

"Of course. You've only just left home and already your father is a vague recollection?" he said with a brief grin.

Eve hesitated, her hand still resting on the coat.

"Don't look so surprised, Evelyn. Information is my business."

"Do you always make a habit of sneaking around digging in other people's business instead of enquiring, as any gentlemen would?

"What else do you think you know about me?" Eve said.

"I know Percy's in a bad state from working in the mines, and that you and he are pretty close."

Eve flushed with anger. "What the hell business is it of yours?"

"It's very much my business, Evelyn. This town was built on mining and will likely live or die relative to the presence of minerals in the ground, or lack thereof-"

"Look, Reynolds, I don't know how you talk to people back where you come from, but here in Vananda we have the good manners to assume one can at least comprehend the basics."

"As I was saying…" Quentin interrupted, his voice even, his face unfaltering, "It's inevitable much of the news we run will have to do with those mines: the men that own them, and the men that work in them. Leave your personal feelings at the door when you come in. And I don't care if you pick them up again on the way out. Always let the facts tell the story. Your emotions have aught to do with it."

"Funny way of getting round to a point."

"I find things are easier to remember when emotions are involved, however... The fact of the matter is, you've got two things going against you, the first being that you're green as a willow sapling in springtime, and they'll smell it from a mile off." He paused. "And by *they* I mean the people of this good town. You'll find that most of them lack good graces even in the best of circumstances."

"You should fit right in then."

"The second... The second, m'lady, rests on what you've not got between your legs. Pardon the expression."

"What I *lack* in equipment, Mr. Reynolds, I make up for in nerve. Besides, this is such a weak... perhaps weak isn't the right word – such a juvenile argument from a schooled libertarian." Quentin stopped mid-stride and turned to face Eve.

"Go on."

"Hannah Green, who assumed the Hartford Courant when her husband died of smallpox in 1777, or thereabouts, was one of the first women in American journalism; Anne Royall who wrote for the *Washington Editor;* Elizabeth Timothy – the *South Carolina Gazette.* If you had it in mind to impress your compatriots with your philanthropy and forward thinking by hiring a woman, you should at least expect them to know more or less as much as yourself."

Quentin squinted at Eve, a strained silence hanging between them.

"Actually, the Hannah you refer to was Hannah Watson. Her husband took over for Thomas Green and she assumed in turn. And I'll agree, you certainly don't lack the venom of any one of them."

By midday the two wagons had been unloaded. Quentin enlisted the men to help him dismantle the old press, to make room for the model he had purchased during his stop-over in Seattle. After they had finished, he pressed a roll of cash into each of their hands and sent them on their way.

When the men had gone, Quentin set to work arranging the equipment and supplies, all the while explaining in painstaking detail the optimum placement of one machine in relation to another, of one type family in calculated disposition to its closest relative. The type drawers were situated at a comfortable distance from the trays; the ink sat uniformly on shelves in anticipation of press plates that would be inserted into the carriage; the sheets of newsprint, once they were cut, would be stacked smartly in proximity to the feed-board.

Several of Prescott's type cabinets remained stacked at the back door ready to be taken away. Quentin selected from one of his own crates, a fitted wood box and slid it open. Inside, the letters, representative of perhaps a quarter of the alphabet, stood in perfect rows, each polished so entirely well, they seemed to pick up the reflected light from the sun that had made its way inside the shop. Quentin wet his finger and rubbed at an imagined aberration on the face of one of the dies.

Two large standing wood cases were arranged near a thick work bench made from sturdy timbers, where, it was explained, the type would be set into the forms appropriate to the page they were printing. Quentin loosened the ropes that had held the drawers in place during the move and slid one of the long, narrow drawers open. Inside were hundreds of type dies. These were coated with dry ink and had obviously been put to regular use.

Eve was given the job of painstakingly selecting one die at a time and stripping as much of the ink as she could manage.

Quentin used a crow-bar to pry open two large crates and began carefully extracting pieces of black polished metal or sparkling brass, each wrapped in cloth, and arranged them neatly in the space that had been cleared.

"This, Evelyn, is called the Grasshopper, slang for Country Press, manufactured by D.G. Walker and Company, out of Wisconsin. Next week, at this very time, she'll be churning out the finest newsprint this town has ever seen."

Despite the monotony, Eve applied herself to the task with such fidelity that she scarcely noticed the time pass.

Quentin cleared some room on the work bench and produced a

small basket. He wiped his hands with a towel from the basket, laid out two plates, and placed a sandwich and a pickle on each one. "Pull up a chair," he said, as he arranged a tall-back leather chair he had just pieced together, behind his own side of the bench.

"Look here," he said, pointing to yet another open wood box on the bench beside him. It too was stacked with clean type. "My good friend Duke Moresby thought we should be on the cutting edge up here in God's country. He was kind enough to send us the latest from Driedeger's, in New York. He's written to us. Shall I read?"

Eve nodded, chewing a bite of sandwich.

Quentin adjusted his glasses.

> *"As this letter finds the light of day, I have every certainty that things are just as you had hoped they would be at your new post in British Columbia. And I don't suppose you'd have it any other way. Truth be told, I rather envy your courage: you remain true to the spirit that brought us to this tireless wheel: our surrogate, seemingly thankless in its voracity and giving back little of what it takes. And we continue to feed on the hind teat and are happier for it; that we might feel satisfied, for a short while, in the countless battles and scant victories it affords. I dare say she is not unlike the ocean you find yourself caught adrift upon. Yet, as Osborne once said, "The reward is in the telling of what needs to be told. It is nonetheless a calling."*
>
> *Curtis Driedeger sends his regards. These are the latest,'*

Quentin rested his hand on the box beside him.

> *'they are called Akzidenz Grotesk, a type face released by the H. Berthold AG foundry just last*

year. I also sent along, if you've not already
acquired one, a roll-film camera. I'm told that
even as I write to you, the best scientific minds
in America are devising an economical way of
using photographic pictures in the
newspapers...

At this, Quentin smiled to himself. "He doesn't think for a moment I would come all this way and not come prepared. If those boys from the police are lucky, they'll be the first to have their pictures on the front page."

Quentin continued to read the last of the letter.

...Remember, you heard it here first my friend. I
trust you are doing well to inform the
uninformed and beseech the ignorant.

Ever Yours,
Duke.

Quentin removed his glasses and set them on the work bench. He contemplated Eve. "I didn't mean to bore you with the letter. I can't expect you to understand the fraternity between two compatriots from the old school. Clearly you must have more pressing matters at hand."

"I was trying to imagine what it must be like there... In New York, I mean."

"The Fates willing, you may just find yourself there one day, Eve...Evelyn," Quentin corrected himself. "Meantime, it appears you've got some homework," he said, pushing the new camera box toward her.

It was almost dark when Eve left the office. She hurried out the front and took in a lung-full of cool evening air before she ran out behind the office.

She'd left Charlie all day, and without his afternoon feed, but she didn't stop to feed him even then.

She would need to ride like lightning if she was going to get home before Catharyn got there. She was not ready for the conversation that would inevitably come. Why was she working? Where was she working? Why ever on earth did she want to be a man? God is just as pleased with women as he is with men. And then the ultimate question: Who will take care of Percy?

Eve closed her book and laid it on the desk. She was restless; waiting, though for what, she could not say.

She listened closely, between the sounds of Catharyn, in the kitchen, and the low, rhythmic thrum of her father's laboured breathing from the downstairs bedroom. She listened, in between, for secrets, for the way life really was, when the veneer cast by the light of day was stripped away and the masks had fallen.

Then it came, a gentle knocking at the front door. Eve followed the sound of Catharyn's footsteps as she scuffed quietly over the floorboards. At the door, it was a man's voice alongside her stepmother's. Words were spoken in low tones, voices fractured and soft-hissing; their words rising, then falling off and melting into silence. Soon, the voices grew careless, but the voice of a stranger it was: Strange, though at times it would catch and hang on some faint chord of recognition.

Her mind reached to make sense of it. There was what seemed an unmistakable tenderness in the words between them: his, rising in bold gesture, then breaking with due respect for... Catharyn, if not for the man sleeping and sick in the next room.

Her voice, in reply, was set at ease falling, slithering, then soft and caressing.

In her heart there began a distant rumble that pulsed and spread downward into the pit of her stomach. And then there was the gentle break: a feeling that would stay with her, but would shrink back when it seemed things were good; would roar to life - a fiery demon in her heart that would not leave as long as she lived.

She pushed the chair carefully away, and crept to the door. She

78

pressed her face against the wall to see into the kitchen, but was careful not to touch the door for its creaking, thirsty hinges.

Through the crack in the door: a sliver of grey coat, or an ear and a whisp of thin brown hair. Black trousers and well-kept shoes. She pressed her face into the wall and caught a glimpse of the man.

Then Catharyn came into view: her hand on his shoulder, slid down his arm; was easy where it lay.

They moved away into the living room, and there was silence.

Eve padded quietly to the bed and there waited, over the aching in her heart, for sleep to come.

She stared at the small sterling crucifix hanging from the bedpost. It had been a gift from Catharyn. She and Percy had just met, and things were still fresh and contrived.

Just beyond the crucifix, sitting atop the desk, was the wooden lock box her father had made for her, before he became too sick to hold on to his tools. She picked up the key resting there on the lid. She dangled it from its string, before sliding it into the lock. Inside, the box was lined perfectly with blood-red silk. Two small shelves and several compartments were all mostly empty, save one that held a doll in miniature, made from intricately woven dry grass. She made the doll when she was ten. The doll was her, and she kept it locked safely in the box, so that, no matter what happened, part of her would always be safe.

She closed the lid again, then opened it once more. She snatched the crucifix from the bedpost and dropped it into the box. She closed the lid and turned the key.

It was true that the things she had allowed herself to love most had caused her the most pain. It was true, also, that she didn't understand the world of appearances.

Ω

THE MANHUNT
FOR
ELI THOMAS

Dulce bellum inexpurtis

✝

War is sweet to the inexperienced

BC Provincial Police Superintendent, Red Sutherland, threw
the saddle over his horse. The horse shifted and pawed the ground, her
breath pluming in the frigid morning air. Red stroked her side with
one hand as he cinched the saddle tight with the other. He had hand-
picked her from the Police stock yards in Calgary. He'd helped out a
fellow officer at one time, and she was his re-payment.

He tested the saddle.

The distant sound of horses broke through the draw. He watched
his men emerge from the trees into the open pasture at the bottom-
north end of his property. Bob Gentry was leading with his quarter
horse, and Charlie Morgan was close at hand with the others trying to
make up time. In moments they had all hit the service road. Red could
see the whites of the horse's eyes as they sprung every bit of muscle
and fibre to take the hill. He'd chosen four of the regulars, men he
knew were good for the job, and another seven reservists, in case the
situation became unpredictable.

Red slid his foot into the stirrup and swung into the saddle. He
snapped the reins sharply and the still air was shattered with the

thunder of hooves pounding earth.

The Salish Village of Si'yat sen was fifteen miles south-west of Vananda. They would arrive mid-morning and make the arrest when the men returned from the fishing weirs.

A mile north of the village, Red stopped where a narrow trail broke off to the right, and motioned Gentry to join him at the front. "You, Pierce and Johnston take the trail," He said quietly. "Flank the village from the south-west," he said, nodding toward the path, "And try to keep out of sight. The rest of us'll come in top-side, ahead of you. If they see us and decide to run, you may be able to catch 'em off guard. If they run down-island, we can cover both sides, push 'em back toward Pocahontas. Keep a steady pace; we'll watch for you."

As they neared the village, the faded grey peaks of clapboard houses flashed through the trees. Red hadn't counted on the forest thinning so suddenly, and hoped the poor cover wouldn't eliminate the element of surprise. He slowed his horse. The others followed his lead. As they broke through the sparse tree line at the outskirts of the village, Red signalled his men to spread out along the ridge. He wanted to make clear to their prey that the decision to run would be a costly one.

The horsemen crested a small hill to find Chief Israel Tomas standing at the trail-mouth, at the edge of town, as if he had been expecting them. Surprise flashed briefly in Red's eyes - a fleeting shadow, like a darting crow in the periphery. Behind Chief Tomas, the streets were deserted. He had come out alone, as a measure of sincerity, to show that he intended everything would go smoothly.

Red stopped his horse in front of the chief, a little closer than he ought.

"Officer Sutherland. To what do I owe the pleasure? Was the meal we served on your last visit so well received you decided to bring your friends?" he smiled widely.

"I need to speak with Eli." Red's face was stony. His eyes shifted from the Chief to the other side of the village, where Gentry and his men would be waiting inside the tree line.

"A good friend of mine," Chief Tomas started, "a white man called Judge Allan Mulgrew, once said that any man who comes to the dance with his gun loaded expects to do more than just dance. How many men does it take to have this conversation?"

"There's been a murder, Chief, and I believe Eli and his boys were involved."

Chief Tomas grunted and met Sutherland's hardened stare. A few moments passed in silence, only the sound of shifting leather and pacing hooves.

"You're certain Eli has something to do with it?"

Red's horse canted, pulling at the reigns. "We found his boat less than a mile from the body, the bottom stained with blood. Eli's knife was also recovered nearby." Red held up the hunting blade and watched the flash of recognition fall upon Chief Tomas' face: the unmistakable blue raven carved into the deer antler handle – Eli's own handy work.

"This is a problem," he said pensively. "Who has been killed?"

"Ernie Tsan."

Pain flickered in the old Chief's eyes, and Red could see that he understood the significance of it.

"Shouldn't John West have come?" he said, his own face now grave and drawn.

"There is no time for formalities. The sooner you round them up, the better. No-one needs to get hurt."

"We don't want any trouble," the chief insisted. "There are children. Let me talk to the boys. They will come in to see you. They will do the right thing. You have my word."

"I'm under orders to bring him in, Chief Tomas. Him and Edward Jack and Jim Charlie - I won't go back empty-handed!"

Chief Tomas looked toward the village and lifted his hand. A man appeared from a small house that stood nearby and approached him. The Chief leaned in close and relayed a message in Salish dialect. The man went quickly back to the village.

"Your lawmakers say that there must be good reason to believe someone has done something wrong," said Chief Tomas. "My ears hear what you say, but my heart does not. Our relationship has been strained these past years, you and I. But I do not want any harm to come to the women and the children. I will call the men you seek."

Then, without warning, a gunshot split the morning. The fabric of time itself seemed to freeze as the shot rang through the valley and rolled across the ocean; to the mountain range, on the mainland, where it cracked off the mountains there too. At once, Gentry and his men came into plain view at the other side of the village. Gentry had his rifle levelled at the tree-line to the south. Red followed the sight line and spotted three figures plunging into the trees. He snapped the reigns to give chase, narrowly missing Chief Tomas as he stormed past. His men followed close behind. They tore through the village to gain on the three fugitives. In no time, they had closed in on the place where they had disappeared. There was no trail, just dense undergrowth among the sparse forest. Gentry and the others fell in beside Red.

"Are you sure that was them?" Red snapped.

"I'm sure," Gentry said.

Red had little reason to doubt him. He was as sharp as they come, ex-American military from the recent Indian Wars, and well trained as a sharp-shooter.

"Check your rifles."

Eleven breeches snapped open and closed. The men sat a little straighter, their eyes burning with intent.

Red surveyed the forest. The horses would be no good in the thick underbrush.

"Everyone but McFee and Johnston, tie your horses. McFee and Johnston, take the trail on the lee side of the island. Morgan and Hughes, you take the shoreline trail to the west and follow it down-island to the draw, to push them out onto the old road. They're on foot, so pace yourselves. The rest of us will spread out along the tree line and move in. If they take the west side of the Island we'll funnel 'em to the beach where we can overtake 'em.

"I want Eli alive."

"What about the others?" Robert Morgan asked.

"They sealed their fate the minute they took up with Eli," Red smouldered.

With his long legs, Red held point and kept easily ahead of the others. Eli was fast on his feet and would be making good time, but with men on either side pushing shoreward, there was little hope of escape. The plateau would eventually drop into steep, untraversable rock bluff about a quarter mile to the left. To the right, the flats ran for the better part of a mile to the base of the foothills, after which rose the steep, rocky coast line – nothing doing, even for an Indian.

By late afternoon they had covered a lot of ground, but there was still no sign of the fugitives. The ground was thick with Salal, and, despite the cool air, the men's faces were glistening with sweat. Red held up his hand, signalling for them to fall back. He made his way to the top of a nearby bluff. A stiff south-easterly breeze kicked up. There was a strong salt tang in the air telling him they were getting close to the western shore.

They started out again and soon the terrain sloped downward, signaling the long, slow descent to the water. Now and again the ocean appeared between the trees. They were getting close, though still with no sign of the wanted men. Red let out a sharp whistle, and the men who were still in sight stopped dead. He strained to hear against the sounds of the forest; the light breeze brushing the pine tops, a raven calling hoarsely some way off, the steady sound of the tide washing the heat off the rocky shore.

Up ahead, something flashed through the trees. Red waved his men onward, quickening his pace. Another movement, closer this time. Red dropped to his knees so he was almost entirely hidden in the salal. It was Eli's friend, Eddie Jack, hiding behind an Arbutus, statue like, framed by the orange-brown of the shedding tree. Red saw his shoulders tense, as if he knew he'd been spotted. He turned slowly, peering around the tree trunk, scanning the forest for his enemy. Suddenly, he shot to his feet and darted into the deeper brush. In a flash, Red levelled the rifle. As he watched Jack down the barrel, through the buck-horn sights, a feeling just short of admiration rose in his chest for the man he was about to shoot. He had spotted Red so quickly despite his thick cover. Red took a deep breath and slowly exhaled, his finger squeezed the trigger. The powerful blast tore into Eddie's back and out through his chest, lifting him forward off his feet and throwing him violently to the forest floor.

Red caught up with his men who were pushing down to the

shoreline. One by one they stepped onto the rocky beach. Gentry was the first to spot Eli. He had run to the end of the island and dove straight into the ocean, intending to swim for the mainland. He would likely have already been out of reach if it weren't for the growing swell and a rising tide.

Then, some way down the shore, there was the faint sound of rocks clicking against one another. It was the third wanted man, Jim Charlie, doing his level best to try for the water. A moment later, Johnston and McFee emerged from the trees on horseback, a short distance behind Jim. The two quickly lashed their horses to a dead-fall.

Red took a quick head count of his men.

"Where's Wiebe?"

"Nobody's seen 'im yet."

Jim stopped at the water's edge to strip off his shirt. Red nodded at Darcy. Darcy levelled his rifle, tracking Jim's movements from left to right. He squeezed the trigger and the man fell hard among the rocks. He reloaded the Sharps Single Shot and turned the sights seaward.

"There he is," Robertson yelled.

Darcy brought the gun to bear on Eli, now some 100 yards off shore. He eased his finger into the trigger, where a faint tell he'd grown accustomed to, whispered that the next stop was all about business. Eli dropped into a breaking swell.

"Wait for it... Just enough to slow him down," Red ordered, "we want him alive.

The shot rang out, and an explosion of water and foam spouted skyward. They waited, watching the water intently. Then Eli appeared again, still swimming madly among the waves. Red raised his eyebrows at Darcy, who'd he'd not seen miss a shot since joining the force five years previously.

"Son-of-a-bitch," cursed Darcy as he reloaded his gun. He found Eli again down the barrel of the gun. After the smoke and water had cleared, Eli lay still on the surface, drifting with the waves.

"Hutchinson! Go in and secure the prisoner."

Red had Eli Tomas on foot, bound between two of the horses. The bodies of Eddie Jack and Jim Charlie were slung over the last horse in the line. It was during the ride back the the way they'd come, Red Sutherland's men discovered the body of reservist, Foster Wiebe. They found him lying in a fern grotto, his throat cut from ear to ear.

Up ahead, they could see the streets of the Village, now lined with people, intent on watching their progress through town, the bodies of their dead draped unceremoniously over the horses. Red dismounted in front of Chief Tomas and loosened the rope that fastened Eddie and Jim to the train, and let them fall.

The Chief stared at Red, his face expressionless. It was in the faces and in the eyes of the young men who closed around them that hatred seethed. But despite their hatred, each remained silent. Chief Tomas held up his hand, signalling that no tear would be shed for their sons and their fathers, whom they could do nothing to help.

Red knew they would not weep in front of the whites. They would not give them the satisfaction of seeing their pain.

Ω

An Unexpected Visit

Obscurum per obscurius

وٌ

*The obscure by the
more obscure*

Eve rested her hand on the door of the Coast Miner. Through the door pane she watched Quentin inspect a test sheet he had just run through the newly erected press.

He peered over his glasses at her as she walked in, letting her know, with certainty, that he was nonplussed.

"Ernie Tsan," He said, finally breaking the uncomfortable silence.

Eve stared questioningly.

"The fella that washed up on the beach. His name was Ernie Tsan. Worked at the Paymaster mine on the North End. Married to a squaw named Heidi, formerly Heidi Tomas, of the Salish Village, at Shelter Point."

Eve's jaw clenched and she motioned toward the door.

"Where you off to so fast?"

"To see Charlie Porter."

"Don't go stompin' the chicken yard just yet, Evelyn. I didn't hear it from Sutherland and his boys." Quentin set the sheet on the workbench. "Clay Grierson here," he said, indicating to the coat rack behind her, "says Ernie was a friend of his."

A man stepped awkwardly from between the open door and the coat rack, wringing his hat with his hands.

"My apologies. I didn't see you standing there."

"After you left last night," Quentin continued, "I got to thinking about how Porter tried to put the run on you at the jail. Frankly, I think the law here is just too damn spoiled from running this town blank slate all these years. I even laid awake mulling over where to start digging. Well. As it turns out, I arrive here this morning to find Mr. Grierson waiting on the doorstep." Quentin crossed his arms and nodded politely at Grierson.

Eve put her hands on her hips and glared at Quentin.

"You're like the Goddess scorned, Evelyn. Don't waste your time. When your source falls at your feet you best strike while the iron is hot. Every second you wait, is a moment Clay here could talk himself out of it. Worse yet, he might make the mistake of spilling it to someone who should not be trusted."

My story, I'll do the striking, Eve fumed to herself.

"Apparently, there was some kind of mess, because Heide'd married a white man," Quentin explained. "That'd be Tsan of course. The story has it the husband was pushing for white status for his bride," Quentin explained. "-or something like it. The Government agent here in Vananda wouldn't touch it, so a magistrate from Vancouver championed the cause – probably looking to make a name for himself. That was last Spring. Is that about right Clay?" He said suddenly, which seemed to put the man on the spot.

"The Indians out there on the reserve didn't like it much," Clay almost whispered, still wringing his hat. He cleared his throat and tried to stand a little straighter. "Some of 'em was pissed off she'd go and do like she'd done."

"So there's your story," Quentin said. "Fighting for white status, community opposes integration, possible bigotry. The husband turns up dead."

"So if the police aren't talking, where does that leave us?" Eve asked. "We still need to separate fact from fiction. And frankly it seems like all we've got is guesswork. You'd have a hard time believing the stories that are already floating around."

"I'd believe it all right. It's the nature of the beast. As for our source on this one – outside of Mr. Grierson, of course - that's where we'll have to earn our vittles. At least we have something to go on... Something solid."

Eve smiled at Clay. He smiled awkwardly in return.

Quentin thanked Clay for coming in to the office and saw him to the door.

"You and Mr. Tsan were friends?" Eve said, just as he was about to leave.

"Friends. That's right," he nodded once.

"Hmmmn," Eve bit the inside of her mouth. "Listen," she said at last. "I'm on my way out. Can I give you a lift?"

"Sure. A ride'd be good. I been walking a lot, of late, due to my horse gone and broke its leg in a hole one of the shitty neighbour kids dug in my field," he explained as they walked to the wagon.

Eve stifled a laugh. "Where is it you're headed?"

"Goin' to work… Out at the Paymaster. Usually get a mile or two along the road north 'fore a wagon 'ats comin' or goin' picks me up."

Eve brought Charlie from his tether and hitched him to the wagon. Once Clay was properly settled, she climbed in and snapped the reigns.

"You ever meet Heidi Tsan?" she asked.

"Couple times. After the two of 'em got married, Ernie pretty much kep' to hisself. Always had some excuse or another and all kindza reasons why not. More often it happened he'd meet us at the beer parlor, or at my shack to play some cards."

"Did he talk much about her? You must have been curious what she was like?"

"He didn't say much about 'er. At first we kind 'a wondered why he tried to keep it quiet. But it pretty much jus' got ol' and we stopped wonderin' about it."

"Maybe he just wanted to protect her... I mean, with her family being angry that she married a white man," she said, glancing at him.

Clay gazed on ahead, his eyes fixed on a single point, with a mind as pure and unaffected as a blinking toad.

"Do you think she might have been in danger? Is that why he

would have kept everyone away?"

"Could as might," he said shrugging.

As they broke from the edge of town and entered the forest, a light breeze brushed through the trees sending a handful of yellow leaves to settle on the dirt road. A passing gust swept them dutifully from their path.

From up ahead, a loud crash signalled the approach of an oncoming wagon. Another crash, closer now, then the wagon careened around the corner up ahead and stormed toward them. Eve pulled Charlie quickly to the roadside. It was a load of men coming from the mines, most of them staring straight ahead, as Clay had done a few moments before. A few of the younger men flashed white toothy smiles from beneath their blackened faces.

"At's a supply lorry from the Northrop," Clay explained. "Our competition for the most part."

As the wagon drew farther away, the silence returned to the country road. It seemed to Eve that the further they went down the path, the more withdrawn Clay became. He was soon muttering one word answers and avoiding eye contact.

Clay Grierson, it seemed, had given all the information he intended to give.

Eve resigned herself to managing the wagon.

"I suppose if you were that curious you'd just go on up to Ernie's farm and ask Heidi yerself."

"Mmmhmmm," Eve nodded, trying not to let her excitement show.

"When yer done takin' me as far as you're gonna, come on back to this here," he said pointing to a narrow side-road that broke off from the main. "The Tsan farm's 'bout two miles that-a-way. Round then you wanna' be lookin' for another path. The road to their place'll be on yer right. Can't miss it. Big old Maple marks it, right as rain."

A short while later Clay put his hand up. "This'll do," he said. "The late morning lorry'll be coming on by. I'll hitch with them. You can turn 'round in that clearing," he said nodding to a point presumably just down the road, but, as yet, unseen by her own eyes.

He thanked her for the ride and tramped down the road, his long

90

arms swinging at his sides.

The big Maple tree was exactly where Clay had promised. Its trunk was two feet through, and the tree itself looked out of place among the lodge-pole pine and cedar. Eve pulled the wagon into a large clearing that was littered with weathered grey stumps, left behind after the forest was razed to make room for the Clemens' homestead.

She brought Charlie to a halt and sat still in the wagon a few moments longer, to see whether anyone would greet her. A fleeting image drifted across her line of sight: Ernie and Heidi cutting trees and shackling them to the horses; breaking roots from the ground, hoisting rocks from the soil to be piled for walls or foundation; tilling the land where a large garden plot now lay - just the two of them making their way.

Across the field, at the North end of the property, the house was well built, and stood on level ground. A good veranda ran across the front and along one side. Behind the house, a large barn with its gambrel roof stood with stern determination against the trees, its sides still faint yellow, betraying that it was a recent addition. Eve dismounted and strung Charlie's lead to an apple tree in front of the deck, where he could pick wind-falls from the ground.

A creek cut through the property and split the pasture before dropping down into a depression in the field and disappearing into the trees behind the barn. To the right, a small bridge, just wide enough to accommodate a wagon, traversed the creek.

With the wagon stowed, and Charlie munching windfalls, Eve fast became aware of the uneasy tension that had settled over everything. A stiff breeze blew in across the field. Branches stirred and clicked against one another above her in the old Maple. It was as if the promise of something good still hung here, but by mere threads, and now, even what hope might remain, was exhaling its last breath.

She stepped onto the porch and rapped her knuckles on the heavy, rough-cut door. The house was still.

She gathered all of the self-respect she could muster and peered into a window.

A soft stream of light pushed between the curtains, into the dim interior. A small table lay on its back, its legs reaching skyward in a state of absolute surrender. An empty rocking chair seemed to think that it might remain in that very place for an eternity. Further inside, almost hidden in shadow, she could make out a dining table. Most homesteads had only the kitchen table, proper: no dining table to speak of. With most families – everyone she knew - this was a luxury to be revered. Atop the table, she could see what must have been a stack of papers that were now mostly scattered across the floor.

She backed away from the window and stood at the edge of the porch. She scoured the property, took care, every now and again, to peer into the shadows at the edge of the forest. Then, from somewhere not far off, came a soft thud.

She glanced back at Charlie, who bit an apple in half and stopped chewing.

"Where is she, Charlie?" His ears perked as he stared at the barn doors.

The thud sounded again. She walked to the side of the house and edged toward the large loading doors at the front of the barn. Her legs suddenly felt like lead weights: they seemed to know that she ought to be heading in the opposite direction: her body's response to the mind's ambition. Self-preservation was paramount.

As she drew near, she saw that one of the doors was slightly ajar. She glanced back at Charlie, who replied by reaching for another sweet apple. "You'd let me know if there was trouble, right?" She said, wishing she could read the horses thoughts as she disappeared behind the house.

"Anyone home?" Eve knocked on the framework surrounding the door.

She pulled the door open and stood back, ready for God knows what. A gust of hot air escaped the barn into open sky. After a moment she stepped forward, peering into the dimly lit interior, waiting for her eyes to adjust. Inside smelled richly of cattle and dust and warm hay.

A loud shuffle erupted from one of the stalls. She drew closer to the source, her feet now all but scuffing through the hay on the dirt floor. Her imagination threatened to run astray with images of Heidi bound and gagged and slow-cooking in the heat of the barn.

Her fingers found purchase atop the stall door and she peered inside, her heart thumping loudly in her ears, her breath coming fast and shallow. Her searching eyes were met with the moist, limpid stare of a young Holstein. The cow paused, amid a long, slow stroke of its massive tongue to stir the flies that had settled about its nose. It continued to stare at her impassively. She exhaled deeply, had not even been aware she was holding her breath.

"Whew," she said aloud, and promptly berated herself for the noise.

A dead give-away.

She checked each of the stalls and counted a horse, two milk cows, and a calf.

Eve had to stop herself speaking to the poor beasts, partly to soothe them, partly to soothe herself.

Every stall had been picked clean of fresh hay. The troughs were dry.

She laid her hand on the Gelding. The horse nosed her impatiently sensing the prospect of food. Two large pails that hung on the wall at the front of the barn would serve the pump she'd seen sprouting from a tuft of tall grass near the creek.

She winced when the bucket clanged against the wall despite her best efforts.

Once out in the sunlight again, she set out across the open field, noting her vulnerability increased with every step. *If anything were to come, it'd come now.*

She forced herself to draw long, slow breaths.

Again she scoured the shadows at the tree line. There was nothing to speak of but the gentle stirring of the breeze in the glowing tree-tops.

Her feet sank into soggy earth as she neared the pump. She purged the handle and got nothing but air. She pumped several more times. When she was about ready to admit defeat, her last attempt brought fresh water spilling freely from the spigot.

The animals were already waiting at their respective troughs when Eve returned to the barn. However, as each trough was filled, they opted against good form, nosing past her and plunging deep into the water, to take as much cool liquid as endurance would allow.

She climbed an old wood ladder to the loft and found good, dry hay in bales stacked four deep against the back wall. She broke open two bales and dropped several quarters through the loft opening, which proceeded to break open as they hit the ladder on the way down. She cautiously descended the ladder. When she stepped from the bottom rung, her heart lept into her throat: the sun was in her eyes. She'd been sure to close the doors when she came back with the water... Leave everything as it was - she'd been thinking it from the moment she'd arrived.

She looked desperately toward the door and was blinded by a flash of bright sunlight. A clipped scream escaped her lips. There, directly in front of her, was a man. A very large man. In fact, this was quite possibly a man of giant proportions. He stood directly in front of her, silhouetted by the light streaming in behind him. Instinctively she stepped backward, almost tripping over the ladder. The man stepped toward her, and she could see he had a rifle. It seemed a toy in his monstrous hands.

"Who are you?" Came a deep, booming voice."

"Evelyn Walker. I don't mean to intrude –

"You are trespassing."

He was a Salish Indian.

"I came to see Heidi Tsan," she almost pleaded, then took a moment to calm herself.

"And when you seen she was not here you should have left."

"I heard something here in the barn... I thought it was her."

The man looked past Eve at the stalls. She watched his eyes take in the fresh hay and the water.

"Come outside."

Eve's nerves bristled again.

The man stood aside and directed her to go on ahead, but he followed close behind.

When she was clear of the barn she turned to face him.

He was the largest man – white or Indian – she'd ever seen. His square jaw was set, his deep brown eyes piercing – probably a violent man... Yet, she sensed what she hoped was a profound tendency toward calm.

She forced a nervous smile.

"Is it normal for people from the paper to snoop around somebody's place uninvited?"

How does he know I'm with the paper?

She swallowed hard.

"I saw that the animals had not been fed, and, considering what's happened…"

He stared at her, his eyes cold and unreadable.

For a moment neither of them spoke. There was only the breeze rushing through the trees, and the creek trickling nearby.

After a moment his grip seemed to loosen on the gun.

"You're absolutely right. I apologize for the intrusion. Please, when you see Heidi, just tell her that I'd like to speak with her. I can be reached at the office of the Coast Miner Newspaper, in Vananda."

"I know where to find you," he said unflinchingly, his eyes piercing her very soul.

A gust of wind rolled again across the tree tops.

Suddenly the man brought his gun close. He cocked his head, listening intently. Eve could hear nothing but the branches clicking in the treetops. Somewhere, off in the deep recesses of the rain forest, a council of crows strategized.

Her eyes combed the shadows again. If this giant man was startled by something it would likely be a prudent measure to pay attention.

"Did you come alone?" He asked.

Eve nodded. "Just the horse."

"Then you should leave," he insisted. "It is not safe here."

"Not safe?"

The man started toward the forest, his footsteps catlike upon the blanket of dead grass and leaves covering the earth.

"Is Heidi in some kind of trouble?"

The man did not answer, and, in a moment had disappeared from sight into the trees behind the barn.

Ω

OBLIGATION

Serva me, servabo te
petronius arbiter

ß

Save me, and I will save you

It was dusk when Eve returned home to find Dr. Alston's buggy in the drive. Behind it was the closed carriage he used to transport patients to and from the hospital. She rushed into the house, afraid of what she might find, her mind pitched with guilt.

Catharyn sat at the kitchen table cradling a cup of tea in her hands.

"Where the hell were ya?" She said, her eyes smouldering. "You were supposed to be 'ere with 'im." The kettle was steaming on the stove, a half-peeled pot of potatoes stood on the counter, peels sticking to the sides of the white porcelain sink.

Eve could hear the calming lull of Dr. Alston's voice in her father's bedroom.

Catharyn picked a slip of paper from the table and held it up. "Woulda been nice to know you were workin' at the newspaper. Then I coulda' got someone ere that'd care enough to do right by yer father." She glared, holding a cheque from Quentin in her hands. Evelyn was careful not to say anything to ignite Catharyn's temper. For now she would simply listen.

"Nice of 'im to bring it by for ya," Catharyn baited.

Eve nodded slowly.

"Hmmppffhh," Catharyn huffed mildly.

"Point is it shouldn't be someone else come into our 'ome and tendin' to 'is needs. Should be you Evelyn." Catharyn's eyes welled. For a moment it seemed she would cry. Then she scowled and, with both hands, tore the cheque in two.

"If 'ee should die, you'll have 'is blood on your hands," she hissed.

Evelyn's face grew hot. It took every ounce of willpower not to challenge her, to say what had been on her mind all this time: '*where had she been through her father's sickness?* It was only *after* he had come home from the mines, unable to work, that Catharyn had been suddenly called to the service of the church. She would leave every morning and not arrive home again until the day was well over.

Eve steadied herself. "Right or wrong Dad needs us right now. Let's let him have his peace."

"Peace of mind?" Catharyn challenged, her voice rising. "What peace of mind could 'ee 'ave knowing your out chasin' a fool's dream – pursuin' a man's job no less, surrounded by men all day long like some hussy in a bawdy house. What do you think people are sayin' Eve? You out there mindin' the affairs of men. It's not proper."

Eve boiled now. The nerve of her. Her and her stuffy Scottish upbringing. This was Canada, and things were different here.

"*And where were you stepmother?*" Eve whispered, unable to keep silent any longer.

Catharyn looked incredulous.

"You haven't lifted a finger for father since he got sick," Eve said, louder now. "Convenient for you to lay the responsibility at my feet. You preach about my duties as a woman. What are yours then? You spend your entire day in town not giving a thought -"

"*God's work* Evelyn Day!" her stepmother growled. "It's God's work I busy myself with…"

At that moment Doctor Alston came out of father's bedroom and closed the door gently behind him. For a moment he stood between the two of them, looking from one to the other.

"I understand this is a difficult time ladies," he said walking further into the room. "I'm the last to interfere with family business, but I think the situation warrants my saying you two need to work out your differences on your own time. What Percy needs right now is for you *both* to be supportive." Catharyn pulled the tea cup into her hands again and stared at the table.

"How is he doing?" Eve asked.

"His condition has worsened, I'm afraid. We know that someone with his condition is sensitive to the weather. As you well know it's been unusually cold and damp for late summer, which suggests to me a poor fall is on the way. Long and short of it is he'll have to be taken to the infirmary where we can do more for him. I'm afraid there's no way out of it ladies... For the short term anyway. We'll see how it goes whether he can come back home."

Evelyn could feel things spinning out of control. A tide of guilt washed through her. She had always known the day would come he would no longer be able to stay here at home. She had always tried to push it to the back of her mind.

Again she steadied herself.

She would busy herself with what needed doing, to keep her mind from delving too deeply. She slipped into Percy's room and pulled a large leather handbag from the closet. She started folding his clothes and placing them with infinite care into the bag. When that was done, she assisted Doctor Alston in securing Percy for the trip and helped Dr. Alston carry the stretcher to the buggy.

Eve watched her father's face as they passed under the porch light. His eyes were closed, and every breath racked his body with obvious pain - pain she could almost feel in her own body.

"I've given him something to ease his discomfort. It'll help him sleep." Dr. Alston said as he got Percy settled in the wagon.

"Catharyn, will you bring Percy's bag when you come?" She nodded and went back into the house.

"No-one is to blame Eve," Dr. Alston said after Catharyn had gone. He closed the wagon doors, and laid his hand on her shoulder. "The sickness is to blame. Nothing else. Your father knows that."

"I could have done more for him."

"He has a warm bed, clean sheets, good food to eat, and he knows you love him more than anything else in this world. More, or less, of any one of those things would not have changed the outcome. The illness will run its course. The best thing we can do is try to get him through this."

Eve hugged Doctor Alston. He climbed onto the wagon and touched the brim of his hat to her.

"You'll help your stepmother bring his things along shortly then?"

Eve nodded.

Alston brought the horses to, making a wide turn in the yard before he started down the drive and disappeared into the darkness. A cold breeze rushed suddenly through the tree tops and rolled away to the East. Through the kitchen window, Eve could see her stepmother fretting and trying to think of things to pack into her father's bag.

Eve hooked Charlie to the wagon and waited for Catharyn. She appeared on the porch, her collar pulled up and looking indignant. She lifted the hem of her dress to manage the stairs. Eve offered to take the bag but Catharyn insisted on doing it all herself, all the while doing her best to make it look as though it was indeed a problem.

They settled into the wagon and Catharyn pulled her coat tightly around herself, intent on maintaining her vigil of silence.

They started down the drive, and a gust of wind bucked against the wagon and threatened to rise to a steady blow. Soon the rain would come.

Charlie plodded along the trail, his head down against the wind. The horse knew his way and could get them where they were going, even in the worst storm nature could conjure. Despite this Eve managed the reigns as though it was she who was responsible for keeping them true.

Under normal conditions the ride was long, but the dark and the wind and the rain made it seem like no time at all had passed before the lights of Vananda speckled ahead of them like stars low on the horizon.

Inside the infirmary, it was dim and silent. Somewhere down the darkened hallways an old man called out, his cries shattering the profound quiet – a brand of somber only the macabre spectre of illness could cast: the silence of men and women suffering and transfixed on clinging to the fine thread of life that might remain. A nurse approached them in the hall, her white uniform catching the light from a wall sconce nearby. She took them down the hall and showed them to Percy's room.

Lying there in the dim, grey light he looked worse than he had when he left the house. Catharyn stood at the end of the bed, unable to look at him, her fingers resting loosely on the bed rail. In a stiff voice she announced she was going to see if the resident Chaplain was in.

The nurse leaned over the bed, checked Percy's pulse, checked his forehead for fever, before fixing his blankets. After she left the room, Eve went to his bedside and took his hand into hers. It felt cold. She held it gently between her own hands, trying to warm him. He might have smiled faintly and squeezed her fingers. Then an unmistakable ease did come faintly to his lips.

"I should not have left you today," Eve whispered. Her father struggled against the medicine to open his eyes. He blinked at Eve. He motioned to a glass of water on the bedside table. Eve brought it to his lips and helped him to drink.

"Your stepmother means well, Eve," Her father whispered. "She has her own way of showing it." He stopped to catch his breath and struggled to sit up.

"Just rest father. Save your strength."

Percy eased himself back into the pillow and took more water.

"With her, tradition is everything Eve. Her father was a stern believer of ultimate penance for one's sins. Better to walk through the briar patch then take the path worn round it." His chest rumbled and he erupted into a fit of coughing. Eve helped him sit forward and rubbed his back until he settled.

"You do what calls you," he said, squeezing her hand. "If God throws a golden path at your feet, who are we to question it? There's nothing..." He struggled to catch his breath, "...I want more for you than to... live your life... doing what seems right. Otherwise, I've worked my hands to the bone for nothing..." His words came slower now. He paused again to fill his lungs with air. "You've given more than I ever would have asked of you. Now you have your life ahead of you. That is what we do for our children, Evelyn. Mine is spent," He paused, his eyes drooping. "No matter what – what happens, Eve... Be patient with her."

Eve caressed her father's forehead as he settled back into the pillow and at once fell into a deep sleep. She was uneasy how fast it had overcome him. To be certain, she left his bedside to find Doctor Alston. She spotted a nurse speaking with two policemen in the hallway. One of the constables stood aside and let the nurse into the room.

Eve approached the officers but didn't recognize either of them. She started into the room after the nurse. One of the officers threw his arm up blocking her way, "You can't go in there."

"I need a nurse," Eve shot back, ducking under his arm.

One of the men followed her into the room and seized her by the arm, but not before she got a good look at what was being guarded there. A young Indian woman sat in a chair bedside a patient. Another Indian – a young man – lay there, staring at Eve, his eyes cutting into her from where he lay. Her mind shot to conclusion: this was Eli Tomas, the man she'd heard Sutherland's men had captured. And, though she had never met Heidi Tsan, if what Norman Hainsey had said was true, Eve was certain it was her.

"Young lady! I demand you stop where you are, or be arrested here and now."

The nurse looking over the young man's bandaged arms looked up impatiently, "Can I help you?"

"I think something's wrong with my father. He's just down the hall." Eve looked again at Heidi, her eyes were big and dark. She saw strength and wisdom there, but her gaze betrayed fear and uncertainty too.

The nurse let out a sigh of frustration and left what she was doing to show Eve out of the room. "Show me where your father's at then."

"Why the police at the door?" Eve asked once they'd left the room.

"Not at liberty to say. Unless you're family. And you don't look a bit like it." The nurse said dryly.

The information was right there, no more than three feet away.

Still, she thought better of pursuing the matter just then.

At Percy's bedside, the nurse laid two fingers against his throat. His breathing had slowed into a shallow, steady rhythm. She lifted his forearm and rested her fingers against his wrist.

"He's doing just fine," she said, the edge gone from her voice. "It's the medication taking hold. He should sleep through the night." With that, she turned on her heel and left the room again.

Eve slipped the extra pillows from behind her father's head and pulled the woollen blankets up around his chest. It was a stroke of incredible luck to have Heidi Tomas just down the hall. She would not pass this opportunity to introduce herself. She would get the story from Heidi first-hand.

With the immediate threat to her father abated, Eve left the room to explore her options. Both officers watched coldly as she drew near. The taller of the two shifted his stance so that he was directly blocking the entrance. Eve ignored him and simply strolled past the room to the next hallway where she'd spotted a trolley stacked with fresh sheets and towels. Heidi and Eli were just on the other side of the thin wall. She strained to hear what was being said. Heidi and the young man spoke in whispered voices, at times Heidi's voice rising, becoming desperate. They were speaking in their native Salish language. But it was as if she were pleading with him, and that he would not give in. She became adamant but got no reply. She then insisted, her voice eloquent and sonorous as she spoke fluently in their native tongue.

Then the young man raised his voice in anger.

"That'll be enough a that," one of the officers barked. "If you want to talk here you'll use English."

"I would not trade my life for the life of a white man!" The young man spoke aloud to the officer. "If I were the one to kill him I would not hide from what I had done..."

Heidi started in trying to keep her voice low: "I will go to father and ask him to help us."

"You are not welcome in the village."

"Eli you must help. I do not know what to do," Her voice desperate again.

"You have made your choice, and now you must live by it. I will

102

be tested by the white man's law, and I will die by white man's law. The elders cannot help me."

"Why do you not look at me?" she pleaded.

"You have chosen to walk among them, and our father has said that now no-one can be trusted. And he is right. Do you see what has happened? I will die because of your decision. They cannot be trusted, and now you must live as one of them."

"Take what you need and move along." Eve was startled to see the taller of the two officers standing directly behind her in the hall. She was swept up by the conversation. She pulled a folded bed-sheet and several towels from the trolley into her arms. The conversation was lost behind her as she carried them back to her father's room. She placed the lot on a chair beside his bed. She dipped a cloth into a small tub of cold water and wrung and folded it neatly, placing it on her father's forehead.

Heidi had been exiled from her village. So it was that the story went much deeper than she had first thought. The adventure of it ran excitedly through her, but there was caution as well. Something she did not understand. Something dangerous.

She would need to get to Heidi, somehow.

Heidi would likely leave the hospital at some point. There was no other bed in the room occupied by her brother, and it was clear the young man did not want her by his side. Eve left at a run to the front entrance of the infirmary. She would stand there and wait for Heidi to leave.

When she came into the foyer it was her stepmother standing by the front doors, staring out the window, watching absently as the rain dripped from the awning. She stood behind her, watching her reflection in the glass.

"How is 'ee?" Catharyn asked in little more than a whisper.

"Asleep."

Silence hung between them.

"'Ee may not come home," Catharyn said.

Again, silence.

When Eve finally spoke, it was to ask if she'd heard from Doctor Alston.

Catharyn nodded.

"It just doesn't seem fair. He's still so young."

"Doctor says it's workin' in them mines that did it to 'im. The damp and the dust. That and smoking tobacco don't help any."

They had never spoken about her father's illness; both had always believed it would pass, just as so many others had through the years.

"He did what he 'ad to do. That's what he always says anyway. His father before him, and his father before that – both worked the mines at Clipstone. They all did what they 'ad to do. That's all any of us can isn't it?"

She turned to look at Eve, her face, for a moment, had lost its edge.

Then something flickered in the glass.

In the reflection Eve watched Heidi whisk past and slip out the front doors into the rain.

Eve left Catharyn standing there, and ran through the doors after her.

"Heidi Tsan?" Eve called out.

Heidi stopped at the top of the stairs. In the light from the door, Eve could see she'd been crying.

"Please, wait a moment." Eve turned to Catharyn. "I'm sorry, I need to speak with her."

Catharyn threw her chin up, and strode back into the hospital, toward Percy's room.

Eve let the door fall closed, watching Catharyn for a moment longer through the glass.

Ω

A MATTER
OF
TRUST

Amicus certus
in re incerta

℘

A sure friend in an
unsure matter

Eve held the lantern to light the path ahead of them. The air was heavy and damp, and the wind blew hard and steady from the south. It snapped at Charlie's mane and pulled at her own rain-soaked clothes.

Overhead, slender cedar branches snapped against the failing canvas of light. An angry gust whipped through the trees and funnelled down the trail, slamming into the side of the wagon. The lantern flickered and went out.

"It's just ahead now," Heidi spoke beneath the wind in a voice that, to Eve, seemed strangely calm for her young years, as though life had already thrown its worst at her and she'd come through it for the better.

The dense forest gave way to a clearing, and the air around them lifted. Up ahead she could make out the house and the barn, both darkened silhouettes against the rain-soaked forest.

"Stay on the road," Heidi said firmly, enough to imply she knew her business and expected the same of Eve.

Eve rolled to a stop in front of the house.

"Your horse can stay in the barn," Heidi said, stepping from the wagon. "You'll find grain and water in barrels, in the empty stall at the front." she said.

Eve was careful not let on she knew her way around a little. She led Charlie to the barn and struggled to work the door latch. The front door of the house slammed closed, and there soon came a flicker of warm light from the windows. Soon Heidi arrived carrying a fresh lantern. She nudged Eve away from the door and struck the latch swiftly. She heaved the door open against the wind and waited until Eve and Charlie were safely inside before letting it fall closed again.

She hung the lantern from a beam overhead, so the room was properly lit.

"Put him in the empty stall there," Heidi said. "There is a tub at the back with water. There should be a bucket."

Eve pulled a dry wool blanket from the ledge and draped it over Charlie's back, to keep him from cooling too fast.

She stepped into the dark room at the back of the barn and waited a moment to let her eyes adjust. With one hand on the wall she felt her way into the room until the toe of her boot rang off a large metal tub. Eve cringed, half-expecting a scolding from her brooding friend. She knelt to search for a bucket. As her fingers combed the straw-covered floor she imagined rat droppings and skittering, hairy barn spiders, among all manner of other godless creatures. She breathed a sigh of relief as her fingers brushed the thin, cold handle of a metal water bucket. She scooped up the bucket and felt her way back to the main tub.

With the bucket full, she turned to make her way back to the well-lit room when something brushed her face. She flinched and swiped quickly at whatever it was, her imagination conjuring the worst. Water sloshed from the bucket onto her feet. Then she felt it brush her face again. This time she caught and held the thick length of rope hanging from above. She let her hand slide down the coarse braids and her fingers came to rest at the knuckle of a tight knot. She set the bucket on the floor and with both hands traced the noose to its apex. Her heart lurched as she recognized at once that it was a slip-knot. She tugged hard and heard it cinch against sturdy rafters somewhere above in the darkness.

She re-filled the bucket and brought it to Charlie, where he waited to wash down oats and bits of alfalfa he'd found in the hay on the floor. When she began spilling the water into the trough, Charlie lit suddenly and heaved the barn wall with his rear hooves. Eve flinched at the thunderous echo and stood aside to let the horse fuss.

"It's okay Charles," Eve cooed. She laid a steadying hand on his side and worked her way up to his neck where she could properly minister to his concerns. She cautiously stuffed another handful of grain into a sack that hung from a nail in the wall, positioned so the horse could plunge his snout in and get his fill when ever the fancy struck. As she drew her hand from the bag Charlie lit again, this time knocking her into the wall and pinning her there. The horse corrected himself the moment he'd regained his senses, and moved to protect Eve from whatever it was that had startled him.

Heidi stood away from the cow and calf she'd been tending and stared at Eve, but it was not impatience that Eve saw there – it something else. It was fear, she was certain of it.

Charlie scuffed nervously.

"He doesn't tend to draw shy like this, I can assure you," Eve said.

Heidi declined to reply.

"I think I'll keep him to pasture. He just needs to find his way after the hard ride." She took hold of his reins and led him from the uncertainty of the barn, into the out of doors.

Heidi waited by the door, having tended to the cow and calf that presided in one of the larger stalls. A gaggle of goats that wandered the barn freely sauntered up to her in hopes of food. For a moment, Heidi held Eve's gaze and, for the first time, her dark eyes betrayed what at first glance could easily have been mistaken for callous deceit. Now, even from across the room, Eve sensed a more profound emotion - a sadness that seemed to reach to the very depths of Heidi's spirit. The fear had kicked something loose and her emotions were on the verge of being laid bare.

Heidi secured the barn door and led the way back to the house.

She stopped on the porch and thrust several quarters of firewood into Eve's arms, before taking as many herself. Eve followed Heidi's lead, dropping the wood on the floor beside the stove. She stood aside as Heidi lit a fire and put a kettle on to boil. Eve moved closer to the stove and held her hands out to warm as Heidi went to the living room to light another fire in a brick hearth.

"You can sit in there," she said pointing to the room where the growing fire now threw shadows around the room. "I'll bring something hot to drink, and something to eat."

Eve settled into a chair next to the fire, staring absently at the growing flames. For a moment she was overcome with a severe longing for home.

Heidi came from the kitchen with a tray of tea and some salted salmon and bread. She poured tea into a cup and handed it to Eve before pouring a cup for herself. She sat easily in a lounge chair next to the hearth: it was her way, subtle but distinct grace.

For a long while, neither spoke. There was only a heavy silence, the fire crackling in the hearth, and the wind trying the stonework chimney. It was the silence of those whose lives have been profoundly changed by things well beyond their control; the silence of losing something that should never be lost, but by some stroke of ill-gotten fate, is lost all the same.

As the warmth of the fire and the tea settled into her bones, Eve thought of her own father, how the damp had affected him last winter, and how she had to be there for him almost every waking hour. She felt her stomach knot, that even now she should be there for him, to give him the medicine that would ease his violent fits of coughing, rub his back to settle his spirit. Catharyn was largely, though claims to the contrary abound, disaffected. She would go about her way, oblivious to his suffering until his coughing became too much to ignore.

"You are welcome to stay the night." Heidi said, almost as though she knew what Eve was on about. "It will be safer to travel in the morning,"

"Thank you," Eve forced a smile, her worry deepening, knowing that the ride home was a losing prospect. "As long as it's no trouble."

"It will be no trouble. I'm sure you can care for yourself."

Eve's smile faded. Again Heidi's words seemed short – almost rude in a way. She thought of the rope hanging in the barn and wondered if it had indeed been for her, wondered at how hopeless it all must be.

"I'm sorry to hear about your husband," she said to Heidi shaking off her affliction.

Heidi stared into the fire, sipped slowly at her tea. "The police believe that my brother Eli killed him," she said holding her cup in both hands.

"How do you know for certain he didn't?" Eve surprised even herself by saying it.

Heidi's eyes flashed.

"Because that is what he tells me! He tells me he is being made an example of, and that he is afraid they will kill him too."

Eve continued on, breathing life into a faint doubt that seemed to rise within her. Surely the police must have had a good reason to suspect her brother. And yet, she was so willing to take his word. It was a trust unequalled to anything she had seen or experienced in her own life; her own people carried with them the same degree of mistrust as Heidi seemed to carry faith in her conviction.

"My brother was taken because they do not like what he stands for. He refuses to take your God," she said, turning to look at Eve. "… Will not take your laws. And for that he will be killed." Her voice was sharp. Eve looked to the fire nodding. To say anything, to ask any question – no matter what side she appeared to come down on – would risk sending Heidi back into her silence, or worse, inspire an anger that might result in her facing the long, wet ride home regardless of better judgement.

"He says he has been made an example to keep our people uncertain and afraid. The same thing has happened to Charlie George. Not two years ago the sick would come from all of the islands, all of the villages, so he could heal them. Charlie George understood the language of the earth and of the animals. And he knew their secrets. He understood people the same way. The whites said he was using sorcery and the priests said he talked to the devil and they told him to stop what he was doing because it was against their God. *Their God*, Eve!"

It was the first time Heidi had spoken her name. Eve felt a surge of hope that she might somehow be trusted.

"Charlie said he could not stop what he was doing any more than the Eagle could stop catching fish, or the Fox could stop chasing mice... But, then the daughter of Elder Galigos became very sick. But the Elder did not take her to Charlie George, because they were afraid for him, that the priests would take him away to be punished. Instead, she took her daughter to town, to the doctor there. The doctor told the Elder that her daughter would soon die," Heidi took her eyes from the fire and stared pleadingly at Eve, that she might understand the implications, and the flood of rage and hopelessness that came with it.

"Back at the village, that same night, Charlie George came to Elder Galigos and gave the girl the medicines he had prepared even on that day, while they had made the trip into town. He gave her the medicines and he prayed for her. But somehow the police had found out what he had done and they came and took him away anyways. Men in strange uniforms came, who were not from here - were not from Vananda, or Texada, and took him into the jail, and none of us were allowed to see him for a long time. And when he was taken to be hanged for sorcery, he was led through the middle of town. We could all see they had hurt him.

"They led him to the gallows, and he was hurt, we could all see it. But we could see that he was still proud, and seeing that, made us proud too... When he was walking up the stairs to the gallows, we tried to leave, to take our children away, but the police would not let us go. They had brought many of their men from other places, so that we were outnumbered... We were made to watch as they drew the rope around Charlie George's neck and they dropped him through the hole. The women and the children – *everyone* was made to watch. And Charlie was hanging there dead, and the children were crying and the mother's were covering their eyes...

"And you know what?" Heidi hissed, staring at Eve, her deep brown eyes suddenly fierce with rage. "To this day, the daughter of Elder Galigos walks this earth. She is a reminder of what makes us

110

different from you. A reminder that we will never be the same. Your police and your judge did not even consider that Charlie had saved her life. The only thing that mattered to them was that he would not take their God."

"It's true that a few of us... we've made mistakes," Eve said quietly, "But not all of us are like that."

"Our people have honour," Heidi seethed, "And yet we are treated like animals by men who have no honour, even among themselves..."

As quickly as Heidi's eyes had flashed in the firelight, Eve could see she struggled to calm herself. When she spoke again, her words were smooth and even.

"When we make a choice there must always be a reason for it. As the rules of the earth, such are the rules of life. There must always be something given in return for what is taken. To take more than you need goes against the earth and goes against the Creator."

Heidi brought the crimson tea cup to her lips and Eve saw a tear glisten and roll down her cheek. She reached out and squeezed Heidi's hand. Heidi tensed and pulled away, wiping the tear away with the hand Eve had tried to console.

Eve sat back in her chair feeling the immensity of the rift between them, between white and brown. A shot of fear flickered within her like a lick of flame. What was she doing here anyway? She was a stranger in this house. What made her think she could come here and pry open people's lives and remain unaffected. For a moment she understood - even if only in some small way - how Heidi must feel being here in this white man's house, in what was fast becoming a white man's world, looking upon the forest and the ocean and the familiar places of her past, as one looks longingly upon childhood memories now long out of reach. Eve searched for familiar ground. What was her purpose? To gather information? To write this story, which had suddenly grown in the last minutes to span the entire rift between her own culture and that of Heidi's.

She longed now for simplicity - if even the simplicity of a story that went no further than those things that were relegated to the world of the gone and forgotten, but were then brought back with the tide.

Ours is not to question: Truth prefers the light of day.

She glanced at Heidi watching the fire, and noticed that, at this moment, in this light, she looked so young: with each flicker of flame she looked at one moment like a child, and in the next, a strong, beautiful, young woman, capable of carrying the immense burden she would need to shoulder.

"Why did you marry Ernie?" Eve asked suddenly. "I mean, you were aware of the potential problems..." Heidi sat quietly in the glow of the fire. For a time it seemed she would not answer the question.

"He worked with my father for the logging company. They became friends. Sometimes, when I was young – fifteen I think - my father would bring Ernie to our house to eat with us. When we had finished eating and the fire was lit, he was invited to sit with us and talk. Father would always tell stories, and Ernie had stories of his own, some of them better than my father's, and everyone would laugh about it because father was the storyteller and it was plain he could see the look of joy on everyone's faces when Ernie had his turn. Sometimes... I could feel Ernie's eyes watching me. He watched me whenever he could. And when he looked at me it was as though something he saw made his eyes shine, like he was looking at the sunrise for the first time. Eli always said it was the way a coyote looks upon a rabbit just before he has lunch," a faint smile broke upon Heidi's lips.

"They remained friends for all those years. Sometimes I would hear them talking, that he would be ridiculed by the other men for befriending an Indian, but that made no difference to him. My father said because he had the honour of our people, that he must be one of us in his heart. They would hunt and fish together, and mother and I would dry the fish they caught and I would wrap it in cedar bark and send it with Ernie.

"Several years passed like this, and all that while he had that same look in his eyes. Sometimes he would take me into the valley with a packed lunch and we would eat there together. He would bring books in English, and he would teach me to read and write in English. I loved the books and often made him sit with me late into the night at our table to read. And I would ask him many questions about the stories and the words and what they meant.

"Then, one day, he came unexpectedly and took my father fishing and I could see that there were grave matters to be discussed. Late that same night father announced that Ernie had asked to take me as his wife, and that my father had agreed.

"What did your brother make of this?"

"My brother was angry," she said quietly, her eyes hardening. "... My husband was a kind man. He did not deserve to die. My people are suffering. We are being killed for living our lives the way we'd always lived. What would it be like if I came into your home, and then, after a while, if I liked it there, I could send you and your families into one small room in the house?"

She stared hard at Eve. "Yesterday my universe stretched as far as your eyes can see. Today, I am kept to one room, and there are imaginary walls I need to try to understand. It is clear that if we do not accept the white man's way we will be made to suffer. We are even now in danger of losing our land and our homes. The elders fear we will be taken from our island." She paused, her eyes welling up. "I thought if I married him... I would learn your ways and of what needed to be done to help my people. I asked for my father's permission and he agreed it might help us to have such an understanding. Eli could not see the wisdom of this."

Eve shot forward in her seat. "Go to your father now and ask his help?"

"I am no longer welcome in the village," Heidi answered, her gaze lost somewhere in the fire.

"When I left I was made to understand it was against the wishes of the Elders and most of my people. They believed I had forsaken the Creator and had become white. We could not tell them the reasons why we saw that it might be a good thing."

As she sat listening to Heidi talk, Eve's mind grew distant. She could hear every word that was said, yet it was as if she was in a trance. Then, in a sudden flash, she could see all of the details laid out in her mind's eye, spreading outward from the centre: veins of experience, arteries of influence - each path pushing to some outer limit, before it dried up or fell back on itself. The influence of one person on another; of man upon the place where he lives; of a culture with lofty ideals, that leaves no room for questions. Something stirred deeply within her mind - a growing sensation, a sudden profound and lucid notion that that there was much more to the murder of Ernie Tsan than she, or anyone else, had guessed.

She was drawn quickly back into the room. The air was static and the light shifted dramatically.

The hair stood on Eve's neck. A bright flash coursed through the room, noticeably bolder than the fire in the hearth. The surging glow came in through the window at the back of the house and coursed and streamed like a dragon - deep red and black and orange and yellow. Heidi hurried into a small room at the back of the house with Eve quick on her heels. Through the curtains, a bright yellow glow flashed against the trees. Heidi gasped.

The barn was ablaze.

Heidi's tea cup smashed on the floor as she ran for the front door.
They ran down the front steps, then, in mid stride, Heidi stopped in her tracks. Eve ran into her. There was a dull thud: a metal pail being dropped to the ground.

The silhouette of a large man drifted across in front of the fire and disappeared into the forest.

$$\Omega$$

COLLATERAL DAMAGE

Acipiti plus ferit ense gula

ΞΘΣώ

*Wine has drowned more than
the sea.*

Luke Faulkner felt a sharp push from behind. "Keep that lantern flush Faulkner."

Luke looked tiredly at the lantern. It flickered and almost went out in the thin air near the ground. He lifted it slowly, so that it sat level as they made their way down into the earth.

Deep inside the mine shaft, the walls glistened black and played tricks with his eyes. He was still heavy with tired. The new baby had upset the night before and wouldn't sleep.

"Hey, can`t you guys smell that?" One of the men asked again.

"Goddam smells like rot."

"That`s the breakfast your wife made you, Deno. Must still be lively." Most of the men within ear shot burst into laughter.

"Don`t get all sensitive on us, Den. You`re fine."

For a while none of the men spoke. The rhythmic sound of their boots falling on the loose, wet ore that blanketed the ground, soothed their frayed minds.

Luke yawned. The rhythmic plodding made it seem alright to

close his eyes a little. It wouldn't hurt. He felt a sharp pinch on his arm, just above the elbow.

"Holy hell, Faulkner. Wake the fuck up."

At that moment, Luke dropped his lantern, cracking the globe inside the protective metal frame.

The men behind him were silent as he gathered the lantern up and stepped out of line.

"You know where we'll be," one of the men quipped on the way by him.

"Yeah. Yeah! I'll catch up."

"Hey wait a sec with that light," Luke shouted to the last man to pass him. It was Corbin Ford, a new hire. He stopped and held his light aloft while Luke settled himself in to fix his gear.

He thanked Corbin and waved him off, trying to benefit from the light before he disappeared into the mine.

Luke stripped his gloves from his hands and calmed himself enough to remove the broken plate of glass by feel and replace it with a new one. That done, he felt for one of the two matches he'd set on the rock next to him. He drew it across the striker several times before it struck. He slowly brought the flame to the lantern wick, but the damp air blew it out before he could bring it to bear. He struck another, and it too sputtered and died.

"Fuck!"

He listened to his voice chasing the men down into the shaft, its distant echo telling him just how much time had passed. He could no longer hear the trudging and clanging of the work crew.

Water dripped from the rock above him, filtering down from the surface, through a mile or more of roots and rock. The shaft was damp and cold, colder on this day than he was used to in late summer.

He felt for his vest, inside his blackened coat. He produced a small cylindrical vial and carefully screwed the cap off, was careful not to drop it in the pitch black. He gingerly pulled a dry match from inside and felt for the sulphur tip. He pressed it to the striker. And, as his mind fired, sending the signal for action to his fingers, he realized at once the reason he was not able to strike flame.

He dropped the match and scrambled up from the rock he was

116

sitting on. He sniffed at the dank air near the ceiling and looked in horror after the men who'd just gone ahead of him.

"GAS!... MINE GAS!... NO MATCH - " He screamed after the crew, louder than he'd screamed before. He could not know that, for many of those men, it was already over.

From down in the throat of the mine came a deep yellow and red flame, roiling and glowing off the moist shaft walls. The massive explosion ripped through infinitesimal cracks in the earth, seeking open air. Where there were no fissures to eat the violent chemical reaction, the blast merely punched through the top of the mountain like a giant crimson fist.

$$\Omega$$

FIND THE LIVING,
CARRY THE DEAD

Ad vitam paramus

ß

We are preparing for life

Eve lay in bed staring into the dark, wondering if it had been a dream – a residual effect from the anguish of saving Charlie and Heidi's animals from the blaze. Outside her window, the wind blasted through the trees. A thin bank of clouds streamed across the moon. Beside her, hanging on the bedpost, the necklaces that hung there began to tremble. Then it happened again: the air pressure dropped suddenly, her ears popped and the room fell deathly silent. Then, a deep roar shook the house. In the kitchen at the bottom of the stairs, stacked dishes clattered in the cabinets.

Somewhere a fateful and unforgiving breach had finally reached the breaking point.

Within moments another tremor rolled ferociously beneath the house. It shook through rock and up tree trunks, through foundations and into timbers.

The effect was grim and inexorable.

As the tremor subsided, and the blast echoed off the distant mainland shore, a memory stirred and pushed in through layers, faint at first, then flooding the avenues of her mind. She was a child, plunked onto a blanket and playing by firelight. There was a distant, violent explosion. The mending in Catharyn's hands fell into her lap; her father looked up from his book and their eyes met in a knowing glance. And in that look, Eve could see certainty and fear.. and relief, that her father was safe at home and not at the mines as he should have been that night.

The explosion that occurred then, and what came after, shook the town to its very core. Though the screams could not be heard from the safety of the warm, softly lit living room, the effect of many lives being ripped from the face of the earth in that single moment sent a tocsin audible - not to the ear, for it was the silent and desperate language of the soul, uttered as countless lives were ripped from the balance.

There were men this night who would lose their lives also. They had given everything they had to give to the thankless mines that, in life, had been their saving grace. Now, in death, it would serve only as their unmarked grave.

Eve pulled the curtains back from the window. At first nothing in the black night betrayed the location of the blast. She flipped the latch and pulled the window open and a heavy gust of wind clutched at her bed clothes. Outside, the air crackled with electricity.

A thunderstorm? She looked at the sky. There was barely a breeze, but the air was phosphor and thick.

She slipped into her robe. Going down the stairs, she was careful not to step where the wood liked to complain. She went lightly through the kitchen and eased the front door open.

On the front porch she pulled her robe tightly and listened for a telling sign of what may have come. But there was no sound, only a faint and dark certainty.

"There's been an explosion," Catharyn's voice startled her.

Eve turned to find her standing there, with one hand on the door knob and the other clutching the door frame. She let go of the frame and shuffled past Eve to the stairs. Eve watched as her stepmother clambered down the steps and out into the middle of the yard. There, she searched the dark horizon, watching, straining to hear the silent language that would, never-the-less, tell its secrets to any who would listen.

"There," she said, pointing a bony finger to the north, her voice resolute. It's Christian Maddox' mine - the Paymaster... Coming from that direction anyhow."

Eve followed the silhouette of her arm until her eyes fell upon the dull yellow-orange glow that purled and spread into the dark above the tree-line.

"You can smell the burn in the air already," Catharyn said as if to herself. "Hopefully they had the good sense to clear them mines out before she went. Else there'll be mothers without sons on this night."

It was still twilight when Eve rode into town. The dull orange plume loomed and billowed on the horizon betraying her hope that it had been an unfortunate dream. Through the dusk she saw the lamps in the office already burning.

Quentin sat at his desk looking apt.

"Glad to see you're on the ball this morning Eve. It'll be a long day. There's been an explosion at the -"

"The Paymaster, I know," Eve finished for him.

"The Paymaster," he repeated, trumping her exclamation. "It was felt clear across the entire north third of the island, and over on the mainland. I'd like you to run up there and see what you can see. Get statements from witnesses and workers. See if you can find Christian Maddox and get a statement out of him. It's rumoured five men were lost. Find out if there's any truth to it, and see if you can put a name to the men. And remember, keep your personal life out of it: They don't teach it in church, but the little known eighth deadly sin is to wield the press as a blade to cut down thine enemy."

Eve barely managed to get Charlie out of the way before a medical cart, loaded with injured men, stormed past. The blackened and bloody men jostled dangerously as the wagon skipped over a protruding rock.

As she neared the mine yard another wagon, loaded to the ground with supplies, stormed by, narrowly missing her.

She stepped down and threw her camera bag over her shoulder. She walked up the hill and into the works yard, where miners were painstakingly moving shredded rock from the shaft, like pebbles from a great stone throat. They had to get oxygen into the shaft, down to the survivors, as fast as possible. Every moment that escaped them was a step closer to certain death for the men who were trapped, and likely scared like nothing they'd ever known.

Staring at the morbid processing before her, Eve lost her bearings and wandered too close to a gang of men fresh from a shift moving rock. They seemed to look right through her with their drawn faces and a hunger to be free of what faced them. Many had their gloves worn clean through from handling the newly broken rock.

The task was painful and slow, and the work gruelling and inhuman. But it seemed they were right in the knowledge that they themselves were the only salvation. For the men in the mine, the knowledge that their brothers would make a show of force, that they would all answer the call, whether they were fresh off a shift or not, would be blessed in itself.

Eve noticed an odd-looking man standing at the tail end of the Hail Mary line. He was kept busy trundling back and forth, taking each stone passed to him and sorting it into one of three piles, clearly arranged according the size of the stone in hand. She laid her hand upon his shoulder. The very act of doing so seemed enough to break him. His shoulders slumped as he broke away from the line, and his comrade stepped in to take his place.

The scene made a permanent impression. She was keenly aware that her job was to write what she saw, to faithfully transcribe the image, the reality, into written word, so that whomever might read it, could see the truth of it: feel the bleak atmosphere, sense the unspoken fear snaking through the line of men; that they hoped to find the living, but expected to carry the dead.

Eve followed the broken man as he slumped away to a quiet spot to rest.

"Excuse me. I'm a writer for the Coast Miner, could you tell me what happened here?" She said, as she dug for her pencil and paper in her shoulder bag.

The man lifted his eyes and looked at her sternly. "Mine exploded. That's what happened."

"Yes," Eve softened her voice, "but what caused the explosion?"

"Some kind of mineral gas - usually," The man said staring blankly at the mine entrance. "Builds up top of the tunnels – usually the deeper ones - and sits there. Usually gets pumped out," he said, bringing the back of his hand across his brow. "The good ones pump it, anyhow."

"Good ones?"

"Yeah... The good ones. There's companies out there 'at take care of their men."

"Were there men inside?"

"Damn right there were men inside. Why'd you think we're doin' what we're doin'?" He shot Eve a look of disgust. "Look lady - what'd you say your name was?"

"Eve Walker."

"Look Eve. I been workin' this line since before sun-up. My arms feels like they could fall off any time now. I'm just plum tired."

"I'm sorry," she said, as she placed her hand gently on his shoulder. "I'm so sorry you are faced with this tragedy... Do you know the men? - Who are in there, I mean?"

"Don't know 'em per se. But I do it any way. We all do, cause if it was me or him," he said pointing at the man who took his place in the line, "We'd want to know it mattered, and that all the men that was able to would be doin' just what we're doin' now to get us out. It's about a measure of faith I s'pose."

"How many men are trapped?" This time no answer came. After a moment of silence, Eve looked up from her notebook. The man was watching attentively, a spot somewhere off to his left. She followed his gaze to a water tower that stood nearby, and saw two men, one leaning against the tower, the other standing with legs apart and his arms crossed. The men stared unabashedly at them.

When Eve turned to speak to the helpful, if awkward old man, he was already walking back to the rock pile.

"Excuse me?"

"I got nothin' to say lady. If you know what's good for ya, you'll go back wherever you came from. 'Sides we don't need any one running around under foot."

She looked back at the men standing by the water tower. "Excuse me?" she said walking toward them. Both men uncrossed their arms and straightened as she drew nearer. One of the men stepped forward and was quickly joined by the other. The bald man was tall - well over six feet. He had wide shoulders - and seemed to know it - and cold gray eyes. His friend was tall and thin, though well-dressed. Eve reckoned, however, that a fedora was over-thinking it, and not at all fitting for the occasion. The bald man crossed his arms again and thrust his chest out. He made a point of chewing a spit of tobacco.

"Eve Walker. I'm with the Coast Miner", she said, extending her hand. Neither man returned the gesture. "You two gentlemen look as though you know your way around. Can you tell me, were there men inside the mine when it went?"

"You're that snipe from the paper,"

"I'm Eve Walker. We don't hire snipes."

"It's like the man said, Eve, straight goods. We're trying to save lives here, we got no time for your questions. As a matter of fact, we got no time for you being here at all." Eve stood her ground. The man with the hat took an abrupt step toward her. "N't you heard what's been said?"

Eve met his gaze unswervingly. "You've got your job, I've got mine. As far as I can see there's news here, and it'll get told with your help, or without it. The people deserve to know. I think that's simple enough, even an ape could understand it."

The Fedora shifted his feet. His eyes flashed and smouldered under the rim of his hat. His hands flinched.

A few of the men who'd taken reprieve from the line-up turned to stare.

The bald man advanced another step, and without warning, he brought his hand back as if to strike. Eve flinched and stumbled out of reach. He moved to strike again, and, at the last possible moment, she felt a hand close around her wrist and pull her off balance... It was the man with the fedora. He had gotten behind her when the bald man made for an attack. He leaned in close to her face. "You've been asked to leave the premises. It's dangerous here, and the men are trying to dig the bodies out. There's lives at stake and they don't need no distractions. So now you been told! If you decide to stick around, there's no guarantees what might happen. Especially to a pretty young thing like you," he leered.

Eve felt her legs tremble unwittingly beneath her. She doubted they could hold her erect for much longer. She hoped the two men could not see her weakness. *Predators always pick the weak one.*

The thought brought little else but cold comfort.

"Is there someone I can speak to later on then? After things are under control?" Eve said, her voice trembling.

"Mr. Maddox says to tell you he'll be in touch. And, by the way, if you even fiddle with that contraption you got there," he said, nodding at the camera, "and it's all downhill from there. And it's a steep hill, so... Understand?" And with that the two men turned and strode away.

She noticed several of the men in the work chain glancing over at her, in between handing off their load of rocks, and reaching again for another. In each of their eyes she saw the spirit of a broken man, like the first man she'd spoken to. She could also see... empathy – in most. In others there was unquestionable hatred. In all, there was fear.

Eve's heart continued to throb in her chest. She could not seem to catch enough air. It wasn't until she had the reigns in her hand, and had begun to leave the chaos of the Paymaster Mine behind her, that she got a hold on her nerves. The churning machinery and the shouts of the men faded behind her. She recalled, then, a strange word she had come across in an old, leather bound dictionary. Admittedly, it was a strange thought to pass into her mind just then, but she noticed that it drew her away from the fear that racked her body. So she let her mind drift...

124

"*Charivari,*" she said aloud. *"A mock serenade of discordant music."* She remembered thinking it odd that the word should describe something so base, and yet sound so beautiful. During medieval times, when a couple was betrothed, it was an age-old tradition that, directly after the priest had given his blessing, it was expected they would pass through the throngs of people to pay their respects. While the two of them passed through this gauntlet, it was the obligation of every soul in attendance to make as much noise as humanly possible. The room would erupt in a hellish cacophony of pots and pans, the crashing of massive pot lids upon anything that came to hand, the stomping of feet, the shrill chanting - all manner of things; but the highlight was the women, who screeched and caterwauled like childish demons, until they collapsed from exhaustion. The couple would make a run through the middle of it, as if for their lives, to find their safe haven in a special bedroom, prepared so they could immediately consummate the marriage...

"Marriage is for creeps," Eve said aloud. She smiled, then laughed. She shook her head and laughed at her own inexperience. Her insecurity. Obviously it was still a problem. There were improvements to be acknowledged, but she made a point of not getting hung up on that. Better to look to the future; don't get caught up in the past. *It's hard enough keepin' yer eyes on yer feet. Double so if yer lookin' back all the time.*

Words of wit and wisdom from Percy. Her heart warmed a little more to think of her father, his warm smile and patient wisdom. Her stepmother, the polar opposite. It astounded her how the two of them ever managed to get on together.

The road narrowed, and the trees crept closer. She felt a lump form in her throat and tried to choke it back down. She would not allow herself to cry. She absolutely refused to cry... A sudden hand on her shoulder quickly changed her mind. She lurched sideways and slid herself down the bench as far as she was able. She pulled hard back on the reins and spun to meet her attacker, fully expecting to see one of the two men from the yard. She was surprised, instead, to see a complete stranger – an oriental man – who'd apparently been hiding in the back of the wagon and was now crawling out from under Charlie's horse blanket. She tried to appear calm, though her heart still raced madly in her chest.

"Miss Walker?"

"After the warm reception up on the hill, that all depends whose asking."

"Miss Walker, my name is Mit Song Loo. Song Loo for short," he said moving closer, his hand extended.

When he moved closer, Eve shuffled away from him on the bench. He was unaffected by her inclination to put distance between them. His eyes curved in crescent moons, seemed to smile with wisdom. White streaks in his black hair added to the effect.

"You wanted to know something about the explosion? Come with me, if you would. I don't intend any harm."

"You aren't worried about those thugs up there?"

"The Maddox men don't scare me. It's the anti-union thugs from below the border that make me a little nervous."

Eve was immediately curious about his clarity of speech. He handled the English language with ease; there was no rounding the "R's"; no clipped sentences, or chopped vowels.

"There are different rules down there," he continued. "...You're with the press? You want a story? We've known this would happen for a long time," he said without pause. "You tell that Editor from New York... You tell him that Christian Maddox has done nothing about it. We told him that the gas is seeping: When it gets damp, the gas seeps out. It backs up in the mine head - everyone knows that. Everyone in the mine, anyhow. Those guys with the inspection, they're in Maddox's back pocket. He pays them to say "no gas", and that's exactly what they say," Song Loo's eyes had her pinned. "It cost too much money to shut the mine down, so they get creative with their bookkeeping, so to speak," he continued. "We try to tell them," he said shaking his head.

"You *knew* this would happen? And you told Maddox?" She said incredulously. "And he did nothing?"

"You jus' kind of get use to it. Maybe it's your friend who died? Maybe it's your brother? You make your peace and keep going, because there is nothing else you can do." Song loo touched her elbow

126

and indicated a narrow trail that spurred to the right of the main.

"You have to feed your family right?" Eve agreed.

Song Loo nodded gravely, "It has been this way for some time. I will show you."

They followed the trail along a cut-bank where the earth fell away steeply beneath them, before rising into a bank of steep rolling hills. Soon the trail came to an end, stopped short by a wind-worn rocky bluff. Song Loo reached up and found a handhold in the rock. In a few moments he was several feet above her on the bluff. He leaned down, "Take my hand!"

She pushed her camera to her side, and stuffed her notebook and pencil into her bag. She reached for the hand hold Song Loo had shown her and nodded that she was ready. Before Eve could make a move, she found herself already standing beside him atop the bluff. He had all but pulled her up unaided.

They started out again, tracing their way up the hill. Eve was careful to follow close behind, and to watch where Song Loo placed his hands and his feet.

As they neared the top, the brush and small trees that clung to the side of the bluff had given way to rock. They crossed over the barren top and were soon back into thick forest. The trees soon opened into a clearing of tall sun-beaten grass. No sooner had they stepped into the field, when they came upon a weathered white cross, fighting for recognition in the taller grass. Nearby there was another, this one carved from hand-hewn stone. Soon they were surrounded by unnatural shapes strewn throughout the field. Crosses - perhaps just under two dozen of them, and easily just as many stone markers. A heavy gust swept in from the ocean and skimmed through the grass. As it did, Eve saw that the entire field was lined with a small, white picket fence.

"These are the men lost in last ten years or so."

"Just the Paymaster?"

"We don't discriminate," he said with a smile. "But, yes, this is just the Paymaster. There are other places like this. It's like I said, we been trying to get Maddox to do something, but he say it cost to much to shut the mine down, we should be happy to even have job."

"But, what about the safety inspections?" Eve was confounded.

"What about the safety inspector?"

Song Loo laughed. "It's like I say, the safety inspector is in his pocket," he said, patting his vest. "Maddox always sees the report first, and if he see something he don't like, he change it himself and everything is copacetic again."

Eve was listening now with rapt attention, looking over the graves, her notebook hanging loose in her hand. A wave of anger washed through her as she thought of her father lying in bed, sick – dying - from his life in the mines. How many others were there out there like Maddox?

"So will you write the story? I hope you say yes. Just so we're on same page," Song Loo laughed.

Eve scanned the field again. Her heart ached for the families, but her mind burned with a desire to rip and tear and hack with her words, to strike out at Maddox. To make an example of him. She cursed Quentin for his well-intended advice.

"*This is my home,*" she whispered.

"What did you say?"

She looked directly into his eyes. "This is my home, Song Loo, and I will *not* stand for it!"

A shadow of sadness, and the ease of certain release fell over him. He reached into his vest pocket and revealed a silver flask – larger than most she'd seen. He unscrewed the lid and offered it to Eve. "Good whisky. The best on the island," he said. "Go ahead. It won't kill you," He drew the back of his sleeve across his eyes. "I apologize. It's just... I never seem to get used to it. And I knew many of these men... I know the men who are trapped back there now..." He looked away from her, and stared out over the brilliant blue ocean that threw itself unfailingly at the foot of the mountain far below.

Eve took a small drink at first, then drank again, this time feeling the draw burn her throat, and warm her stomach.

She passed the flask back to Song Loo, and knelt down in front of a cross that lay in the grass, almost at her feet. "Justice Gainer," she said aloud, and wrote the name carefully, lovingly into her book. As she moved on to the next cross, Song Loo took up behind her, replacing the fallen cross.

"Felix Ortega... William Jantz... James Taupin..."

Ω

THE TRIGGER
AND THE
RUNNING MAN

Victoras, non veritas,
facit legam

Victory, not truth,
makes the law

The hoe cut into the earth, breaking out the dark soil from beneath the grass. John West lifted and swung again, methodically breaking up the square of land he'd marked. He stopped to wipe the sweat from his brow and looked over his garden plot that lined the fence at the south-west of his property.

The sweet corn had come ready, and the Tomatillos he'd experimented with turned out to be a good bet. Seemed he never had quite enough to satisfy the appetites of his neighbours, as well as the many resident deer and raccoons that dropped by to visit after dark.

The sound of horses plodding on the dirt road caught his attention. He shielded his eyes against the sun and saw Chief Israel Tomas approaching on horseback, leading a procession mostly of women and children from the village. Chief Tomas was in full ceremonial dress, and was flanked by three men. Behind the men, two women rode on small horses. The rest of the procession followed on foot behind them.

John swung the hoe a few more times before setting it against the fence.

When the procession reached the gate, Chief Tomas dismounted with the grace of an old grizzly, and stood holding the reigns in his hand. The three elders also dismounted and approached the fence. John went to the gate and welcomed them into his yard. He shook hands with the men and suggested they let their horses graze in the field behind the house.

"On what occasion do I owe the honour?" John asked Chief Tomas, noting that none of the young men of the tribe had come.

"We have come to see the Indian Agent, John West. We request council, to help us with a matter of grave importance."

"By all means," John said, inviting the chief and the men inside his home, while the women laid blankets out on the grass. Several of the young girls stood at the edge of the garden reaching for the ripe tomatoes that shone in the sun.

John showed the men to his sitting room and asked his wife to bring some refreshments. He pulled a window up for some air, and inclined his guests to seat themselves in the high-back leather chairs he'd just had re-finished.

"I hear Miss Calder is doing good things with the reading program in the village," John said, offering cigars to each of the men. "From what I understand, her young assistant will be ready to take over the classroom soon. Your support in helping us get that program up and running, Chief Tomas, is going to favour well with the Minister of Education in Victoria."

"Sadly this is not a pleasant visit John West," Chief Tomas said gravely. "Sergeant Sutherland brought his men to our village looking for my son and two of his friends."

John selected a cigar for himself, and slowly closed the box. He set it on the edge of the desk.

"I was not made aware of this. Where are the boys now?"

"Ethel Paul has lost her two sons," Chief Tomas said gravely. "Eli was tied up and made to walk behind the horses all the way into

130

Vananda to the jail."

John West looked at the floor for a moment. "Is Miss Paul here with you?"

"She would not come. She is mourning the loss of her sons. She said coming here now, in this time, would do nothing. She says that it is only a sign of what is to come. Many of my people have been saying the same thing; that the land we have been promised will not come. That we will be like our neighbours and our friends to the North, whose village now stands empty... We don't see them anymore."

"We are doing the best we can, under the circumstances Chief Tomas. I personally have taken an interest in what is happening here on this island – your home – and intend to see that justice is done."

"Your justice, John West, is very difficult to understand. It is always changing. Our young men are not here, because they are angry. They also say that coming here will do nothing. I fear they will allow their anger to drive them to do something foolish. This will only make matters worse, for them... For us."

"I see." Inside, John was seething; angry at Sutherland's arrogance, that he would challenge the fragile relationship it had taken the last two years to establish, and even then only by the skin of his teeth.

"Did Corporal Sutherland give a reason for apprehending the men?"

"There is no good reason to kill a man. These men were unarmed. When they saw Corporal Sutherland come with all his men, they ran into the forest to protect themselves."

"I understand Chief Tomas. But why did Corporal Sutherland tell you he intended to arrest the boys?"

"One of your people was found dead - drowned in the sea - and the police believe that these boys were to blame. They say that Eli's stag knife was found nearby."

"Did they tell you who it was they found on the beach?"

Chief Tomas hesitated for a moment. "Ernie Tsan, the husband of my daughter..." he said, as he leaned forward, his hands on his knees, his feet apart. "It seemed strange to me that you would not come -"

John leaned forward as if to speak. Chief Tomas held up his hand, that he should continue. "We have always been friends. Why were you not there with them – with Sutherland when he came?"

The man sitting to the left of Chief Tomas had red lines painted high on each of his cheeks, along the contour of his cheekbones, and stared, with his dark eyes, unblinkingly at John.

"I was not informed," John repeated himself, picking up a pad of notepaper. He went to his desk and took the cap off a bottle of ink. He poured a measure into an ink well on the desk and laid two fountain pens neatly on a writing tray before returning to his chair. He seated himself and arranged the tray on his lap, careful not to put the large oak desk between himself and the Chief. He intended to defuse what had fast become a potentially explosive situation to the best advantage of all concerned.

"I hesitate to say that, had I been there, it might not have happened. I can't speak for Sergeant Sutherland. I can't speak to why I was not informed. I'll admit, it seems a brash move, even for Sutherland," he said, almost under his breath. "You have my assurance that the matter is of the utmost importance to me and will be pursued immediately. The harm done cannot be undone, but once the facts are in front of me…" John looked pensively out the window, watched the children coaxing his dog to try the tomatoes.

"You said you specifically requested my presence before the arrest was issued?"

Chief Tomas nodded, his steely grey eyes never leaving John's. "John West, you have always been fair. You have always made sure our friendship with your Government is reasonable. Before you came there was no discussion, we were made to do what the Government thought we should do. The police did as they pleased – even before Red Sutherland came. Much is happening that we do not understand, and the answers are not easily at hand." Chief Tomas, paused, stared, unmoving at John West.

"I once visited the city of Victoria, when it became necessary. I was taken, there, to a grand building called the Empress Hotel, built for your Queen. It did not occur to me what the meaning of this was, until I stood before a picture in stone, in the floor of the hotel, of a

132

crown. The others continued on ahead, but I could not take my eyes from this crown. Beautiful as it was, as I stood there for some time. And in my heart there grew a deep sorrow, that somehow this crown, there in the floor, cast a shadow far and wide over this land; that what was once ours, is no longer."

John West smiled tersely. "I can assure -"

"It used to be a long time would pass before we would see a white man," Chief Tomas continued. "Now strangers pass through our village many times a week. Many tell us that it is not our land and that we should leave. Men I've known to be steady and true now seem vexed. Their thoughts are troubled by something that affects them deeply. When this happened I feared for the safety of my people. I have not felt that way for a very long time – since the time I first saw that crown. The spirit of uncertainty has settled beneath my village like a dark pool, and now that pool is stirring and threatens to become a river. I can feel it. My people can feel it. When you were not present during the arrest, the boys did not trust the situation and they ran for their safety."

John grimaced.

"Why do you make that face?" Chief Tomas asked.

"Red Sutherland is a hunter. A running man to him is like a rabbit to a fox."

Chief Tomas and the three men stared at John, their eyes cold and unmoving.

"The rabbit is certain of his innocence," Chief Tomas started, "And wonders why the fox should threaten to take his life. Sutherland and his men chased them and soon we heard gun shots and I feared for the safety of my people. It should not be this way. My son is to have his ceremony – his day in your courts – in two weeks time."

"I share your concern Chief Tomas. You understand my duty is to fairness – on all counts. My heart tells me this was wrong. But I am obligated to follow due course."

"What is *due course?*"

"My apologies. I have to follow the rules."

"Red Sutherland did not follow the rules."

"I should have been there."

"What would cause him to change his own rules in such a way? Two boys are dead. If this is what it means to live under the Government that you preach to us then we will not accept it. We are proud people and will not be treated like prisoners. The young men in the village are outraged and I fear will try to do something on their own if they see that nothing is being done to protect Eli's freedom...

"...It has become a matter of your word, John West."

"If you choose to fight, you will lose everything," John flashed, a hint of panic showing in his voice.

"I am beginning to think the same will be true if we do nothing."

"Did Sutherland present a warrant for the arrest?"

Chief Tomas pulled the folded piece of paper from his vest and handed it to John. John looked it up and down. The required signature of the magistrate was in its place. It appeared to be authentic. At that moment the maid came into the room and set a tray of cakes and tea on the table.

"Bring some to our guests outside, would you please?" John said. "In fact, you are all invited to stay and have dinner with us. Is there enough for extra portions?"

"I'll need to have Mary come and lend a hand if it's to be done by dinner time."

"Please do whatever is necessary," John smiled.

Chief Tomas held up his hand. "I thank you for your offer, but we will not stay. Our people are in mourning. To enjoy ourselves in comfort would be to dishonour our men who were killed. Until the matter is put right it is in the interest of our people that we exercise caution. It would not be wise to provoke the situation."

"Of course. It was insensitive of me -"

"If Eli was guilty," Israel Tomas continued, "If he killed this man, then he would answer to your law, as we have always tried to do. But in my heart I do not believe he has killed Ernie Tsan."

John was quiet, puffed on the cigar and looked at his hands for a moment. "Did Eli approve of the marriage?"

"That makes no difference. He said he did not do it."

"I understand," John said sharply, then corrected his manner.

"I understand. But for now we must try to get inside Red

Sutherland's head, to know what he is thinking."

Chief Tomas straightened himself.... "Eli did not approve of the marriage."

"Did he make his disapproval known?"

"He carried himself with honour, as did all others who disapproved."

"Did you disapprove, Israel?"

"Chief Tomas leaned forward resting his elbows on his knees, a profound tiredness came across his face. "Any father knows it is no easy thing to let a daughter go to just any man. In my mind I could not approve, and I spoke the will of my people. In my heart I wanted to give them my happiness. I could see they were happy together, that he treated her good. I could not ask for a better man to have her – only one of her own, perhaps... But this was not to be."

"What was the will of your people?"

"That if she went with Ernie Tsan, and she married him, she could no longer come back to the village. She has forsaken her ancestry, her people."

"Were there others who were angry with her?"

"There were many, just as there were others who were not angry."

"I'll ask only once more, and then never again on the subject: was Eli angry with his sister?"

Again Chief Tomas looked pained, with the understanding of how things must look to Red Sutherland, to the Government.

"Eli was angry."

"And you're certain he would not have killed Mr. Tsan?"

"Eli was my first born. He passed from his mother into my hands, his spirit would not allow him such a liberty as taking a man's life, unless in defence of his own. It would not have happened that way."

"Why are you so certain?

"Because Eli and Ernie were friends."

With that Chief Tomas and the men rose to their feet and made ready to leave.

"You have my word," John said red-faced, "I will get to the

bottom of this," he extended his hand to Chief Tomas.

The chief hesitated a moment then accepted the handshake firmly. "We have always known you to be fair."

John West stood in the yard leaning on the wrought iron gate watching his guests leave. When they were a good way down the road, he stormed inside to the closet and reached for his coat.

"Carmalita, prepare several baskets of food and some gifts to send to the village," John shouted to the maid. "I won't return until late."

He cursed under his breath as he got on his horse. He wasn't going to let some Redneck military washout ruin things for him, for the country. Sutherland had better have a damn good reason for threatening the entire process. They'd worked too hard for too long to have things go on all fours.

Ω

ABYSS

Facilis descendsus averno

The descent to Hell is easy

The three boys raced through the untended field at the back of the old Lambert property, holding their fishing poles above their heads. Their feet skiffed through the tall grass and the sun was high and warm, and the hoppers flung off in every direction. Miss Clarendon let them from school early, and they didn't even stop at home to change, or eat dinner: A day like this had to be used for every possibility.

They ran for the woods at the south-east edge of the field. There, not too far into the trees, the earth peeled back from the limestone cliffs, where the ocean had stripped them bare. They followed a natural stone path that traced a jagged ledge along and above the shoreline, to Paton's Creek, where it played over the bluffs and into the sea. There were fish here like no other place. Jake Hamilton's pa said it was on account of the feed washing down off the hillside into the waiting mouths of the rockfish and Greenling. Sometimes, if a guy was lucky, he'd even hook into a salmon.

The hours passed by like minutes, and the sun wandered down toward the western horizon. A healthy stringer of rockfish and a good sized Greenling lay out on the sun-warmed rocks. The day was well-spent.

It was Peter Oakley who commented that the light had shifted, and that they ought to cut straight over the bluffs, back to Paton's field, and take the old pasture to the road.

The boys collected their rods, and their catch, and started for home. With a little luck they could be back before dusk.

The climb over the bluffs was not dangerous, but the weather-worn outcroppings, where the rock was exposed, made for slow going. Under the trees, the rock was slick and covered with a blanket of moss, still damp from a recent passing storm.

They had almost come to the edge of the field, to a thin strip of trees that lay between them and the old Paton property, when Jake Fulton stopped. "Hold up fellas. I gotta piss."

The other two boys dropped their gear on the ground and found a rock to sit on. Peter laid the stringer of fish upon the moss. Arthur snapped a dry branch off a fallen lodgepole pine and poked absently at them.

Jake hopped down from a small outcropping and dropped out of sight. A few moments later his voice erupted from places unseen, *"Come and see this fellas!"* The two boys scrambled down the bluff and stood beside him, all of them staring into a cave, gaping and black, its opening lined with jagged rock, like an old man's worn, broken teeth.

Arthur moved in to have a closer look. He rested his hand carefully on the cool rock wall at the cave entrance before leaning in. "There's some old timbers. I bet its one of them old mine shafts."

"Finder's luck," Jake said pushing past Arthur. He stepped into the opening so that he was now almost entirely inside the mine. The other boys watched as he inched his way further inside.

"Wonder how far it goes?" Peter asked absently.

"No way of knowing unless we go on in, right? Jake said.

"Peter stood back from the entrance. "I don't know fellas. Doesn't seem safe to me."

"Wonder if there's any gold left over?" Arthur said, ignoring him.

"Probably ain't no gold," Jake scoffed, his voice echoing into the mine. "Them miners didn't leave a drop for no one else. They took everything they could get their greasy mitts on."

"I ain't goin in," Peter stepped back again.

"Aww come on. It ain't nothin' if you were a man about it."

"I'm man enough as it is, just not stupid. That's all there's to it!"

"No-one's gonna get hurt," Jake said inching further into the dank blackness.

"Dang what's that smell. Smells like someone dropped their fish in the sun and left it to ripe."

"Could be a bear lives in here," Peter said.

"Dang it Peter, why don't you run on home to your mom, let the men handle this here."

"Go on ahead then," Peter retorted, "World'll be a little brighter without your sorry ass around anyhow," Arthur burst out laughing at Jake's expense and Peter joined him. At once there was the sound of loose rock falling away as Jake lost his footing. His hands shot out to the side of the cave seeking purchase. He continued to slip – faster now – as the ground grew steeper and steeper beneath his feet. The skin on his fingers was sheared away as his hands were ripped from the rock wall. At once the ground opened up beneath him and he was falling down, down into a blackness he had not known possible. A desperate terror-filled scream escaped him. Then all was silent.

Peter and Arthur looked at each other in horror.

"Jake!" Arthur screamed. But no answer came.

"JAKE!" he screamed again, louder this time. Again he was answered only by the echo of his own voice, deep and full, and the sound of a few small rocks letting go, betraying the vast dark labyrinth.

The boys strained against the silence and the realization that settled upon them. There was only the faint smell - as if something had gone off badly - which grew stronger from time to time, carried on a cold, anonymous draft.

"Sweet Jesus, what are we gonna do?" Arthur cried.

Peter stood, his mouth agape in disbelief, unable to move, staring wide-eyed at the spot Jake stood running his mouth only moments before.

"I'll go get help. You wait here," Arthur insisted, and, before Peter could object, he scrambled down the rocks and out into the field, lifting his legs as high as he could as he bounded through the tall grass. When he reached the far edge, where the grass gave way to forest, he stopped and brought his hands to his mouth. "Mark for us when we come back," he called, his nerves showing in his voice.

Peter scuffed the rest of the way down the hillside, through the ferns and salal, and watched as Arthur disappeared into the trees.

After a time, he dared to look back over his shoulder. He stood there hoping, with every wish he had in him, to see that Jake might have found his way out. His eyes traced the shadows and set upon the black sliver menacing him from just inside the edge of the forest.

Alone now, he could feel the cold, damp air spilling from the earth and slithering along the ground, crawling up around his ankles and up into his pant legs, over his shoulders and into his shirt.

He shivered and moved a few steps further into the field.

$$\Omega$$

LOST SOULS

Tarde venientibus orsa

ㄱ

For those who come late,
only the bones

Peter was still alone when night came. He stood in the field shaking from the cold and the fear of what had happened. Several times, just before dark, he had been watching for the men to come when something, a movement, he thought, caught the corner of his eye in the dim twilight.

He shivered violently.

He sat on the grass and pulled his legs up to his chest, trying his best to keep warm.

After what seemed like forever, he heard noises - voices in the distance. He stood up and peered into the blackness. At the other end of the field several specks of light emerged from the trees. Now there were ten. Now, easily twenty and counting.

He heard the men calling. He tried to call back, but his voice cracked and was lost in the rising wind. He tried again, and hoped they would hear.

The lights grew closer, the voices louder. He could see, now, how quickly they came, by the way the lights jerked and swayed as they cut through the dark. Then they were upon him. One man with a

141

lantern – a policeman – leaned next to him, to see that he was alright. The rest followed Arthur into the trees.

Some of the men carried ropes, others carried hooks and blankets. Their serious faces flashed in the lantern light, some of them glancing at him as they passed by; most staring ahead into the trees. Arthur felt a hand again on his shoulder. He turned to see his older sister, Gladys, as she wrapped him with a blanket, and promised food. She hugged him close as he watched over her shoulder, through streaming tears, the lanterns trail into the trees, to the entrance of the mine.

Jake's father bellowed down into the mine shaft, that Jake might hear him, that he might still be alive.

"How we gonna get him out?" Asked a man standing nearby.

"Only one way. Go down after him," Gendron said, loosening a stringer of rope. His voice was steady, but as he turned to hand the loose end of the rope to another officer, it was clear in the lantern light, that his eyes betrayed his fear.

"Tie a double half-hitch around a good sturdy tree, Portman. And you," he said, nodding at a man the boy did not recognize, "help him reel in the slack when we need it."

Some of the other men came to help, each taking a place along the rope.

Nate Fulton, Jake's father, insisted on going down for his own son. He fastened a knot around his waist and cinched it tight. He hung a lantern from his belt.

"Make sure she's good n' tight," Someone down the line called out.

"Alright, let me down boys. Let 'er out a bit at a time, on my say so... Portman you stay here and relay my instructions once I'm in."

"Got it," Portman nodded.

Once inside the cave, Nate cautiously worked his way downward, letting his weight fall back onto the rope, to let the men feel what it was like. He found the edge with the toe of his boot, and he called up for the men to steady themselves. Trembling now, he reached down with one foot and found another small hold.

Nate leaned back into the rope harness, to keep the lantern from catching on the rock wall. He could see at once where the rocks had

142

been newly disturbed. He began inching his way down when suddenly his feet plunged forward into open space and his weight fell full upon the rope.

The added weight jarred the men up above and the rope slipped several hands before they could regain themselves.

He held the lantern aloft and saw at once that he was dangling before another shaft that cut deeply into the wall directly in front of him. He peered into this new brand of black – darker, somehow, than what lay below. He brought the light around and then, some distance beneath him, something shimmered.

"Jake?" He called out.

Nothing stirred. He was met only with deep silence.

"Quiet a minute up there!" He called to the men above.

"Lead out more rope. Hand-over-hand fellas," his voice boomed and echoed in the mine shaft. "Keep a tight grip!"

"*Hang on Jake, I'm comin'*," he whispered to himself as he began his descent. Soon he could make out a ledge jutting from the side of the shaft. Now, caught in the light, he could see, almost clearly, what he could only glimpse from above. The ledge had been sheared smooth by the miners that worked the shaft years before it was abandoned. A heap lay in the middle of the outcrop. His eyes sought familiarity, but found none.

"A little more," he called up, holding the lantern out over the ledge.

In a moment he brought his full weight to bear upon the ledge and carefully made his way toward what appeared at first to be a mound of refuse. He leaned in closer and saw at once the morbid grimace of a human skull. He reacted instinctively, fumbling backward, away from what horrors lay there. He felt the ledge beneath his feet. Panicking now, he reached ahead to steady himself, falling forward again into the body as he did.

A handful of small rocks broke free and trickled down into the shaft.

"Goddam!" He yelled, despite himself.

"You ok down there?" the call came from above.

"I'm fine... It's..."

His gaze followed the rope upward, to the glowing entrance that seemed miles above him. He forced himself to look down, at the grim scene that lay at his knees. His eyes followed the contours of the body, and where its legs were turned beneath itself, an arm lay draped overtop at an impossible angle. Another corpse. His eyes traced the arm to a rotted hand and then back behind it, where the skull of the second body lay, still with a full head of red hair.

"Whad'ya see down there? Ya find 'im?"

"Hold up," he called back, forcing himself to take stock of the situation before calling up to the men.

His gaze continued along the contours of the second body and he made out yet a third, lying beneath; further on there was still another. His mind reeled. Had these men fallen into the shaft? One after the other? Or had they all met the same perilous end, each on their own terms?

He pulled a stone from the wall, held it out over the shaft and let go. Some long way down there was the distant click of rock on rock.

There was no hope for the boy.

He turned to the bodies again and held the lantern high. "Dear God," he whispered.

To the right of the ledge another shaft bore into the side wall. Inside - near ten feet in – Jake sat huddled against the seeping mine wall, shaking to his very core, and covering his eyes with his hands.

"I've found him!" Nate screamed, his voice cracking. "He's alive!"

A roar of cheers erupted from above and spilled into the shaft, tumbling eerily down into the darkness.

In moments, he had guided the men above and set foot into the second shaft. Nate went to Jake's side and knelt beside him.

"Jake," he said, resting his hand on the boy's shoulder. He did not reply. His body shuddered with each breath.

"It's alright now Jake. You're alright, son," he laid his hands upon the boys shoulders. He pulled him close, hugged him and kissed him on the top of his head.

Jake's knuckles where white, pressed into his eyes.

"Go on and keep your eyes closed, son. I'm gonna take you home

144

now."

Nate untied the rope from his waist and fastened it securely around Jake – under his arms, and passed twice between his legs. Once the rope was tight, he carried Jake to the ledge. The boy clutched at him, desperate to remain in his arms, his eyes wide with fear.

"Jake's on the rope now boys. I want you to pull 'im up slowly."

"Jake. If you can hear me, boy, I want you to try to help the men out a little. I want you to use your hands to keep the rope off the wall ok?"

Nate thought he saw a faint nod.

He watched for the slack to be taken up and held onto his son until the men took his full weight onto the rope. Slowly he began to creep upward, toward the beam of yellow light. Jake's body brushed against a wood support beam and Nate was pleased to see his trembling hands come out and push nervously off the wall. Nate ran over in his head whether he had tied the lead correctly, whether the knots he had fastened would hold.

At last he could see from the shadows that the men had him now safely at the top.

"We've got 'im, Nate. We've got him! ...Rope's comin' back down."

Nate watched the rope unfurl into the shaft ahead of him, and dangle above the abyss.

He wondered how he would tell the men what he had found.

Ω

DEATH COMES TO LIGHT

Amor tussique non celantur

*Love and a cough are
not easily concealed*

Warner McLeod stood in Paton's field, with one hand on his hip and the other holding a pipe to his mouth. He had the sultry look of a general surveying the field of a losing battle.

"Over here. Set 'em down next to the others," He directed two policemen, each half-carrying, half-dragging a body wrapped inside a dull gray blanket. He watched impatiently as they pushed their way through a large and still growing crowd that had gathered.

The lawmen insisted on handling it themselves; but the men that rescued Jake insisted on being a part of it too, arguing, the job was half done, and they weren't about to leave it that way. Others from town were inclined to go too, on account of they had family or friend who had not been seen for some time, and, by their vicarious experience, felt they were elect. They believed the opportunity held promise of closure.

As it is in a small town, many others who, for one reason or another, felt inclined to accompany the men to the mine, if for nothing else but to see the bodies as they were dragged from the depths.

Once word got out, there was no stopping them from coming.

And they came in droves, most hoping to catch a glimpse of the unthinkable.

A yell came up from inside the cave to signal that another body was ready to be pulled up. "Biggest one," Darcy added from down in the mine shaft. The men heaved and pulled the rope one hand over another. The loaded carriage swung back and forth, tracing a large arc over the dark pit. It hooked on a protruding beam and Darcy yelled for them to stop heaving so the carriage could correct itself. As it came near top the crowd pushed in to get a better look. Constable Hutchings bumped into the last man on the rope who stepped sideways and lost his footing on a moss covered rock. He fell hard into the ground and started the next two in line falling back over top of him. Jim Hamilton and Gendron lunged to the rope, caught it, but the rope started slipping through his hands. Evelyn dropped her notes and fell in behind Jim and grabbed onto the rope, one of the officers jumped in behind her and the rope held fast until they could get it to the surface.

Two of the officers let Jim and Nate take their place on the rope and turned on the crowd, driving them back to the field.

Down below, Darcy had taken care to cover the body but when the rope had slipped the blanket fell away partially revealing the corpse lying beneath. They dragged the carriage out of the shaft onto the forest floor.

One of the officers leaned in close to Eve. "You step off now, give us the room we need to work. You shouldn't even be up here – should be back there with the others. Not getting underfoot."

"Take it up with Quentin."

Evelyn glared at him met his stare – the two of them stood there glaring at each other. Evelyn dropped the rope. "Your welcome. It was no trouble at all," she said dropping the rope. She walked back down to Charlie who was grazing at the edge of the trees.

As the body was dragged down into the field, the crowd closed in again. Red Sutherland's face turned crimson as he started yelling and pushing them back. He took his baton out and started waving it around. The others did the same spreading down the line of civilians who had gathered to watch.

"You *all* better get the hell outta here before I lose my good humour," he bellowed, sending the bystanders scattering homeward. "Anyone who's not helping better leave now if they know what's good for em. As of *now!*"

"We got every right," one lady near the back of the crowd yelled back. "Some of us is missin' family. We want to put our worry to rest."

"You're interfering with police business. Go on home. You'll all find out in due course. Besides you oughta' know better than to bring your children out here. Mrs. Philpot, you're a good mother, why don't you take those kids on home."

"Just like Heidi Tsan found out about her husband? She had to hear it from gossip after two weeks a you guys not saying a thing."

A rustle of agreement rolled through the crowd. Red Sutherland strode to the edge of the crowd and pulled a young man into the open and threw him to the ground instructing one his men to arrest him.

The crowd was pushed further into the field and one by one started to turn and leave. As the crowd shifted, Evelyn spotted a man she recognized craning his head above everyone else, to see the bodies as they were pulled on old sheets to flat, solid ground, where they could be covered and prepared for the trip to town.

Warner McLeod, Vananda coroner, crouched beside the first body to come out of the mine, with furled brow. She watched with growing curiosity, her recognition starting faintly at first, then growing; concern fluttering faintly in her mind like the wings of a black butterfly seeking escape. The man watched as Warner pulled the sheet back bobbing, his head from side to side to get a clear sight line. Suddenly his gaze found Eve's. He noticed Eve watching and ducked into the crowd where she lost sight of him.

The mothers and their children, fathers, and grandparents moved away from the trees, out into the field on their way back to town. Evelyn watched the lanky form of the stranger, his faded yellow shirt trailing untucked – he walked alone with his head down in front of him and shoulders hunkered around his ears as he strode easily across the field, ahead of the others, with wide lurching steps. It was then she realized she'd seen this man once before, at the Paymaster mine collapse. Her pulse quickened.

148

She looked back at Warner as the second body was slid in beside the first.

Eve dismounted her horse and strode easily across the field of trampled grass that, only this morning, stood to her waist. Captain Sutherland took sentry at the perimeter to maintain some semblance of order. His cool stare remained fixed upon a group of onlookers who evidently were not acquainted with the notion of empathy. With one swift movement, in which all of his training and physical prowess was evident, Sutherland had the baton from its sheath and made for one of the young men who had just delivered a glib punchline to his friend. A sharp blow above the left knee was painful enough to leave the boy begging for death, but still more-or-less ambulatory and well enough alive.

Warner yelled over the crowd, suggesting they all make for homeward and tend to their own business. They made way as he moved through the crowd, some of them side-stepping so they could still see what they could of the corpses laid out in the make-shift clearing.

Seven bodies had already been pulled from the mine and were arranged side-by-side so Warner could ply his trade. He knelt in the grass beside the first body and pulled the blanket back to expose it from the waist up. He proceeded down the line until each of the bodies had been partially exposed. Some of the women who put off their departure until the last possible moment gasped in horror. Others clung to their children trying to cover their eyes.

"This is no place for a child anyhow, woman," Hutchinson snapped. "What the hell is wrong with you?"

Some of the bodies had been inside the shaft long enough to have been partially mummified. The climate and atmosphere offered nearly perfect preservation in some cases. In others, that, by happenstance, were exposed to a damp cool breeze, or moisture from the mine walls, experienced putrefaction to some degree – enough to properly horrify the onlookers. Thin lips were pulled tightly over perfect rows of yellow and black teeth. Tufts of hair exploded from cracks in skulls. Menacing grins and empty eye sockets cast complacent stares upon whoever passed before them.

"What in hell'd they think they were gonna see anyhow?" Gendron muttered as he stormed off to the mine again. He brushed past Constable Hutchinson, who struggled with a body that was partially wrapped in a heavy wool blanket. He was trying to move the body - a surprisingly fresh corpse that must have been left there recently - and he'd gotten hung up trying to navigate a mass of roots and salal. Eve strode the short distance across the field, stepped into the trees and grabbed a corner of the wool blanket, not waiting for an objection from Hutchinson.

"Let's try bottom-side first," she said already pulling toward a faint slope that broke down toward the end of the log. Hutchinson had to hurry to catch his corner of the blanket. Together the two of them muscled the corpse out of the forest and laid it beside the others. Hutchinson wiped a dirty sleeve across his forehead and tried to catch his breath. Eve attempted to make eye-contact, but he seemed content to look anywhere but directly at her.

As noon approached a light salt-breeze drifted inland and rolled through the trees, stirring a stench that had, until now, remained hidden in the earth. But, one by one, as the bodies were wrested from their tomb, the damp, stale air from inside the shaft roiled to the surface and poured out into the forest clinging to trees and creeping low over the grass. It was a drift that brought with it the distinct odour of death that, until now, had been kept secret and hidden in the earth. Were it not for the three boys, it might never have been unfettered.

Eve stood among the seven officers and several of the men who'd helped in the recovery. Warner stood again with his hands on his hips surveying the corpses, which now lay arranged alongside one another.

An eerie silence hung in the air.

The slow, warm wind stiffened and whipped across the field. Untrammelled tufts of standing grass waved and snapped over the bodies in a bid to lay claim.

Eve noticed Hutchinson looking at her, "You oughta' be on your way with the rest of 'em," he said, nodding to a few stragglers still making their way through the field.

Evelyn caught and held his gaze.

"Don't like being showed up by a girl, Constable?"

150

"Nothin' doin'. You got no business here is all."

"She's with me," Warner said, calmly handing his notebook and pencil to Eve. She looked at him and then at Hutchinson.

"This one's been here about three months," Warner said nodding to the notebook.

Hutchinson turned abruptly and strode awkwardly away through the grass.

Warner knelt and pulled the blanket away from another body. Eve's gaze fell immediately upon the face. Before taking up with the newspaper she'd not seen a dead body to speak of. Only one week into the job and already she'd laid eyes on no less than eight. Roughly one a day, she thought to herself, hoping her odds would improve.

She wondered if it ever got any easier as she studied Warner's face. He handled the bodies as though they were nothing more than a vague curiosity.

She noted Warner had been staring intently at one body in particular for some time. He looked up at Eve, then back at the corpse. At that moment two officers stepped from the trees and walked toward them.

"Are you alright?" Eve whispered to Warner.

"Quiet!" he hissed, and let the blanket drop again.

"Body number seven is partially decomposed, less so than the others…" He looked at Eve intently, then at the notebook in her hand. She fumbled to flip the book open to a blank page and started scribbling notes.

"Present in the mine – by my estimation – eight to twelve weeks, given the slowed rate of exposure and decomposition due to low oxygen levels. Male," he said reaching into his bag for a tape measure.

"Here hold this," he handed Eve the loose end of the tape measure.

"Keep it up near the top of the head - as close to the top of his head as you can now." He pulled the tape down toward the feet, until it ran the length of the body. He pinned his end alongside the bottom of the black rubber-soled shoe.

"Six foot," he said glancing up at Eve.

"That's all of em."

"You're sure none went over the edge?"

Hutchinson chuckled and looked to the other men who'd now

gathered to watch. "No damn way of telling doc. It's gotta be three hunert' feet if it ain't twenty."

"Is that your professional opinion then?"

Hutchinson smiled dryly.

"Make yourselves useful and help me lift them into the wagon," Warner said, nodding at the string of bodies.

"Why? You've got you're little Miss there to help lift haven't you?"

Eve opened her mouth to snap back before Warner waved her off.

"Can the smart-alec routine Hutchinson," a voice boomed from behind her. "You're here to do a job."

She turned to see Red Sutherland striding through the grass toward her.

Hutchinson's face flushed as he quickly busied himself loading corpses into the wagon.

Red strode into Warner's personal space, his boots nudging up against one of the corpses. "Constable Gentry's packing a case of dynamite and a charge into the mine. He's going to set the charge and make sure the mine can't be put to further use – whether good or bad."

Warner glanced at Sutherland's boots and then back up to meet his gaze again.

Red spat in the grass next to Warner and headed off toward the mine.

Warner leaned toward Eve as they walked toward Charlie, where he was hitched to a solitary fence-post – remnants of the profitable pasture that was once there. "Come to my office after dark tonight," he paused. "After eleven..." He hesitated another moment, as if to say something, then thought better of it.

Hutchinson eyed them suspiciously.

Eve untied Charlie, climbed into the saddle and wasted no time breaking across the field as fast as he'd go.

She was a good way to the forest, at the north end of the Lambert property, when the dynamite blast shattered the air behind her.

Ω

A MESSAGE
FROM
THE DEAD

Obscurum per obscurus

π

The obscure, by the more obscure

There was something about this night that had Eve on edge. It was quiet, the air was still and close. The very night seemed to tremble, ready to snatch up even the slightest noise, and broadcast it to the universe.

Warner had asked her to come to his laboratory after dark. He cautioned that she avoid becoming a spectacle; a young girl travelling in the middle of the night, to the office of an elder gentleman, would serve that end. But, despite her best efforts, the moon flashed arrogantly between buildings like a giant, stubborn spotlight tracing her every move as she and Charlie made their way through the middle of town.

Charlie's hooves scuffed the gravel. A movement drew her gaze to a second story window, above a portico. A silhouette peered from behind a thin veil of curtain. Eve tensed, then, and just as suddenly felt foolish for her nerves. All the secrecy was nothing but a farce; a childish innuendo. Still, the nagging truth of it - that people were dead - and that a shadow of suspicion seemed to shroud the minds and intentions of what should be the town's most trusted, was hard to deny. She would be a fool to think she were beyond reproach.

Eve pulled on the reins, steering Charlie into the alley that cut between Quartermanche's and the apothecary. Once she was away from the lantern light, and beyond the reach of the moon, the darkness descended quickly, and the air grew cold and damp. A breeze funnelled from one end to the other, seemed to whisper that, if anything were going to happen, it would be here, in this very place. Up ahead she could see the narrow strip of light where the alley spilled into Warner's yard.

"Don't be a bloody fool," she said aloud. Though she'd intended to soothe herself, the sound of her own voice, echoing between buildings, startled her again. She urged Charlie onward.

Warner's stable lay awash in the moonlight. She slid from the saddle and led the horse to the hitching rail. She loosened the tether on a small leather bag. The sweet oats were for Charlie, to keep him interested that, at any turn, there might be something in it for him. She let the horse see her pour some into her hand. He snuffed at her hand and reached for the payoff with delicate, velvety lips. He snorted and wagged his head at her in horse-approval. When he was finished, she let him see her tie the bag and tether it to the saddle again.

She loosened the saddle bindings that held the camera bag and tripod securely in place. With her arms full, she made her way to the top of the trim cement steps leading down to Warner's office, beneath the apothecary. An understated District Coroner's sign hung by two lengths of chain high above the door.

Eve shifted the weight of the camera on her shoulder. The metal feet of the tripod clicked on the steps behind her as she descended. She knocked on the door and waited. No answer came. She knocked again, and instinctively looked around to see that she was still alone.

Warner's door burst open, sending a spray of light into the dark.

"I wasn't sure you'd come," he said, pulling her inside.

Even in the dim light, she could see his face was ashen with concern.

"Did anyone see you?"

"I don't think so. But the moon…I might as well come in the middle of the day for how bloody bright it was."

Warner went to a small window over the bookcase and pulled back the curtain.

"Hunter's moon," he said. "We get rain twenty-nine of every thirty days in this god-forsaken place. I suppose it's too much to ask for a little cloud cover this one night."

Warner let the curtain fall back.

The office was arranged in painstaking detail, laid out like a surgeons tray. A barrister's bookcase stood against the wall, behind the desk. It was lined with leather-bound tomes, each standing perfectly erect, as though they had been tuned with a compass. There was a stack of writing paper on the desk, its edges perfectly aligned. Two fountain pens and two mechanical pencils lay side-by-side, ready for use at a moment's notice. Beside the pens and pencils, a writing tray offered a full ink-well, and a small glass box filled with metal clips.

Across the room, a renaissance-style floor lamp stood in the corner with dignified air, throwing its light pragmatically over the oak desk and chair.

On the wall. immediately behind the lamp, hung a thoughtful portrait of an intelligent looking, bearded man.

"John Moore," Warner said, glancing at the picture. "An ancestor of mine. He practised anatomy, then medicine in Glasgow, last century, before becoming a novelist. They say it's in the blood," he said smiling.

"And on that note... You can set your things there for now," he said, pointing to the filing cabinet. He stood aside and waited while she settled in, then walked briskly to a narrow door at the back of the office. He drew the door open and stood aside, allowing Eve to enter the heart of the laboratory.

Inside, the air was cool. It was a large, windowless room, dimly lit, with a single bulb centred over each of seven narrow, metal tables. The tables themselves were strung across the length of the room. Upon each, lay one of the bodies they had pulled from the mine, each covered with a white sheet. The faint smell of ether mingled with the subtle stench of decay.

"Can I ask you about Ernie Tsan? I mean can you tell me anything?"

Warner handed a cotton mask to Eve, then proceeded to tie a cloth mask over his face. "Tsan's body was never delivered," he said, turning to the table closest at hand. He pulled the sheet back to reveal a blackened skull that grinned a macabre jest, defying the man to unlock its truth.

"I don't understand. Don't all bodies come here, to the morgue?"

"Most do, but there are rare occasions where I get a firmly worded letter from the police explaining why I won't be receiving so-and-so -"

"Is that unusual," Eve interrupted, "I mean don't you find it strange that Ernie Tsan wasn't... didn't arrive?"

"Mine is not to question."

"Yes, but -"

"Do you know something I don't, Eve?"

Eve found herself at a loss for words.

"I mean, if you have a suspicion, more than that, if you have some kind of proof there's something not right, some breach of etiquette?"

"It seems strange," Eve spoke in measured tones, "after the way they were acting when I found the body and all."

"By 'they' you mean the police?"

"Obviously."

Warner shot Eve a look, to let her know she was venturing into uncertain territory.

"There are rules, Eve. Things are done a certain way. Until the laws are changed, there's nought anyone can do about it," Warner said turning his attention to the corpse in front of him.

Eve thought it wise to heed his body language and bit her tongue.

Warner pulled the sheet fully away from the body. It was partially mummified. Flesh had dried to form a thin, ribbon-like coating entirely true to the bone beneath it. Most of the hair was intact and gave the impression that rats could easily have been nesting in it.

He slipped his hands beneath the head and propped it up onto a wood block with a deftness that might easily be mistaken for compassion, but was simply borne by a desire to preserve the evidence.

The sheet slipped from the table and fell to the floor, revealing the feet: one was bare, and leaned awkwardly against an unlaced boot still covering the other. The trouser pockets were turned out against what faintly resembled faded, yellow and black checkered wool pants, the kind her father used to wear to the mines when she was young.

"It's been made to look as though he was robbed before he was dumped into the mine," Warner said calmly, glancing at the turned out pockets. "His right index finger's been cut off," he said lifting the hand.

"You think a thief did this?"

" Not a thief. In fact, I don't believe any of them were *robbed* at all," he said, looking over the row of dead men. "None of them likely had anything worth stealing."

His gaze followed the contour of the hand, the fingers, the palm, and then the tattered, stained shirt sleeve.

"Lack of oxygen in the mine slowed decomposition considerably." He coaxed the sleeve back. "See here," he said pointedly. "Coal, or some other carbon residue from a mine," he said, showing her the dark stains. "And not the one he was found in either."

Eve looked at him with surprise.

"The mines on the Paton land were dredged for gold. This man worked in the coal mines. So did his friends," he nodded at the others.

"Who are they?"

"We'll know in a moment," A disembodied voice sounded from just behind Eve. She darted away from the table side, and turned to face what ailed her. Her hand went instinctively to the gun beneath her coat.

"Eve, this is Drew Kellerman. Drew, this is Evelyn Walker. She writes for the Coast Miner... Eve, Drew is on our side. Please, put the gun away."

Eve regained her composure enough to accept a hand shake.

Drew draped his jacket over a chair near the front of the laboratory and set his leather physician's bag on the chair. He popped the straps on the bag, snapped open a clasp, and pulled out an eye-piece. He then pulled on a pair of gloves, taking care to cinch the cotton down between each finger.

"So, who's the trouble maker?" he said, looking over the bodies.

Eve looked questioningly at Warner.

"I'll explain in a moment," Warner waved her off.

"This fella here is the one I told you about," Warner said, pointing at the body two tables in. "But, there's nothing at all stopping you from looking at the others too while your here."

"Not sure you can afford me, Mcleod."

Warner explained to Eve, that Drew Kellerman was one of only two dentists practising in Vananda – but only for the company men. He'd come with the influx of professional men who'd first arrived when news of the mineral boom reached the mainland. It was generally agreed that Wentworth Forman was the town dentist. To him, Kellerman was a late comer and presented needless competition. The truth of the matter was - as Eve's father was often fond of saying - Forman was a dentist with traditional leanings and couldn't hold a candle to Kellerman. Once word got out that Kellerman had a gentle way with his means and his ends, and had drugs that made things properly bearable, it was only a matter of time before he'd got the lion's share of the town kitty. However, owing to his allegiance to the company line, it was all kept under wraps. It was Forman's good fortune that Kellerman was a savvy competitor, a man of real compassion, and took only what was fair. He sent the rest on to his compatriot.

"Let's have a look," Kellerman went to the head of the table.

He slipped his hands under the corpse's neck and inserted two fingers into the mouth. With a slight flick of his wrists, a dull snap split the air, and the jaw fell loose, but not detached, from the skull. He adjusted his eyepiece and leaned closer, peering into the gaping, morbid mouth. "There's some dental work alright. I may recognize the work. I'll look further in a moment."

Warner moved to the next table and pulled the sheet back. He tilted the head to the side and shifted his stance to let the overhead bulb shine full on the corpse.

"See this hole?"

Eve leaned in for a better look.

"Shot in the head. Probably a 32 Winchester." He picked up a lead slug from a metal tray and held it next to the entry wound. "Someone

158

had these men at their mercy."

Eve pulled her notepad from her bag.

"This can't go in the paper Eve," Warner said. "Make no mistake, Charlie Morgan made it clear he'd be the one dishing out information. You print this and I'd be out of a job. Maybe worse."

"What do you mean worse?" Eve asked incredulously.

"We'll know shortly," He said looking gravely at Kellerman.

"What do you need me here for then?"

"Get your camera," he said, nodding toward the office where she'd stowed her gear.

Eve glanced at the overhead bulbs dangling from the ceiling. "I don't know if we'll have enough light, but we can try."

"We oughta' do better than try. If this is who I think it is, we have a real problem on our hands... Put all this other stuff to shame. We'll need these photographs, Eve. We're here 'til we get it right."

Just then a bold knock came at the office door. Warner and Kellerman looked at each other, then at Eve. Warner put his finger to his lips and left the room, closing the door quietly behind him.

Kellerman glanced at Eve and turned his attention to the body again.

Eve stared at the cocked feet. Her eyes followed the entire length of the body and settled on the face. A faint recognition stirred. High cheek bones, pronounced brow. She looked closer, trying to place it, but, just as quickly, any recognition that might have come, had faded.

"That was the lady from upstairs," Warner announced, as he entered the room again. "Says your horse slipped its noose and was nosing around for grass on the next property."

Eve winced. She thought she had tied a half-hitch.

"He's safe now," Warner smiled faintly.

"UL3 extracted," Kellerman spoke into the room, still peering into the second corpse's mouth. He tilted the head back with care and exactitude and peered inside. "UR2 - gold cap." He closed the mouth and ran his fingers along the jaw bone, on either side of the head. He pulled his gloves off and looked gravely at Eve and Warner.

"It appears the former editor of the Coast Miner, Mr. Jonas Prescott, has returned from his hiatus."

Ω

A GIFT
FROM
UNCLE SAM

*Accipe sume, cape sunt
verba placestra papae*

II

*Take, have and keep, are
pleasant words from a Pope*

Eve followed closely behind Song-Loo, over the moist, slippery path to the foresters' bunk house. Eve slipped in the mud and reached for Song-Loo to steady herself. He paused, offering his arm, before continuing on.

The windows came into view and glowed warm with yellow lantern light. The meetings were always held after dark and the men were expected to know the route well enough they could find their way without the aid of a lantern.

Despite being a spurned minority, Song-Loo walked with pride and self assurance. As a young boy he had been adopted to a well-educated white couple in Vancouver, after his parents died on the Komagatu Maru. The ship was caught and got turned around in a terrible south-east gale and sank miles from where it had any right to

160

be. Later on, with the benefit of propriety and a good education, he left the comforts of home to try his hand at mining, when word of a mineral strike on the island got out. He had intended to pre-empt a few land claims, if he got in early enough, but there were unexpected delays and later complications in processing the paperwork. It was this unexpected wait that kept him out of it. Song-Loo could see that, with a few minor adjustments, these unreasonable and inexplicable delays might easily be avoided. But despite the unshakeable hope that propriety and congeniality would result in reward, for him, the benefit of advantage was not to be.

Song-Loo stopped at the foot of the stairs. "Try to relax, Eve. These men can smell fear. If they do you'll be done here for good." He kept just ahead of her and reached the porch. He tapped on the door and waited. A few moments passed before he knocked again. This time the door opened quickly and a ribbon of light fell across their faces and cascaded down the stairs behind them.

Inside, Eve met the grizzled stares of some three-dozen men who peered at her through wafts of smoke from rolled cigarettes and loose tobacco pipes.

"This is Eve Walker, the newspaper woman I was telling you about," Song-Loo introduced her to the men who sat in chairs, loosely arranged in groups of three or four. A few of the men nodded an aloof greeting. Most peered coldly, as if challenging her for intruding.

The room was warm and well-lit. The welcome smell of coffee, and wood, and sweetly-sour pipe tobacco permeated the air.

Song-Loo directed Eve to a chair against the wall, near a podium at the front of the room. She set her papers and pencils out on the chair while the men settled in to talk among themselves.

A stately man dressed in a black Stetson and oil skin coat, stood at the front, with a man at either side.

She felt a hand on her shoulder.

"Glad you could come, Miss Walker."

"Just doing my job," Eve replied curtly. "Tony Watson isn't it?"

"Guess you're right about that. Suppose that's why you're doin' what your're doin'. You get paid to know everyone's business and all."

Evelyn hesitated. "I suppose that's one way of looking at it.

Taking the catty gossip women are inclined to and putting it to an art form," she smiled tersely.

Tony smiled awkwardly in return.

"Please be assured, I do aspire to greater heights than what you might expect, Mr. Watson."

Around the room many of the men stared conspicuously before looking away abruptly and trying their best to look distracted.

"Anyhow, it's good you're here. You'll have to excuse the men, they tend toward over-cautious," Tony explained. "I'm sure you understand... Ernie always said we gotta use the modern conveniences and innovations to better our cause. And I'm guessin' your newspaper's one of 'em right?"

Evelyn eased a bit, showing a spark of pride.

"It's a shame about that Indian killin' 'im. What with it bein' her brother and all. You just wouldn't expect it... I bet Ernie didn't even know it was comin."

"Nothing's been proven one way or another," Eve said calmly. "We'll have to wait and let the courts have their say."

"And the God above after that I s'pose," Tony said leaning in with a smile.

"Look. I know it's difficult, but we're not doing Ernie Tsan any favours by spreading rumour and disregard." With that, Tony took a step back, the smile leaving his face. "Who'd a thought a pretty thing like you could be all spit and vinegar," he smiled again, dryly.

Song-Loo made his way through the crowd, to the front of the room, and stood at the podium waiting patiently for the room to quiet.

"Evening gentlemen, ladies," he said nodding at Eve.

A few of the men who were still standing moved slowly to fill the few chairs that remained. An old man was led carefully from the doors, with a man on either side, and a chair and some space was made available. Those who remained found an empty spot along the wall at the back of the room.

"It's good to see we have a good turn out for tonight's meeting. Means there's a lot of support for what we're trying to do... Firstly, I want to thank you all for coming. I know you all work hard to make your living and would like nothing more than to be at home with your

162

families – those of you that have them. But just your being here says to me that you all know how important this is." A murmur rustled through the crowd, some of the men nodding in approval.

"None of us is any good on our own, but together, we can get results. As you know, in the field, what one man can do in ten days, many can do in one. And that's why we're here. We're here to tend the field today for prosperity and fair working conditions tomorrow."

A louder vote of approval rang through the crowd.

Someone stood from his chair and shouted over the noise, "Why ta hell will it be any different this time? Seems to me we done this all before and Maddox and his men coulda' give a damn. Besides, what about those men who was found in the mine. They was all men who worked with us. So who killed em? It was Maddox and George Sutton, 'at's who!"

The room fell silent. And it was obvious, from the silence in the room, that the truth was likely not far off.

Song-Loo hesitated, appeared to be deep in thought... "It's a good question. One that needs to be asked," he paused again. "As well as cutting a trail through the thicket, we just as well take a look behind and see where we come from. Do you all remember last year, down on the docks at Westminster Quay? No battle worth fighting - worth winning - was ever won in a day. They – all who've ever fought for just labour laws - were pushed back to the edge of defeat, before they found it within themselves to rally and break through to a measure of success. And I ask you now... What would have happened if they hadn't kept fighting? The truth is - that fight – it was worth fighting and worth winning. And our fight carries that same truth."

When Song-Loo stopped speaking the room erupted in applause and there were shouts from the men. The man who'd asked the question of Song-Loo looked around, his cheeks flushed with embarrassment.

"There are no bad questions, my friend," Song Loo assured him. "In fact, if any of you have questions, or concerns, now is the time to voice them."

"What about in Victoria not six weeks ago. I heard Dunsmuir's man, Porter Jackson, got the government to call in the militia. It wound up a bunch of men getting killed – just for standing against Dunsmuir for better pay."

"At's to say nothing of dangerous conditions in the mines," someone shouted. "It's our second home down there. A guy'd want it to be safe."

"I read it in the paper," said another, "Dotty's Pa sent it from the city. They got the government in their pocket down there. We're losing men in the mines, and we're losin' 'em on the street, just on the question of fair workin' conditions."

The room erupted again, this time louder than before. Eve's attention was drawn to the front doors, where a man had come in late. His long moustache stuck out from under a tan bowler hat, with a black ribbon tied round it. He wore a fine deer-skin jacket, and shiny black boots. He walked a short distance and stood against the wall, looking calmly over the room.

"And what did the paper say about the workers? Was their voice given equal representation?" Song-Loo asked, trying to keep the meeting focused.

"Cut the legal-speak Song-Loo we ain't lawyers. Ya might as well be talking through a mouthful a cotton." Many of the men laughed.

"In that newspaper, did it tell what the workers had to say about the government being called in?" Song-Loo went on.

The man who'd brought it up shrugged and settled back in his chair.

"*No.* It did not. You're talking about the Victoria paper. It's been a common complaint, aside from Mr. Higgins' term as editor, that it's a paper owned by people in big business, and owned by the colonial government. You're getting only one side of the story. And that's the side that favours business. Favours the Government."

"What's the damn point of it all, then. If we've lost before we even got going," came a shout from the crowd of men.

"You gotta have money. We ain't got no money," someone else piped in.

"Ee's jus' blowin' smoke up our asses."

Song-Loo stood before the crowd with his hand raised for

164

silence, and waited for calm to descend.

Just then, a man standing at the back of the room stood away from the wall and shouted over the din: "I heard it wasn't no Indian that killed Ernie Tsan." The shouting died quickly beneath his deep, resonant voice.

"I heard it was Maddox got his men to kill 'im, cause he heard what Ernie was up to. Folks are sayin' that Tsan was killed 'cause a his bein' involved – bein' an organizer with the union and all. They're playin' with our heads, people. And truth is, could be any one of us that gits it next."

Eve tried to get a look at who'd said it.

"Don't be fooled," the man next to her drawled quietly, as he rolled a cigarette on his lap.

"What do you mean, exactly?" Eve asked.

The man calmly placed the cigarette between his lips and struck a match on his boot.

"That's right. Don't be fooled," he said, the cigarette dangling from his mouth," The day Tsan decided to marry that squaw. That's what got him killed."

Eve sat forward and bristled.

Some of the men around them overheard the conversation and now waited to see what she'd say.

"We oughta leave that to the police to figure," one of them offered.

"The police are in Maddox's shirt pocket jus' like in Victoria. Ain't nothing gonna be done - even if it was the chief's son that did it."

The men's voices were loud, many now arguing among themselves.

"Calm down," Song-Loo yelled over the crowd. "Calm the hell down. We sure as hell aren't going to get anything done fighting among ourselves," he paused to let the men settle.

"Look. I know it's hard. But we have to stay tight. You all have a choice to make. If we start to break rank and they catch wind of it, it's all over. They'll get tight. And each and every one of you will pay for it in other ways. Of that you can be certain."

165

"You think they know what we're up to? It's possible. Is there risk involved? The answer's yes. It's more likely, with the new labour strike in Victoria, that Maddox is just trying to play his cards, to keep it from spreading. The mine owners meet in rooms just like we meet in rooms, to keep things going, one way or another. We *must* keep the pressure on. Sooner or later they'll break. It is the right thing to do. Because if we don't do it, we just pass the whole thing on to our sons, and their sons after them. I'd rather leave them with something to be proud of."

The man with the bowler stood chewing tobacco. His eyes were shrewd and sharp and he watched from under the brim of his hat. Then he shouldered his way through the crowd to the podium and rested his hand on Song Loo's shoulder.

"Song-Loo is right, people. Whether you know it or not, you've got numbers on your side." Quiet quickly descended upon the room once again, as all present waited for what he'd say next.

For a moment, he let the silence reign.

"It's not just you, and it's not just this town, people. It's workers in every town, on every island, on the mainland, in towns stretching clear across your country... Every town that's got a town and a mine on it. It's every island with a forest that's roped to be cut. And then too, it's over on the mainland – all up and down the coast, and as far inland as you can go. And we're all comin' together. Not a dozen, not a hundred, but thousands upon thousands of men, all working the same cause."

"You said, '*Your country*'," came a question from a man standing at the back of the room.

"Pardon me?"

"Your country... you said, *your country*. That's meant to imply you are from elsewhere. Where might that be? And what in hell do you know about what we're up against here?"

The man looked at Song-Loo and then back at the crowd. Song-Loo stepped in. "This is Lester Freeman, people," he shouted over the crowd. "He's the head of the United Workers' Union, on the West Coast of the United States."

Almost at once, a profound silence fell through the room. The

166

very moment seemed to hang upon a hinge.

"As the man said, gentlemen, my name is Lester Freeman. I'm here on behalf of the United Worker's in Seattle. We are affiliated with and have a large chapter in San Francisco. And believe me, I *do* understand the situation you're in. It's simple enough for a guy to stand up here and say what he thinks. But, I have the advantage of battle scars. Scars from wars fought on the labour front - for the working man. And, chances are, they're the same battles your fixing to fight here."

All at once the room exploded. Conversation and conjecture ran rampant – most of it rumours and guesswork; very little of it resting upon the sound pillars of truth. Fears of assimilation into the United States, ran rampant. Fears of a conflagration of American business interests, come to feast upon the wealth held by the Dominion in the West, were cast about with complete hubris.

"Rest assured, I stand united with Song-Loo – with what he says about being able to win this fight. It's been done before. And it can be done again. I'm here to tell you you have our full support."

Someone coughed at the back of the room. Outside, a gust of wind blasted the side of the bunkhouse. One of the lanterns swung on its hook. "I can say with confidence the fight is worth winning."

A few of the men clapped, and the others joined in. Lester waited until the mild clamour died down. A few of the men who were on their feet allowed themselves to sit down again.

Eve looked over the room, taking in the important details. She could see the newspaper falling on doorsteps, at the first sign of dawn; the papers lying there waiting to be picked up and spread out over the breakfast table and taken with coffee. The importance of implication, of what she was witnessing, was not lost on her. The realization of her responsibility was paramount. It struck her as odd, in some way, that Lester Freeman... spoke the words of a well-thought businessman: sharp-minded and a wit and intellect sharpened on experience – hard-fought, hard-won battles through which American business had emerged the victor, for the most part. Then there was the fact that the United States, with their railroad fast on the heels of the Canadian intercontinental railway, now stood in a position to fast overtake the vested Canadian interests, but here he was speaking in terms of unity, of a profound joinery, who by their experience would assist their Canadian neighbours – their competition. It was profound, it was unheard of, and yet, still, it made sense, such that it brought this room full of opinionated men to utter silence.

"The men who own these mines, these production plants, and these companies have one thing fixed in their sights: the almighty dollar. Loss of life is a human-cost of doing business, and one that, so far, has not *cost* them anything. We agree with them, that without money there's nothing, but we also believe in equity, safety and the long-term fix. We say that without the working man there's nothing to be gained. Successful business is a union between business interests and the safety of the men who risk life and limb to keep the well oiled machine spinning its wheels. We are part of the equation – not in spite of it. The business man who cares - not only about profit, but the well-being of his common fellow is the man with his sights set clearly on the future."

There was a raucous round of applause.

"It's about relationships and affectations, men," Lester went on. "One thing affecting another, one man supporting the next, doing his part, so the next man can, in turn, do his part. Take care of your people, we say, and profits go up. Treat the working man like he was expendable and two things happen: if it weren't for the fact of jobs being so scarce we'd take our loyalties somewhere else. But most men would choose to stay on, on account of family obligation. Second thing is this: productivity goes down when your workers are dead. Safety for our men is paramount – not negotiable," Lester pounded his fist on the podium and the room was up on their haunches. They hung on his every word, some of them allowing themselves to believe there was hope.

"What if those good men down there in Victoria are being killed for standing up for their God-given rights? The government is doing nothing. In fact, there is every sign to indicate that government and big business are one in the same. And, men..." Lester waited for quiet enough to speak. "Make no mistake. Blood will be spilled again."

168

Some of the men stood and put their hats on, and made toward the door. Others followed.

Lester spoke a little quicker now, as if throwing a net to draw them back in. "How many men did you lose last month in the mines here?" He asked. "What about the month before that?"

The men who were making for the door, stopped once again.

"What about last year, gentlemen? I'll tell you how many – twenty-three men, last year alone. By my account that's twenty-three too many. You there," he said pointing at a middle aged man with a long beard, who appeared to be leading the small procession of men to the door. "What's his name?"

"Spencer Williamson."

"Mr. Williamson! May I ask, have you had the misfortune of having a close call in the mines?" Williamson showed no sign of slowing his pace. "Got a wife at home Williamson? Sons? Daughters? ...What if one of them twenty-three men was you? What if tomorrow there's another pocket explosion like you had here, and you leave, never to come back home? If your loved ones are lucky, they'll have a pit-side burial for you, because odds are they'll never recover your body from that mine shaft."

Spencer Williamson stopped, fists clenched: "You best shut yer mouth 'fore I shut it for you," he spat on the floor.

One of his fellows piped in: "He just lost his wife to sickness not three weeks fore."

"Please accept my humble apologies Mr. Williamson. It was not my intention to offend, only to appeal to your sensibilities.

"All of those lives," he went on, "the lives of your brothers and friends, could have been saved with a little money spent on safety. That's what we're trying to do here. Last year we only lost four men in our region. Compare that to twenty-seven over the two years prior - before we got our initial labour laws instated. It is NOT negotiable! Safety must be paramount on the minds of management *and* ownership.

"And, as I said, lives may be lost in the fight, but with perseverance, you will win, and those lives and the lives of men lost in the mines, will still mean something. If you do nothing, every man that's been killed before, and those that will certainly die after this moment, will be for nothing.

"In Washington this last May we got the six day work week passed, and we can help you try and do the same here. Bear in mind it'll take some doing. You'll pace yourselves and take the small victories with the grand, but it'll all come in time."

"The way I see it you're asking us to throw ourselves headlong into the mouth of the beast," came a question from one of the men sitting near the front. "Maddox's men got bats and go about thumpin' anyone they see fit, that's makin' noise about things not bein' fair. Or, for that matter, anyone who looks at him wrong."

Lester stepped off the podium and nodded to two men who were standing at either side of the door. They both stepped outside and returned a short time later carrying a large crate – a man on either side. They waded through the crowd and set it down next to the podium. One of the men handed Lester a crowbar. He jammed the business end of crowbar under the lid, and, with a wretched creaking, wrenched the nails from the green wood. The men nearby closed in to have a look at what lay inside. On top, on a layer of straw, were laid at least two dozen shiny black pistols. From the size of the crate one could only guess there might be three or four more layers packed just like it.

"What the hell are we supposed to do with those?" someone asked.

"It's like I said. The men we're dealing with aren't above taking a life. We've seen it again and again. With the kind of money we're talking, some men in their position wouldn't give it a second thought. They see what we're doing as a threat to their livelihood; like we're stealing food from the mouths of their wives and children. Things aren't getting any better, my friends. Our sources tell us that ownership to the south of here has already stepped up their patrols, that they intend to squash the movement before it starts. Your colonial government has promised to send in the militia if another strike breaks out like the last one. Already three workers turned up dead in Vancouver and Steveston over the last two weeks."

Another man stood from his chair and made for the doors, "I, for one, ain't no murderin' fool. What they're doin' ain't right, but it don't make it right for me to go killin' them too. What... pretty soon we all got guns and go round shootin' everyone else. There won't be anyone left. What they're doin' is plum wrong, but I ain't gonna kill a man over it. No better n' them if I do." The man made for the door and was followed by several others.

"And I respect that..." Lester hollered above the men. "I respect your right to say so. But don't go putting yourself in harms way then. Because you'll be asking for trouble. I ask only that you respect the will of your fellow-workers, your brothers, and speak not a word to anyone about this. If it gets out, the militia will be down so fast, it'll all be over in a shake, and blood will be on your hands whether you want it or not."

"As for the rest of you," he said - "Jack, help me hand these out." "Use them only with great discretion, only when the alternative is your own peril. If you must shoot, dump the gun straight away into the ocean and get on home, or somewhere else you've got an alibi."

He placed his hand on Song Loo's shoulder and leaned in close, "Make arrangements for a care package to be sent along to Mr. Williamson for his recent loss: food, coffee, a little whiskey to ease the bite... Money if there's need for it. Write-me up an invoice for costs. I'll cover it before we leave tomorrow night. In fact, do the same each of those seven families who had their loved ones dug out of that mine as well... Make it: care of Canadian Workers' Union, and with a tip of the hat from their brothers to the south..."

Ω

PREDATOR AND PREY

Ad mores natura recurrit damnatos,
fixa et mutari nescia

ᚼ

Human nature ever returns
to its depraved courses
fixed and immutable

The Maddox estate was perched on a barren hill-top, the highest point on the sprawling property. The trees had been cut away on all sides, to open the view, so that the excessive grandeur of the estate could spill out the windows and doors, and splash across the backs of mountains and down into the valley, there for whomever might care to notice. The silver-blue ocean glittered as it caught and held bits of the sun,

A cinnamon-skinned woman dressed in a pleated servants dress answered the bell. Though she was only an inch or so shorter than Eve, she was dwarfed by the great double-oak doors. She crossed one foot over the other and dropped her gaze before stepping aside to allow Eve into the hall.

"Musn't worry about yer shoes missus. Nobody else does," She turned to lead the way past a staircase wide enough for a small brass band to navigate at once, if there were call for it. They skirted down a darkened hallway, lined with elaborate portraits and fine art. It seemed at first that each piece was hung ad-hock, with no fore-thought given as to size or subject. There were handsome portraits interspersed with random historical subjects; Robert Gibbs' impression of the Scottish charge at Balaclava, an oil painting of a kingly, hot-blooded Arab horse standing atop a country knoll; portraits of Sir John A. Macdonald and two preceeding Prime Ministers... Perched upon the wall, in the middle of the run, was an oil portrait of Christian Maddox himself, trying his best to appear every bit a statesman as the fellows whose company he kept there on the wall.

Eve chuckled.

The maid flashed her a look that warned of the importance of propriety, despite obvious realities.

The maid's soft-soled rubber shoes padded on the polished tile floor. She hesitated outside an interior double entryway. Inside, came a boil of laughter, betraying a roomful of men who were all intent to talk at once.

Eve's confidence faltered a moment, but she fixed her gaze and kept her mind sharply upon the object at hand. There was a more noble cause to be accomplished here: the base requirements of the ego had no place.

The maid turned the glistening brass latch and carefully walked both doors open at once, so the men inside could stand aside. A thick curtain of cigar smoke drifted out into the hall. It seemed every man in the room – upwards of fifty in total, by Eve's estimation, turned to stare at once, as a hush fell over them.

She fixed her gaze and followed the maid through the crowd.

Each guest was in perfect attire, and each turned to stare as she passed them by. Some of them joked with their fellows, and a hearty laugh was had at her expense. She could sense their undisciplined libidos, their misplaced sexual tension... She stood straighter, shoulders back, and noted the more dominant personalities in the room becoming a little louder, no doubt to ensure their brand of artful brilliance could be properly appreciated.

Some of the men stood with hands tucked cleverly into coat

pockets, holding drinks, and with cigarettes or cigars tucked neatly between their fingers. Smoke hung at the ceiling and the servant stopped at a tall window to let the fresh air in.

Maddox spotted Eve and, excusing himself from a small gathering of men all sporting moustaches and canes, made his way across the room.

"I wasn't sure you'd come."

"And miss this? A journalist is only as good as her sources Mr. Maddox."

"Journalist? Yes. Well we'll see about that," he said laughing, so that anyone who stood nearby could benefit from his own good humour. He placed his hand on the small of her back, compelling her through the crowd.

"I couldn't help but notice that you seem to dress the part. Like a man that is. I suppose, the fact that it *is* a man's job, that stands to reason." He said smirking at the men nearby.

Eve smiled dryly: "And I suppose *you* are dressed like a man because you don't look particularly good in a dress." Several of the distinguished spectators broke into boisterous laughter. Maddox pressed his hand more firmly now into the small of her back. He was in a hurry to get somewhere. A flash of nervous tension snaked through her.

They walked across the room, directly through the sea of men, again drawing the full attention of almost the entire room.

"And what, in your knowledge, makes journalism solely a man's domain? Surely a woman can be as intellectually stimulating as any man?"

The room quieted. They were all poised for Maddox's reply.

"If it were not a man's job, Eve, then why on earth would you pretend to be one?" The room erupted. "At least let your hair down and let us know we are in the presence of certain beauty."

Eve flushed, her cheeks hot now with blood. She stopped and pushed back sharply against him. Maddox came to a halt beside her, his jaw flexing. Indeed this was a man who liked to be in control.

"I'd like you to meet..." he said aloud, sweeping his arm across the room: "Evelyn Walker," he paused: "Journalist." A low chuckle

174

bubbled through the crowd.

"Why, thank you Mr. Maddox," she managed to spit through clenched teeth.

"Please, refer to me by my first name," he chuckled with smug self-admiration.

Eve felt her face turning ever deeper shades of red. "I can't say, for certain, but could it be that Christian, here, seems threatened in the presence of a woman?"

"My dear Evelyn. I welcome any woman into my home... In fact, just now, as you can see, I have several maids present."

A murmur snaked through the room, coupled with a smattering of applause. Eve sensed Maddox's guests were growing uneasy with the sparring, which had now, in her opinion, descended into little more than childish bickering.

"I dare say we need a few more men like you around, to set an example for the rest of the us," Eve said, trying for the last word anyway. "Perhaps you should let one of your maids run your business too, given you even need help running your own household."

This time Eve was granted a wash of applause that equalled the admiration Maddox had gained. One of the maids smirked as she made her way to the door, her hands and fingers burdened with empty glasses.

"I think you may have met your match Christian?" someone shouted.

Maddox grunted, now visibly annoyed, but still managing a terse smile. Eve was prepared for him to take things further, but instead, he raised his drink in the midst of the laughter. Maddox took Eve by the arm and lowered his voice. "Thought I should tell you, I had a nice chat with your man there at the paper. Says he's sorry he couldn't be here." Maddox's jaw flexed, his eyes simmering with rage. "He assured me he was looking forward to a healthy working relationship with Christian Maddox Enterprises. Assured me that all of our fledgling industries here on the island would be well represented... For the good of the town. Thought I'd tell you that... Just in case," he said with a wink.

"Excuse me," he said, turning to the crowd before Eve could

respond. "I want to thank you all for coming, for taking time from your hours of industry, to hear what I have to say." Maddox allowed a moment for the men to settle.

"At this moment, gentlemen, you are on an island -"

"There's a notch for the public education system," one of the men shouted, "It's a good thing we've got 'im around." This earned the man a round of heartfelt joy.

"Yes, yes. Have your fun. Then be sure and find the back of the line, Foster, because you'll get nought from me," Maddox smirked, noting the response was somewhat less than he'd hoped with his reply. "So, back to the matter at hand. It's not just your run-of-the-mill geologic protrusion we're speaking of, but an island quite unique in its character, steeped in tradition and history. And," he paused a moment for effect, "I have the privilege to tell you, an island that contains enough mineral wealth to power a small empire..."

Every face in the room was now riveted on Christian Maddox. The murmur of conversation died as they all hung on his every word.

"For one, Texada is one of the largest of all of the islands on the B.C. Coast. The local Indians say that, a long time ago, there was a great shaking of the earth, and that when it had passed, this island had newly risen from the sea, and stood glistening where it stands. They say that, one day, it will again return to the ocean depths. Whether or not that is true, this day – and always – the fate of our island, our Texada, remains the will of God." He paused to sip at his drink. The crystal clicked loudly when he set it on the table.

"When I first came here, I was skeptical. I was trained in the Empirical sciences, which, by all accounts, would argue that such an event was highly improbable. But, given time to learn the island, to understand her nature, I came to wonder whether, on occasion, does not a man's reason interfere with his faith? I would suggest that, being a man of faith, it is entirely possible that she *is* in fact a gift from God. A gift of such rarity and wonder, it would not be unbecoming to have her burst from the sea... After all what really do we know of the ways of the earth?"

Most in the room listened with rapt attention. A few men on the fringes, shifted uncomfortably.

"Most of you, I assume, are aware of the success we've had with mining on our island; we've discovered copper, silver, iron ore, and very recently, limestone, to an extent unequalled in the empire. It's as if God himself dug a hole and dropped his treasure into it. The copper mines in the north, the silver mines to the south and to the west, have fast come to provide for a good chunk of our territory's Gross National Product. Demand for goods produced to our neighbours in the South is growing, and thanks to our resident provincial foreign investment adviser..." A chuckle rose into the room; one of the men patted a short, well-dressed man wearing glasses, on the shoulder.

"...We've had fans in the Motherland for some time, whose impression is nonetheless adoring. Most of you are probably not aware we've only very recently found an audience in the United States, ports in South America, and, there is demand all through Eastern Europe. These are all expanding nations, whom we expect will become great friends as the extent of our mineral wealth is proven over time."

"Hear, hear!" someone yelled, and the room erupted with applause and adulation.

Maddox paused to allow another turn of boisterous applause. He raised his hand and waited for quiet. "But that is not all, gentlemen. It is clear we, in this room, are all kindred. We are the very men who will deliver this province, this country, into this next great age of prosperity. But... That is *not* what I've called you here for." The cheers fell to a low murmur, then almost to a silence, as they waited for Maddox to let them in on his secret. Maddox was a brilliant speaker. He had the entire room on a string.

The two maids slipped noiselessly into the room and cleared empty plates and crystal tumblers from the serving table. He let the quiet hang, almost a moment longer than he should. He waited with the skill of a fox eyeing a hare for the precise moment when the light, the angle of approach, the anticipation, all things converged in a moment of perfection, and success was the only possible outcome.

"There will soon be an announcement, a *new* opportunity, one that may well cast a shadow upon all that we've done to this day. But as much as I would be pleased to be in a position to present the paper to you here today, I cannot." A volley of shouts went up, Maddox's audience was visibly shaken, expressions turning from approbation, to concern, and frustration; even mild anger for the thought of being led to pasture.

Christian Maddox only smiled, awaiting his moment. He would not have wasted their time.

"All I can say to you now, is that I've spoken with some of the best minds in science, in industry and I've confirmed that, very soon, there *will be* an opportunity unlike any other you have been kin to. It is upon the dawning of this new era of industry, that we here in the west, we here on Texada, will have our hand firmly upon the rudder.

"A man - some of you know of him by the name of Chase Whitney, was hired by the government to survey, identify and confirm the discovery of a limestone deposit here on the island. Plans have been underway, behind the scenes, beyond common knowledge and the prying eyes of those who would work to deny us this grace. It was almost a year ago today, from the time Whitney advised us of the prospects of just such a find. We immediately set about preparing to identify the source and extent of the deposit, to see where we might stand.

"We understand," Maddox shouted over the conversation running among the men, "that there are still... issues with the Indians here on the coast. While we've been changing the course of our economic prospects here in the West, Macdonald's government has been busy drafting laws that would give the land outright to the Indians.

"Marion, please," Maddox said to a maid standing nearby. She handed him a fold of documents. "I have here, Mr. Whitney's report which outlines his findings. They state, and I paraphrase: 'there is enough limestone beneath our island to supply a large proportion of the world's demand in the coming years'."

Decency and candour were now an afterthought, as the men fought to shout over one another. As it seemed on the verge of imploding upon itself, a stranger stepped forward. "Please, gentlemen. Please!" He shouted, holding his hand aloft. "My name, is Gavin Cartright. I am a representative of Amor De Cosmos, Premier of the Province," he announced, and waited again for silence to descend.

"We are about prosperity here in British Columbia. I want to confirm that the Provincial Government has taken a stand. The Federal government is *not* welcome to stick its nose into the affairs of men that have made this place habitable. They are fixing to have a hand in the wealth here. Of course, they are welcome to bring their money: just leave their opinions at home is all."

A mild wave of applause met Cartright's candour with approval.

Eve made her way through boisterous crowd until she stood at the back of the room, trying her best to make sense of who was whom. One thing was certain, the self-imposed self-importance of everyone there made it next to impossible to tell one from the other. Most had an extra notch or two worked into their leather belts; the Bodega in Vananda must have a run a special on grey pin-striped suits.

She noticed a man standing near the entrance way, a reasonably tall man, well-dressed, but not quite like the others. He looked to be taking an inventory, just as she had been moments ago. She tried to get a look at his face. He adjusted his hat, interfering with her intent.

"As we speak," Maddox continued, "delegates from Japan and China – even though there is a moratorium on trade in both countries - and the United States, are securing agreements on good faith, with our provincial government, to obtain supply agreements for limestone, copper and iron ore for the foreseeable future." Maddox paused to let the appreciation of his words settle into the crowd, before continuing.

"By now the purpose of it should be clear why I've called this congregation. *If* you take anything from this opportunity, take just that: the promise of opportunity. At the moment, some of us have our hands full. Others of us have fulfilled our economic goals and aspirations. And yet, among us still, there are those who are ever-hungry for prosperity, who are waiting for the next Utopia... And this, gentlemen, is it." The room was poised to spill over.

"From this meeting, we will plot the course for our future, and the future of Vananda. I will not take anymore of your time, other than to say there is excellent food and drink and, good conversation. Take from the company in your stead, everything you can."

Men closed around Maddox in a flurry of back patting and

adulation.

Eve looked again where the stranger had been and was startled to see he had gone. She searched every face that came to her in the crowd trying to place him. At last, through the milling sea of men, she spotted him: a flash of olive skin, a large moustache, a glimpse of blue eyes. But it was only for a moment. Then he slipped from the room.

She followed after him into the hall and pulled the doors closed behind her. To her right the foyer was empty. To her left, a long darkened corridor led to the East wing. The man was no-where to be found.

She stepped quietly down the hall, to a narrow staircase that led up to the second and third floors.

To proceed - to climb the steps - would put her half-way into the fox's den. If she were caught, she would tell them she was simply trying to find the ladies room. It made perfect sense, and would work – certainly with the staff, or any of the guests, but Maddox didn't trust her worth a damn. To be discovered would only serve to deepen his misgivings.

Soon she was at the top of the first flight, peering down a second story hallway.

No going back now.

Perhaps he had simply gone to the men's room. Quite possibly the look he had given her was nothing more than a flirtation, or misplaced recognition. What would she say to him, a complete stranger, even if she did find him? It was of no matter. She was going purely on... journalistic instinct.

In any case, she would see it through. She was committed now. She would find something to say, to make it seem a natural consequence that they should meet. And if there were something to it, she'd know. Somehow she'd know. Then again, it could simply be a fool's notion, that would lead to nothing but trouble – that would come soon enough on its on.

Eve stepped quietly down the hall, pausing to check each room. She strained to hear movement but none came. She placed her hand on the door and pushed it open. A room for textiles. It was empty. A yellow cotton curtain stirred in front of an open window.

She searched the entire floor and found nothing. It was only a matter of time before someone should find her.

She hurried to the staircase and skipped up to the third floor. There a movement caught her eye, just down the hall. It was so fleeting that she couldn't be sure it wasn't just her own eyes playing tricks on her.

Some way down the hall a door drifted open.

She had to will her legs to move, as if they had suddenly conspired against her. She grabbed the door latch and slipped into the room. It was Maddox's study. The walls were lined with tall book shelves hewn from thick, dark wood. Each shelf was arranged with books that looked as though they had each been placed for effect rather than utility; not one looked as though it had been read, but they were there simply to look fine on the shelves.

A monstrous barristers desk sat presumptuously in the middle of the room: the centre of the universe.

Here was an opportunity she had not expected, the man she had been searching for, now all but an afterthought.

The desk was littered with papers, some stacked in half-formed piles, that demonstrated a half-hearted attempt at organization. Others simply lay wherever they had been dropped - on the desk, over pens and wax seals... and a pair of eye glasses that might now have been missed for some time.

She began leafing though the pile closest to her, the pile that would presumably lay close at hand when Maddox was at his desk. She hadn't much time before she would be missed: being the only woman in the room had its disadvantages. She rifled the pages, skimmed the first few lines of each, hoping not to miss the finest of telling details.

She was through the first pile of documents and onto the second, this one she guessed was a hundred pages or more. Half-way through the fourth document, a word leaped off the page. It was an assay and a mineral report sent to Maddox from Victoria. Two alpha-numeric codes marked what she guessed was a serial number. She slipped a pencil from the holder and began scribbling them onto a scrap of paper.

Voices down the hall signalled an approach. She recognized Maddox' voice. He was with at least one other man.

Eve plunged the paper into her pocket and rushed for the door, hoping to have enough time to make the hall, where she could enquire where the ladies restroom might be.

She took a deep breath and was about to leave the room when she was grabbed from behind and pulled into a dumbwaiter, a hand planted firmly over her mouth, the other firmly around her throat, so that she couldn't scream. She stopped struggling. He loosened his grip and allowed her to face him. His eyes were severe and pleading as he put his finger to his lips, warning her to be silent. Moments later, Maddox and two other men entered the study. The two of them watched through the small crack between the closed doors as Maddox unlocked his liquor cabinet to retrieve a bottle of whiskey. That in hand, they retreated from the room again.

"You were careless to follow me," he said as he lowered the dumbwaiter, hand over hand, in almost perfect silence, to the ground floor. With a curt gesture, he showed Eve into the service hallway whereby the kitchen was kept stocked.

She turned in time to see the doors close again behind her. She watched dumbfounded as the small elevator crept back up to the next floor.

Despite the unexpected outcome, she counted her lucky stars that she had survived her enquiry – even had something to show for it. She slipped back into the library where the men were still engaged in boisterous conversation at future prospects.

Eve helped herself to a glass of champagne and watched as a maid found Maddox and whispered in his ear. As she spoke, Maddox turned red-faced with anger, and turned at once to address the crowd.

"It seems," he hollered, then waited for the noise to die down. "Gentlemen, it is my regret to inform you that it seems we have a thief in our midst. Now -" he was cut off by shouts of indignation, and he allowed his guests time to properly weigh in with their support. "Now, if you'd all like to come with me, we can set things to rights, and then be done with it."

182

The absurdity of the entire congregation waddling after Christian Maddox through the endless hallways of his mansion, out through the double-oak doors and around the house to the caretakers grounds, like a flock of lost penguins, was laughable. But there the levity came to an abrupt halt, as one of Maddox' henchmen – the bald man from the mine – had his hand wrapped tightly around the back of a young Salish Indian boy's neck. He said he'd caught the boy stealing dynamite from the supply shed.

The young boy, no more than fifteen, stood with his shoulders up around his ears, and his long hair hanging down over his face as he stared hard at the ground. Maddox, who'd been striding with the confidence of a schoolyard bully, lost his composure and stormed at the boy. He swiftly tore the shirt from his back and ordered his man to bind the boys hands and tie him, arms above his head, to the clothes line.

A hush fell quickly over the men, their faces lined up like a committee of fools, and reflecting the entire spectrum of human emotion. Many remained salient, and holding fast to their convictions. These men, it seemed, felt the punishment fit the crime.

Christian Maddox stripped his belt and raised his arm. He held there for a moment – about the time it takes to pull a trigger - before bringing the belt down hard across the boy's back. The boy's body stiffened in a contortion of raw pain. But no sound escaped his lips. The silence seemed to multiply as Maddox brought his arm up again.

Eve shoved her way through the crowd of gawking men and caught Maddox's wrist before the next blow could be wagered.

"You will NOT strike this boy again!" She yelled in his reddening face.

The bald man was quick to respond and slid in behind Eve, to catch her unawares. With one lightening-fast arc of his long legs, he swept her feet out from under her. Maddox moved in quickly and struck her a blow with the belt. Eve caught most of it on her forearm, but the stinging lash of hard leather came down hard across her face. The blow stunned her.

Maddox moved to strike again, but was halted by a booming voice that seemed to descend upon them. All heads looked to the treeline, at the edge of the property. There a massive Indian – a truly magnificent specimen of humanity - emerged from the forest, followed by a few better than twenty men – all of them Salish – running now at a steady pace toward them. Few among them carried guns. They did not need them, owing to the thoroughly impressive aspect of their procession.

Maddox stepped back involuntarily.

The bald man straightened himself and looked over each shoulder for help that was not to come.

The crowd of men parted effectively as Big John strode through their midst. Several of his men followed his lead. The others split evenly to the left and to the right of the gathering and fell in around Maddox and his man.

John held up his hand, signalling the others to stop. One of the men went immediately to Eve's aid.

John approached Maddox, who found himself scaling great heights in order to meet the stare of his attacker. He looked instead at the massive waiting hand that hovered inches from his throat.

The negotiation was over. He surrendered his weapon without further conversation.

With the belt now safely in his hand, John leaned in close to Maddox and let loose with his booming voice: "Untie the boy!"

Somehow Maddox managed not to flinch.

"Stevens! Let the boy down."

The bald man looked past the Indian, opting to avoid direct eye-contact, as he made toward the boy.

"I said YOU untie him," John bellowed again at Maddox.
Maddox held his gaze resolutely upon John. He bit the inside of his cheek and nodded slowly.

His man Stevens made as if to try and spare his benefactor added humiliation, but one further look of concern from John convinced him to rescind his offer.

"I'll need a knife, big man," Maddox spat, shifting his gaze to the boy. John made out as if to produce his knife from its sheath, then smiled almost imperceptibly and slammed it back home. "Do not make the mistake of thinking me a fool, Christian Maddox," he glared. "You will untie him with own your hands."

Maddox opened his mouth to protest and was again silenced with the sound of a finely honed blade on its sheath. John now held his exposed blade down at his side. "I am losing my patience... Christian Maddox. And, as it is, there is still the problem of your ill treatment of Miss Walker."

John nodded slowly when he saw the first flicker of fear cross Maddox's eyes.

"That's what I thought."

Maddox corrected himself, having taken a moment to regain his aloof composure, which, to him, seemed right, given the circumstances.

The boy was freed from his bonds and stood beside Big John; his hair was brushed from his face and his gaze level, fierce, for his age. John laid his hand upon the boys head as he set out across the yard, the procession following in noble repose.

Several strides into the forest, the boy broke from the group and disappeared into a large rotting stump. When he returned he was carrying two canvas bags each stuffed with dynamite.

Ω

A CAVE
IN
THE FOREST

Ab uno disce omnes

From one, learn all

After ensuring the boy was delivered in safety to the village, Big John led the way over a narrow but well-worn path through the deep forest. It was an ancient place, shrouded in shadows that were given life, from time to time, by a faint breeze; or sprays of light breaking through the high canopy.

The air down among the trees was dense and quiet. Time seemed measured in the subtle movements of the plants and of the trees themselves.

Eve startled when a Kingfisher alighted on a branch next to her. John chuckled.

"She knows the way. If you lose me, you can always call on her."

As they went, the underbrush grew dense, and they had to use both hands and both feet to scale a small mountain that seemed out of place, as if it had failed to heed the call of progress, and so was swept over by the myriad lifeforms that clung to the forest floor. She reached for a tree to steady herself and felt something she did not recognize – texture – ridges that were carved into the bark and plied into the flesh of the tree. It was an ancient face staring back over the path from where they'd come. She looked questioningly at John, who merely nodded, indicating they should continue to climb.

Before long, Eve could see a light emanating from near the top of the forest bluff. Then, almost at once, the ground levelled off and they stood at the lit entrance of a cave. She followed John inside, where the air again grew close and quiet, save for the crackling of a fire.

"Hey whitey, you forgot to take your shoes off," a voice ushered from the dark and rocky throat of the cavern. A man then appeared as Eve peered into the darkness.

"Joe Martin," he introduced himself. Eve guessed he was in his late fifties. His long, black hair was streaked with silver and tied back into a ponytail that gleamed in the fire-light.

"Sorry, I'm not that used to people coming and going. Forgive me if I seem odd at first... Mind you that won't change. I'm almost sure of it."

"Consider it forgotten."

"Yes, but forgiven as well then? ...Just so we know, between the two of us, where we stand." He looked at Eve for a moment, then continued on, not waiting for a reply. "Without a doubt, I can see you are a woman of... well, there is something there. Let's just leave it at that. Okay?Okay!"

"Hold your horses Mr... I mean, Joe. Is it ok to call you Joe?"

He nodded earnestly. "No horses, I'm afraid to say. A few resident deer though."

"Fine..." Eve smiled, then broke into a laugh. "Hold your deer then." Joe chuckled too. Big John stood stoically beside the fire, his arms hands folded in front of him.

"There you are. I suspected you were in there. Just needed a little coaxing."

"This is not what I expected," Eve looked around.

"Times are changing young white lady. And you should know - you must know, really, that change is coming for you too. You are following a thread of logic, because it is your job. Because you are doing what is true to your heart. And that is well and good. That is *good* change... All of us in this game," he paused and nodded to the cave entrance, where his quiet solace spilled out into the world.

"Well," he paused to look around. "Come here, with me," He said, taking Eve by the hand. He led her further into the cave, where a fire warmed several large stones that were arranged around it. He let go of her hand and walked to the cave wall, where he ran his fingers over the rock there, its rough surface long-since tempered by the winds of time. When her eyes adjusted, she could make out – faintly at first – primitive paintings on the walls there.

"I was lucky to find these. They were covered with soot, from years of burning here," he waved at the fire pit.

"What do they mean? I mean, what story do they tell?"

"The one on top there, we believe, tells of another location where there are more paintings, much older than these here - unrecorded hieroglyphs in vivid red paint, on a cliff along the Homalthko River. The shaman who left these ones, indicates here," Joe pointed to a group of figures at the bottom-left of the painting, "that he was told the information by a two hundred year-old woman, who remembered the time before the white man came." The fire snapped loudly.

"They tell, also, of a place up on top of a mountain, where a man and his son had found quite a few big war canoes hanging up in the ancient trees there." He stared calmly at Eve. There was a long pause, as though he were challenging her to say something about the nature of myth and realms of possibility; that the two never tread the same path.

"The ocean has never gone up that high. At least as long as we've been here. It was a mystery for a very long time, until some of our people – a hunting party – found the huge bones of the people who must have owned the boats." Joe looked at Eve again, appearing nonplussed. Then he smiled. "Okay, I'm sorry to burst your bubble, but they are not the bones of giants, as it might sound.

Eve nodded.

"I've seen them myself, and they are the bones of a creature of some kind – that walked the earth long ago. They are very similar to some of the Smithsonian reports."

"I'd love to see them myself some day," Eve said.

"That is out of the question."

Eve knit her brow.

"Well, it's been forbidden to bring people there. Even among our own kind, to go there is a rare gift."

Eve stared calmly in return.

"Well, given you insist, I will see about it, maybe."

This time Eve smiled.

"Time changes when it wants," Joe continued, "Maybe sometimes it is wise if the rules change too." He picked his way between large stones and sat again, poking at the fire with a carved staff. "The other painting there, the one on the bottom, says that on... Estero Peak – I think it's Estero Peak – there is also evidence of a great flood that came long ago. So long, it is almost beyond the memory of my people... Our people," he nodded at John.

He looked back at Eve, then at the blaze in front of them. A shadow seemed to fall over his eyes.

"There is a storm coming that I am afraid may be beyond us at this moment." The tip of the staff was now glowing red-hot, but seemed to hold its own against the flame.

"The grizzly has wandered from its den. After months of nothing but sleep it is near starvation. But it is yet a young grizzly, a three-year-old," He explained, "they're the worst. And this young Xawgas has caught a scent that will take him far from home, and he does not yet have the good manners to know his place. That he *has* chosen, will come at great cost," Joe paused to look deeper into the flame. "But not all of the burden will be on his back. The cost – in lives, in the land, in our story, will lay at the feet of the Indian. But be certain that you will bleed too. Don't mistake it." Joe leaned in closer. "Whispers come from Victoria, and from Vancouver, and Prince George, that the government wants more land – more control," he met Eve's gaze now.

"There is more going on than what it would seem, young Eve. In the Government they are working to drown our culture in grief. They are writing big, long pieces of paper and then they blame the words there on the paper for what comes after. What happens to a tree when you start ripping away at its roots? Damn right it does, Eve! It bloody-well falls. They will say that we have no claim here, that the land is not ours. They will torch our roots and the Great Creator only knows what else."

"How do you know this? Do you know it for sure?"

"A woman who I trust was there in the big city and heard some of these conversations."

"Who? Who is the witness?" Eve sat forward on her rock. "And who came up with this plan?"

"That is your job, Eve. To find out."

Eve gaped at John, then back at Joe Martin. "But you know the names. Why not just tell me now? That way I can get to the fire as fast as possible, no?"

"It is important that you find the string by yourself, Evelyn."

"Eve," she corrected him.

"What was that?"

"It's Eve. Not Evelyn. Sorry to interrupt."

Joe stared a moment into Eve's eyes. "Evelyn is better for you. I will call you Evelyn."

Eve gaped at Joe, uncertain whether he intended it to be funny.

"Where was I?"

"Tracing the string."

"Yes, thank you. So it is important you follow the truth yourself. Sometimes, if somebody has planted an idea in your head you get lost in the words, and they make you blind to the thing itself."

"Yes, but with all due respect -"

Joe lifted his hand to stop her speaking.

"What do you know of our people?"

"Not enough."

"Go with John. He will tell you what you need to know. The questions to ask are up to you."

Eve looked from Joe Martin, to Big John.

"Victoria." John said. "That's where you will start."

"Victoria." Eve affirmed.

"I will tell you this as well, Evelyn," Joe followed, "There are those that will tell you to go for the throat."

Evelyn started to nod.

"But, there is another way. We must learn to negotiate, to move like them. Study their ways and learn their weaknesses and their strengths. Like the young grizzly it is his inexperience that will unsteady his balance."

190

"Play the game by their rules," Eve agreed.

"That is just what I said. Yes?"

Eve smiled warmly.

"Okay then. I am glad we understand each other."

Eve turned to follow John from the cave into the darkening forest.

"Oh," Joe said behind them. They both turned and looked at him expectantly.

"I lied. There is one more thing," he turned and disappeared into the cave. He returned a moment later holding something heavy, wrapped in deer hide.

"This," he said unfolding the hide, "was found lodged deep inside a tree at Shelter Bay." Joe revealed a ball of solid black iron.

"Go ahead, it won't bite," he said offering it freely.

Eve took the weight of it. She inspected it closely, then looked back at Joe.

"It's a cannon ball."

Eve's eyes shot from Joe, back to the ball of iron, then back at him.

"A cannon ball? But -"

"It was an ancient tree. Four hundred years old, at least."

Eve was about to speak.

"Wait!"

She closed her mouth and shook her head in disbelief.

"There are many questions now to be answered." He clapped his hands together, satisfied he had offered what he could, then held up his hands to usher them homeward. John started immediately into the darkness. Eve hesitated, looking expectantly at Joe Martin.

"Don't worry young woman. We will talk again... And one more thing... John is right in his thinking, about the Kingfisher. She is young, too, but knows the ways of her kind. There is wisdom, if your eyes are clear enough to see it." Joe Martin paused, watching her closely.

"She is the mother of the forest. She will endure great hardship and danger to protect her family. She protects them at all costs. And she brings this wisdom for you today: that the things that trouble us every day are small, and do nothing to help us when it happens that our loss seems too great to bear."

Ω

A
MAN
AMONG
MEN

Fortis in arduis

¤

Be strong in your difficulties

It was drawing toward dinner time, when it caught the corner of her eye, as she sat at the desk in her bedroom. The deep orange and red glow thrummed and pulsed and spread itself across the open sky. It purled across the dark clouds and flickered across tree tops.

Her body tensed. She'd seen this before. Forest fires were not altogether uncommon at this time of year. In truth, it had been some time since the last blaze had ripped through the chaff littering the forest floor.

A blast of hot wind tore through a bank of trees high on the hill, somewhere ahead of the blaze. She knew without a doubt what that first blast of dragons breath felt like on the skin.

A siren blast erupted from town. It was a full alarm.

Evelyn stood abruptly and sent her chair toppling behind her. She pulled the window fully open and leaned out on the sill. The menacing glow roiled and scudded through the low ceiling of cloud. A chill horror snaked through her body. It was too close to town! She thought of her father in the infirmary.

She charged for the stairs.

The house came alive around her as she blasted through the kitchen. She pulled her boots on and grabbed her jacket. She could hear her stepmother behind her, already aware of the danger. Something not right here either. Her voice was tight. That, and the worried look in her eyes.

Eve made for the door. She ran across the yard as Charlie eyed her from beneath the apple tree. His equine mien was alert and responsive as Eve pulled the harness over his head. She grabbed the reins and in one fluid motion Evelyn was on his back compelling him onward.

The faint outline of the path and Charlie's good sense kept them true.

As she broke toward town from the edge of the forest, the full spectacle loomed before her. Flames billowed into the black night sky. The shadows of men silhouetted against the blaze, were harried with water buckets and scrambling and fumbling against the dark; four men dragged a hose from a pump wagon that was likely brought from the nearby Copper Queen mine.

The wagon was still rolling to a stop as the men tore the hose from its mount and worked their way toward the heart of the blaze. Liberated ground came hard. For every foot earned it seemed a yard would again be lost. But, at last, the spigot was spun wide, and cooling water set upon hungry flame, sending steam and smoke billowing skyward.

Eve leaned into Charlie as far forward as she dared, urging him faster through the centre of town. The horses hooves threw up dirt and dust that hovered momentarily in the fire-light before falling again back to earth.

The city was on high alert now. Men poured from their homes and from the living quarters above the shops on Halliburton, pulling at suspenders as they hurried to aid the men already fighting the blaze. Women stood on the boardwalk, their night caps and camisoles pulled tight, some with hands over their mouths in disbelief. Still others, thinking how they might help the desperate effort, and who pushed those more helpless than themselves on ahead shouting orders for drink and food to aid the men.

When Evelyn reached the infirmary two of the night nurses stood sentinel on the new verandah awaiting the sick and injured to emerge from the battle. An old man propped on a cane stood nearby half leaning on the balustrade as he watched the fire through narrow, keening eyes – eyes that had seen this all before, and knowing that nothing good would come of it save for a few new buildings after it was all done – a penance for the mass of life that was sure to be lost this night.

Evelyn dismounted and lashed Charlie to the rail. One of the nurses – the older of the two – drew her attention from the fire, to see who had come. Eve ran through the doors, to her father's room, but there she stopped short.

His bed was empty.

Had she passed him by on the steps when she burst in through the doors? She ran back outside, where there was now only one duty Nurse at the foot of the steps watching the fire.

"Pardon me?" Eve asked.

"The other nurse, she went to find yer father, ya know" she said nodding toward the blaze. Eve looked from her to the shadows of men struggling against the fire.

"He came up out of bed and dressed himself."

"Insisted on helping..." she said again, her hand, her fingers shaking as she pointed to the inferno. "Said he would not let himself stand by while so much might be lost. He felt he could still do some good."

Eve's mind reeled as she turned toward the fire. She searched the silhouettes for the recognizable form of her father.

She started running.

He would simply not survive... Perhaps was already dead. The smoke would kill him... And yet, part of her was certain he would have it no other way. She felt sluggish and useless at the immensity of it.

She was still a good distance away when she was forced to withdrawal from the intense heat. She shielded her eyes and gaped

194

desperately for her father – for a hunkered old man barely able to carry himself through and among the strong, the young, and the able-bodied. He would perhaps be dragging a bucket - maybe able to throw one half-bucket of water for three or four of a healthy man. She scanned the fires edge, closest to the infirmary, where he would likely take up alongside the others.

Then, some 100 feet down the line, barely afoot among exhausted soot-soaked creatures, she saw him where he rested, his clothes fire-scorched, his face covered in soot. It was indeed, Percy. But not as she had expected to see him. His white bed shirt trailed, half-tucked into his trousers. His pants legs were gathered and tucked into his boots. She ran to him, lurching in her hesitancy: her fear that the mere act of her *discovering* him would take him by surprise and shock him into collapse.

It was imperative to get him back to the hospital! He would surely understand that it was in his best interest... But, as she looked upon him she saw not a hunkered, dying old man, but a man like any other, bravely doing what he could – his level best - to battle among his fellows.

It was in that moment that he appeared as he had once been - how she remembered him as her father: *strong* and *able*. He was there in mind and body and spirit, not only *among* them, but *with* them. He was, again, a man among men.

Together the force of men fought to push the flames back, but the blaze roared with pleasure now, fed by dry timbers and a steady shore-ward gale. When the heat became too much for them, the men in front would throw what water they could before finally relenting. No sooner had they stumbled away into the cool night than another douser would replace him.

Those who were natural leaders had taken stock of the situation and assessed the fire: lines should form an arc East to West, thereby facing into the wind and throwing his pail deep into the heart of the fire. Others who were on the outside perimeter would throw water onto the buildings that surrounded the stubborn inferno. It was here that several pump and hose fixtures were brought to bear upon the buildings that remained standing, thus keeping them wet and cool that they might be saved.

The flames made a steady gamut for the Coroner's laboratory and, beside it, the Landry Hotel.

Eve could not bring herself to pull her father away, even as she saw him hesitate. The second bucket came quickly and her father, sensing hesitation in the man next to him, thought to unleash a whip tongue. But, as he turned to snatch another bucket into his hands he saw her standing there. For a moment what was almost certainly fear, was replaced at once with profound pride.

This was his daughter. Evelyn Rose Walker.

The silver-blue mist of first light hung over the charred remains of the Northern quarter of town. In total, fifteen buildings had been levelled. Quartermanche's boot shop, Bartlett and Wharton Surveying office... Even the coroner's office could not be saved. All that remained of Warner Mcleod's laboratory were the charred corner posts jutting from the ruins - caught and held in the morning sun.

A breeze struck and stirred the lazy tendrils of smoke that spiraled up from the ashes. Exhausted legions of men stumbled home, many not feigning to hide that it was not only sweat they wiped from their faces. They, each one of them, felt the loss to their very core. They had blistered their hands on those buildings, just as their own sons had done in turn. Now to have it spirited away by flame...

There were perhaps those among them who did not acutely feel the pain as most others did, but inevitably, they all knew someone, who knew someone, and in this way not one life in Vananda was spared the profound loss.

Eve recalled the Kingfisher then, and Joe Martin's gentle warning about hurts too great to bear.

Ω

AFTER THE FIRE

Acta sanctorum

Deeds of the Saints

Through the night, Percy had worked as hard as any of the men. He was finally overcome by heat and smoke, had collapsed at the fire's edge, and all the men around him, who realized his state, rushed to his aid. While several took him up and carried him to the wagon transporting the injured to the infirmary, others fell in to take his place against the fire. Though all of their hearts were with him, the men assured her, later, that the fire refused to relent, even for the moment's admiration and respect they'd wished for.

As the wagon made toward the infirmary, Percy had insisted he be able to stay and carry on. He insisted on being there, much as a general would remain in the field of battle - a perfect symbol of strength and courage. The men had taken to him in such a way that it meant something to them. Eve joined the nurses in rejecting the notion outright, while the men made their case for him to at least remain nearby, where he could provide them with courage against the long night ahead.

Percy was made comfortable, propped against several wood pallets that were stacked against a pump-house safely beyond reach of the fire.

When the silver light of dawn broke over the mountains to the east, he had already slipped from consciousness. Eve travelled beside him in the wagon, holding his hand as the doctor tried at what little he could do. It was expected that Percy would not live to see another sunrise.

The doctor's words echoed in her mind as she watched the sun break over the cedar and fir forest. To the left the sea was looking glass calm – an almost perfect black surface, unbroken by the shipping traffic that would soon come.

Her father's face was drawn, but still held a hint of the pride of purpose that had, for a short time, been his.

Eve snapped the reigns and dug her heels into Charlie's side. The horse dropped his head, coaxing every ounce of vitality from his legs. Eve leaned into him, her hands low on the reins, as his hooves carved deeply into earth.

The sun threw its first light over the far mountains and caught the mist in the back field as she wheeled up to the house. She jumped from the wagon and ran inside.

Catharyn was nowhere to be found.

She went to the neighbours, and hesitated before knocking, on account of it being so early. June Porter answered the door, pulling her robe a little tighter against the cool morning.

"It's you Eve," she said, trying half-heartedly to draw her fingers through her hair. She said she hadn't seen Catharyn, and her eyes widened when she was told about the fire, and how her father was now near death.

Eve turned to leave.

"Eve," June stopped her, and dropped her gaze for a moment when Eve looked back. After an uncomfortable wait, June looked up at her again. "Check the church."

Eve looked at her expectantly.

Catharyn was with Reverend Millen, at the church last night, June explained. And when she had left them there together, they had expected to be quite late. Evelyn thanked her and left in a hurry.

She rode Charlie bare-back into town and barrelled into the

church yard heaving to a stop in front of the front stairs leading up to the double oak doors. She tried the doors only to find them locked tight.

She went behind the church, to the back door, and put her hand on the latch. It opened easily.

The hallway was dimly lit, with wall sconces still burning from the night before. She went down the darkened hall keeping one hand on the wall to find her way.

She called into the quiet of the empty church. There was a faint bump somewhere in the dim twilight.

Light broke beneath a door at the end of the hall.

Eve went to the door and burst into the main body of the church. It was empty, but for the lonely Christ looming above the pulpit, looking down upon her with a shade of pity. Or was it irony?

A memory flooded her mind. She was a girl of eight, or nine years old, and she was made to join Catharyn for one of her weekly visits to the church, where it was intended she would repent her foolishness; that she was a dreamer, and that her head was always in the clouds. As such, she required firm counsel from the Lord, as her constant dreaming and listless revery were like an open door to the searching mind of the Devil.

Eve recalled that, at the time, Catharyn had to use both hands to open the church doors. She then grabbed Eve by the wisps of hair on the back of her neck and led her to the altar where she was made to kneel on the hardwood plank floor, before the very figure of Christ. She was instructed to remain kneeling until God was assured of her repentance.

Catharyn had disappeared through the curtains behind the altar.

She had remained there on her knees for far too long: forever, in fact, as was evidenced by the two blood stains she had left behind on the floor. An emblazoned icon of Saint Christopher and numerous silver and bronze crucifixes all seemed to glare from the walls. She kept thinking that, any moment, her stepmother would come charging back into the church, and, with furled brow, chide her for her lack of good judgement. Either way, the hoped for conclusion seemed not to be forthcoming. There she remained, her knees, and the blood, and the rise and fall of her own breath, echoing through the empty church, bereft, as it was, of any brand of forgiveness.

She waited for a sign, then, if not from her stepmother, from God himself, advising that she had successfully purged her misgivings, and her base animalistic nature. How long would she have to remain before what seemed an angry, unforgiving God? Would there be a sign? Would "He" tell her "Himself" when she was again suitable to stand before her stepmother and him? Or, would her stepmother be the self-proclaimed conduit of Divine grace? She waited patiently, but still no answer came. Finally, when she could bear the pain no longer, she struggled to her feet and left the church by her own recognizance.

She had walked home alone, in the pitch dark.

A door slammed somewhere in the church startling her from her reverie. But it did not sound as though it came from the hall. It sounded like it came from beneath the floor.

She ran behind the altar and pulled a red felt curtain back, to find a staircase leading to the basement. She stepped quickly down the stairs, her heart beating in her chest at what she was certain she would find.

The voice she'd heard weeks before, in the kitchen, while her father slept in the next room, rattled around inside her head.

It could not be.

Eve hesitated at the bottom step, where a single lamp hung from the ceiling and cast a dim light down a dark and narrow hallway, lined with doors on either side. She opened each door as she went: priests quarters, and rooms, she guessed, for those in need of asylum. She neared the end of the hall and heard muted words. Eve turned the knob. Catharyn sat on a desk at one end of the room, her dress pulled back leaving her legs completely bare. Reverend Millen sat with his back to Eve, his hand resting casually, dangerously on Catharyn's thigh. His face was close to hers, so that she was the first to see Eve. In one fluid movement she slid from the desk and yanked her skirt down below her knees.

Reverend Joachim Millen scrambled to his feet and reached for his pants.

Catharyn's eyes were wide with surprise.

200

Reverend Millen's face changed from swollen pink, to pale white in the blink of an eye. He stopped for a moment and then lurched again to move behind his desk, as though he expected Eve herself was going to invoke the penalty that was sure to come one way or another.

For the moment the outcome hung in the balance. Catharyn stared at Eve. The priest looked down and struggled feebly with his pants. Then Catharyn's nervous smile transformed. A flash of anger came into her eyes. "What the hell are doing down here anyhow?"

The Reverend smiled sheepishly, having affixed his demeanour, and placed his hand piously upon her shoulder. "Perhaps we have lost track of time somewhat," he said, with the same somber and reverent tone he used on Sundays. "I'm sure God in his infinite wisdom has seen fit to grant our Evelyn here the guidance we have asked of him Mrs. Walker."

As Eve watched, she was scarcely able to comprehend what she had walked in on. She closed her eyes to the image of the Reverend and the look of fire in his eyes, and his hand on her thigh; that he wanted to take something from her, which she could never again get back.

Catharyn continued to regain her countenance. "For God's sake. Have you no common decency Eve? Bustin' in on us that way?"

Eve turned her disbelief back upon Catharyn, who stared coldly in return.

Such brazen aplomb.

Still, Eve sensed a flicker of guilt.

It was useless, however. Her misgivings had no currency. This, that lay in front of her now, stripped Catharyn's affect, like the first fall wind that stripped the old Oak of its leaves after they had turned.

Eve's eyes narrowed. "Goddam decency?" She spat on the floor beside the desk.

The Reverend Millen looked up, "Evelyn please."

"Please what Rev – ...Millen!"

"Eve Walker," Catharyn hissed, "You'll address Reverend Millen by his proper title."

"You're both hypocrites," Eve snapped. "Spare me your sanctimonious tripe. You're fornicating in a house of God... AND

YOU'RE MARRIED! Your husband – the MAN YOU LOVE – is in the hospital - Dying!"

Catharyn stood agape.

Reverend Millen's face turned a deeper shade of red as he hastily checked to see that he was in order before things turned from bad to worse.

After a moment of apt silence, Eve delivered the news: "There was a fire in town last night."

The two of them gaped, waiting for what would come next.

"Father went out to help, against the doctors wishes. He'll be lucky to see tomorrow morning," She turned to leave, then hesitated. "But rest easy in knowing he died with a smile on his face." With that she turned on her heel and walked out.

Her father needed her.

She would wait at his bedside for as long as it took.

Ω

THE SWORD
IS
MIGHTIER
THAN THE PEN

---

*An nescis mi fili quantilla
sapientia mundus regatur*

*Don't you know how
little wisdom rules the world*

The corner of the Victoria Times Colonist newspaper sagged to the table as Eve sipped at her coffee. Gregory Fairbanks, a senior reporter for the Colonist, had written a piece on the burgeoning town of Vananda; The Little City, as it was affectionately noted. It's a fair town, so he writes, which was not so little anymore, according to word of mouth slopping in on the Red Line and Royal steamers, plying waters southward to Victoria from as far north as the Queen Charlotte Islands. Vananda, it seemed, was fast becoming a destination among famous prospectors, high-rollers looking to risk their stake, all for a second chance at fast fortune. The Klondike was in the last throes of glory. For miners drifting back down the Chilcotin Trail empty handed it was another chance for redemption.

The people of Vananda, according to Fairbanks, went from place to place, going about their business and in no hurry to get there before the next fellow came along. Everyone here knew it would all get done, and that there was, for the time being, enough for all, just as there always had been. And so, life went along at the only pace they had known since the first foundations had been laid some forty years earlier. If it weren't for the lumber mill churning without pause, and for the mines churning to the rhythm of industry, and progress pulling the town along with it... It all combined to offer a vague sense of moving toward something. Further, it seemed, by all counts, it – the town - had always been lucky, generally and collectively. All the same, he wrote, we in Vananda seemed to have our collective finger on the pulse of industry and the forward way of progress.

Eve came to the end of the story and let the paper down on the table, deep in thought.

She was startled by a loud rap at the door.

She looked up to see Warner Mcleod offering a curt nod at her through the door pane. Eve stood quickly and went to the door, watching his face carefully as he came inside.

"I'm sorry about your place. I'm sick about it."

Warner nodded.

"Anything salvageable?"

"Nothing. Burned to the ground along with everything in it. Funny thing is, I feel worse for those people who'll not get to bury their kin. Give them a proper burial. That's worse than anything."

"Coffee, or chicory?" she asked filling her own cup with coffee again.

"Black coffee, please," he said, slipping his jacket over the back of a chair nearest the door.

"I don't suppose any of the families have been around yet?"

"Surprisingly they have. Lorna Thompson. Had a son brought out of the mine there."

Eve set the coffee in front of him. "Must have been an awful thing being there to tell her."

"Nothing needed to be said of course. It was all very plain to see. Hardest part was we were standing there, neither of us saying a word, you know, silenced by the gravity of it, and she took my hand and held it there for a while, and then just walked away."

"Lord."

"Lord is right. Makes a guy think. I poke at dead bodies for a living without a second thought. I'm in there myself until late at night no matter the weather outside or time of year. Some nights'd be worse than others for nerves – for most people anyway. Not me. Doesn't shake me in the least. But that boy today. That shook me a little," he said turning the sugar spoon between his fingers, staring. He took a drink of coffee.

"And there's the rest of them too."

An uncomfortable silence drifted between them. Eve sipped at her coffee and set it down, the rim of the heavy mug hitting the oak table sharply. Warner looked up and stared at her blankly for a moment and brought the back of his sleeve across his mouth seeming to regain himself.

"Somebody didn't want those bodies found."

Eve looked at Warner abjectly. "You think it was deliberate?"

"I expect it had something to do with Jonas Prescott turning up in the mine. Those others are bad enough together. But they're miners," Warner explained. "I say that with all the respect they've got coming, mind you. But the way they live and carry on, it's not a wonder sometimes more of them don't turn up cold. But Jonas," Warner shook his head. "He wasn't your run-of-the mill miner."

"He was eccentric though. People thought he was a little off didn't they? At least that's what my father always said."

"Sure he was off. We're all off. But he wasn't a push-over, Eve. Don't kid yourself for a second."

"I'm listening."

"Jonas had clout. He wasn't unlike your friend Mr. Reynolds, from a big city, come up here to get away from it and have a quaint small town paper, in a community where the worst that happened was some of the right people didn't get invited to the right party and maybe the wrong people did. Whatever the case, I suspect part of it was the lure of money, held out by the fist-full like it is sometimes on account of the mines, when the mines are turning a good profit, which is most of the time these last years. But, I don't think he ever shook the big city. Would make trips south to Seattle, sometimes as far as San Francisco. Where he went in between was anyone's guess. Sometimes he had visitors come in from other parts as well. Handsome, good looking folk. Powerful people. You could see it in them. He picked them up from the steamers in his carriage and took them out to his house, and that was the last anyone ever saw of them for days on end, until the trip back to the docks. My guts tell me all the conjecture about Jonas' company back then wasn't all off-key. Seems now more than ever."

"It's a little unsettling to think of it in those terms isn't it?"

"Damn right it is! Look around you. If what I'm saying is true, Eve, someone around here is wielding an awfully big hammer. And they've got a lot to lose. No-one is really safe if that's the case. Best stay on the path straight to and from, and keep your eyes peeled and your feet in front of you."

Eve furled her brow.

"What?

"Jonas turning up dead has got someone stirred. The trail of suspicion doesn't fall too far from home neither."

"Who do we talk to?" Eve stood from her chair and walked to the kitchen window, looked out over the yard, damp from the rain.

"That's just the thing. I wouldn't trust anyone. Least as far as the shores of this island. Any one of 'em could be the viper. Likely more than one at that. The way everyone in the police has been carrying on, what with the code of silence and all the rest, I would say they're bloody well all in on it."

"I think you're onto something," Eve said still staring out the window. "We need a sympathetic ear. Someone that's not from here and that's got some influence in Victoria. Tell them to get their shit-kickers on."

"I'm not an investigator by any stretch," Warner said, "but the scenarios – I mean, the practical application of medical science appeals to my sensibilities, but never-the-less, I'd say, if one were to find out what Jonas Prescott had that could stand to get him killed, we'd know what we were dealing with. I still believe in the sanctity of the Sovereign. We were given the opportunity – MacDonald granted us the opportunity - to make something of ourselves to protect the ideal. Men like Sutherland and Maddox are opportunists. They only see what's in it for themselves. They'll damn well ruin it for the rest of us."

A light breeze jostled the brush at the edge of the yard sending a shower of drops to the ground. The wind carried the scent of salt air up from the low-tide line right the way through town, the turgid, earthy smell of life coming and going - thriving... flourishing.

"Wait a minute." Eve looked at Warner. "Quentin said the cellar was packed wall to wall with Jonas' things. If there's anything telling, chances are it may be there."

"How the hell do you get to it. You just ask him?"

"Didn't you just say not to trust anyone until we know who the players are?"

"You made my point for me." Eve smirked at Warner.

"I don't like that look you got on yer face."

"Quentin told me -"

"I don't want ta hear it."

"I'll just go and have a look. See what turns up."

"That's goin' a little far ain't it? You're going to get yourself in some trouble."

"You have any other ideas? Let's be clear about this. Just what have we got to lose? It's not just about the freedom of one Indian. He's a brother, a son – of the Chief no less – Do we care what happens to the union? Do we care what happens to this young man?"

"I applaud your womanly sensibilities, Eve. Admirable in their own right. But not reason enough to risk life and limb."

"Where to start though. There could be scads of paper to go through. You'd have to bloody camp there, well enough."

"It can't hurt to have a look."

"Let's hope not. Seems that whoever we're dealing with has an appetite for journalists. I'd hate to see you wind up like Jonas."

Ω

A SLOW LEAK

Arcana imperii

א

Secrets of the empire

It was still this side of dark when the Monday morning paper was dropped on the doorsteps of Vananda. One by one, as the day started to make its appearance, doors opened and papers were brought in to be read over breakfast.

In the Lobby of the Red Tassel Hotel, Judge James Harper, and business owner, Harley Braithwaite, sat eating eggs and bacon at one table, while beside them sat Quentin Reynolds and Red Sutherland at another; an additional plate between them sat unattended.

Harley rubbed the crust of his toast in the leftover egg yolk pooling in the bottom of his plate, "We need someone in the legislature who can push for the working man, that will speak to labour," he said with a mouthful. "You know, to balance things out."

Judge Harper squinted at him, finding his manners disagreeable. "Well you can forget anyone from around here, or anywhere else between here and the capital for that matter. Anyone with inroads to the government is likely on the gravy train already in some fashion," he said thoughtfully. "Or men of like mind are thinking they may need to call on favours at some point, so had better not run the dog up a tree."

"Yeah well I ain't givin' up," Braithwaite said. "There's gotta be someone whose willin', down Victoria way. A man 'ats paid for is apt to get the job done faster 'en someone whose bridled heart and soul with the notion. Takes ones like 'at a while to come to the point

208

usually."

"There will be laws in place that'll make things better on the whole," Judge Harper stated. "The Labour Union isn't the solution. We've seen more than enough what it's done already."

"Yeah, well, some of us that was not even in the line got sent out. Hard to make pay when you're sent out," Braithwaite complained. "It's a fine thing. Just goes to show what kind of sway Ernie Tsan had got. And Song Loo was right in the thick of it. He had that former newspaper editor – no offence, Quentin," he said, glancing at him with a mouthful. "... he had 'im in his back pocket. That's about the long and short of it."

"Yes," Quentin stated boldly, "And now the tools of the state are properly on the side of right!" he said, pointing at the newspaper that lay open on a nearby chair.

"Only person that's got anyone in cahoots, from what I'm seeing," Judge Harper said, "is that Maddox has got is nose half-way up De Cosmos' backside."

"What do you mean?"

"Looks like he got to him first, is what I'm saying. Meantime, while De Cosmos is busy looking in the mirror, Maddox is fixing to jump claim," Judge Harper wiped his mouth with his napkin. "We should have bought up more ourselves the moment Jonas took leave of his senses." Harper gulped a mouthful of food with his coffee. "Speak of the devil himself," he said, wiping his mouth again, and nodding toward the door.

Christian Maddox apologized for running behind, as he slipped his jacket off.

"Getting right to it, though," he said, directing a blow at Quentin, "That girl of yours, Eve, is to stay off my property, Quentin."

"She grows on you, doesn't she?" Quentin said, before leaving his order to the waitress.

"I admit to having high hopes, but after meeting her, my desire for growth of any sort came to a rapid halt."

The men laughed.

"I don't like her," Maddox said. "She's too cocky. Thinks she 's a man. Just look at her -"

"I've been lookin', and I can tell you, she ain't no man," Braithwaite put in.

"Goddamit Braithwaite. Let the men talk," Maddox retorted. He looked back at Quentin. "The way she asked her questions – *her* questions, mind you, not the ones you gave her - if you hear what I'm saying. And she looked at me with those eyes of hers; like she already knew what she was gonna hear."

"She's a smart one alright. Smart and pretty," Braithwaite said again.

"Knock it off, or you'll find yourself looking up from down the bottom of a mine shaft like the others," Maddox threatened. Maddox's face turned red as he squinted at Quentin. "Just keep a collar on your young tyro is all I'm saying."

"He's right, Reynolds." Red Sutherland said, sitting back in his chair. He had been quiet until now, biding his time, listening to what was said and taking stock of the mind and temperament of the others.

"It's one thing to have your finger on the flow of information, but Eve Walker is not that."

Quentin moved to speak again, but was cut short when Sutherland produced a folded document from his coat pocket. "Read this, before you say anything else."

Quentin unfolded the sheet.

"It's a request written by Warner McLeod, to the ·Government Agent in New Westminster, requesting permission to dig up Ernest Tsan's body."

Quentin stood and lit a cigarette, paced across the rug and stared cooly back at Sutherland. "It's out of my hands."

"I can see that it's out of your hands," Sutherland raised his voice. "If this isn't handled, be assured your cut will be out of your hands as well." He took a cigarette from the case in his pocket and lit it. His face was hot. His eyes narrowed. He scolded himself for sitting in the corner - a position of psychological disadvantage.

"None of it could have been avoided," Quentin stated calmly.

"It all could have been avoided," Braithwaite cut in. "You should have done the job yourself," he said glaring at Maddox, "instead of letting some half-brained Pinkerton's flunkey handle it. Not only did you fail to remove the bodies, you picked an Indian. Of all the -"

Red stood from his chair with a deft agility that startled Braithwaite. He was not one for being talked down to. He had a fistful of Braithwaite's shirt, while the other hand rested on the handle of his side-arm. The document floated to the floor.

Maddox sat, and stared calmly at his empty plate.

Braithwaite struggled to regain himself.

"Need I remind you, gentlemen, we're in the middle of an arrangement that will see us all very wealthy men," Quentin made an attempt at reason. "It's a fragile relationship... This," he said waving his hand over the lot of them, "could kill the whole thing. There are policy issues to be enacted – to be carefully put into place, so the whole does not shatter and blow back upon us. There are numerous grants written to people who do not even exist. And even though you may have the paper in-hand today, there are applications pouring in weekly for that same piece of paper. That means that somewhere down the line someone in the land office is looking at that piece of paper... *again!* That is why we said, from the start, that we needed smart people, who could think on their feet. You do all remember that?"

"That's why." Red smouldered, letting go of Braithwaite's shirt.

Braithwaite chuckled nervously. "Why what?"

"The murder charge'll stick. It'll turn things in your favour. You said yourself they're looked upon poorly."

Braithwaite stared at Red for a moment before he turned and walked to the window, smoothing the front of his shirt. He folded his hands behind his back, bringing the shirt-tail that was now untucked sharply into focus.

"You may have a point there," he paused. "There is a bigger battle at stake. If the Indian is found guilty it may turn the tide in favour of the government. Give them Indians enough rope to hang themselves. It'll take emphasis in our favour, while having the effect of everyone looking the other way while the deal goes through."

"What do you mean, enough rope to hang themselves?" Harper asked.

"What I mean is, if you back a bear enough into a corner, he'll ignore the gun and come straight at you."

Red gritted his teeth at Braithwaite taking ownership, but opted to keep quiet, realizing it might suit his needs.

"Meantime, we have this other little problem," Braithwaite said, nodding at the document now lying open on the floor among the chair legs.

"Move the trial up." Maddox hadn't spoken for some time. He slid his chair back and stood. "So much of this depends on everything falling into place. Well, I'm sure it *would* help if people were looking the other way when this all comes down. We need a conviction. Otherwise, if word gets out before we've had a chance to go to trial, it'll all come down around our bloody heads. Meantime, you're the damn Judge," he said looking to Harper. "Reject the application to exhume Tsan's body."

Judge Harper smirked dryly. "On what grounds?"

"On the grounds it would undermine faith of the general public in the competence of our provincial police force. That's what. Tell 'em you have every assurance that due course was followed, and lay it to rest."

"Warner is a smart man," Red parried. "he'll find a way around it."

Braithwaite paced the floor again, waving his cigarette in the crotch of his fingers. "The issue will be scrutinized. We're under a magnifying glass right now. The reason better be good. Where did you say the body was found?"

"On the beach, near Vananda," Maddox offered, looking at Red as he spoke. Red stood, feet apart, glaring at Braithwaite.

"Was too far-gone by the time we got him to town, so we by-passed the coroners shop," Red stated. "That's about all I can tell you." He plucked his hat from the chair. Then he looked into Braithwaite's eyes, and what he saw there told him things had already begun to unravel. He saw unfettered greed. He saw that this man did not care about his fellow, in any circumstance. It was true that a fair bit of greed played in on all parts. But at some point you had to at least appear to care for your fellow man. Any prudent businessman could see that.

"As for your girl, Eve," Sutherland addressed Quentin, "I told you, it's out of your hands. Do not mistake me on that!"

Ω

KNOWLEDGE
IS
POWER

In Propria causa
nemo debut esse ludex

No one should be the
Judge in his own trial

"What happened to my bloody story?" Eve said as she came through the door.

"One of the greatest advantages growing up in a small community," Quentin pontificated, "is that everyone is in some way acquainted..."

"A soft news story on lumber shipments to the mainland?" Eve interrupted in a carefully measured tone. "People are dying needlessly, Quentin. People have died. And it *is* news. It should be in the paper."

"...but," Quentin continued on, as though Eve hadn't said a thing, "this is also it's greatest flaw. You need to be careful what side you appear to come down on - "

"I don't much care to be lectured right now, Quentin. I'm angy. Where is my story?"

"You make it sound as if we failed to mention it. We did cover the story when the accident occurred. Your secondary piece on the need for job security and protection for workers, is superfluous. It's as I've said, if the movers and shakers perceive you are acting as power broker to a position of advantage -"

"Wait. Wait a minute here. I'm confused: We're not favouring one side over another are we? You just finished lecturing me about not wielding the newspaper like a weapon to smote thine enemy, and all that horseshit. Is it not *you* who are now choosing what gets printed, one thing over another?"

"Deciding what gets printed, Evelyn, is a daily chore. I do not pick and choose, as you suggest, to what end serves *me* best!" Quentin snapped, his emotion colouring his words now. "It's a valuable lesson you've learned here. Sometimes things get pulled."

Eve flushed with anger.

"What the hell is it we are doing here?" she snapped now, her eyes blazing behind clenched teeth. "Aren't we supposed to report the things that matter to people?" She stopped herself what she would say next, and took a deep breath. "How in hell is a mine collapse *not* news. That's what I'd like to know? This is not some freak occurrence, *Reynolds*."

Quentin straightened at hearing his last name used in such derogatory fashion.

"We live in a hot climate here, Evelyn," he said, his voice had lost its edge. "From what I gather Prescott had an appetite for writing about society ladies and allowed all that favoured one set over another to shine bright as day in this journal."

"That's bullshit!"

"I'm just saying, that's what the talk about town is. I don't necessarily give it much credence."

"You might not be so quick to find your peace with it," Eve said, struggling now to keep her cool. "I don't know if you've picked up the sense with your keen journalistic prowess, that there are people that think Jonas disappearing may not have been an accident."

Eve tensed. She realized the power of the information she had. She was one of three people who knew that Prescott was not only missing, he was dead: he did not die, he was killed. Whether it was a case of murder, remained to be discovered.

Quentin held his hand aloft to silence her. "Decide what side you want to come down on, Evelyn. This paper does not pay for itself. It's

214

paid for by people who pay for advertising. And the people who pay for advertising, as a general rule, own businesses. And those businesses are all connected – like mycelium is to mushrooms - by the relationships people keep. Maddox money runs a fair sizable chunk of this town, and therefore, is responsible for a good part of the advertising revenue. In short. He pays your wage."

Before she realized what she was doing, Eve spat on the ground at Quentin's feet, a precise exclamation point to end the conversation. She turned and walked out of the office.

Eve did not wait for the ride she had arranged from Tess. She started walking, needed to walk, to breathe, to get her head straight. Despite her early excitement and willingness to trust, suddenly there was this something about Quentin that did not sit right. He refused to be pinned down – always side-stepping direct questions, and using ridiculously long-winded explanations for the simplest things. It created an opaque atmosphere where words and meanings could easily be lost. And now, with this shattering blow to her pride... At first she thought it was all done exclusively for her benefit – part of her education as a writer - but it was obviously much more than that.

She walked for some time, unaware of time or place, and when she took her eyes from the ground in front of her, she was home. She went immediately to her bedroom and pulled a box from under her bed. There were questions that needed to be answered. Here she kept copies of the Coast Miner that she had worked on with Quentin. Until now, and due to her over-arching joy at being part of an actual paper, she had not bothered to read Quentin's work.

She pulled a paper from atop the pile and began skimming stories. By the time she'd gone through three of the papers, there began a sinking feeling in her stomach. After two more issues, she was convinced there was credence to her suspicion that Quentin might be towing the company line. He was on their side - a funny thing, she thought, because, until this moment, she wasn't aware that sides existed. In fact, it seemed there were two distinct camps: those with money, and those without. All of his stories were quaint, though verging on literary in style: they were watered down versions of the truth, all slanted, but giving the artful impression of being even-handed and God-like in their apparent omniscience.

It seemed there were, in fact, times when it did not pay to tell things as they were.

Ω

A HEN
IN THE
FOX HOUSE

*Acta deos numquam
mortalia fallunt*

*Yet if mortal actions
never decieve the Gods*

Quentin was meticulous in his profession, prided himself on the journalist's code of ethics, to which he so strictly adhered - a brotherhood, he often chimed: He would not have destroyed the documents.

After the meeting in Gillies Bay, Eve knew that Quentin often stayed late at the press office Sunday nights, to set type for the following week's paper. That was her best chance to gain access to his home. Setting the type was something he insisted on doing himself, though twice she was made to sit and endure the slow, painful process of unwrapping and setting each letter into the carriage plates.

Crisp edges were paramount. This was so the carriage inked and printed even edges, even lines, thus giving the printed page the look of authority. It was something he'd criticized the Colonist – Victoria's paper - for, not taking pride in a well-printed page, skewed lines and over-blacked letters being the norm, as far as he was concerned. Amor

De Cosmos, the paper's owner, was a loud-mouthed slacker, who was also in government – a lethal combination as far as Quentin was concerned.

The paper arrived from Victoria on the steamer once a week – Saturdays for the most part - and would often lay untouched on the bench: a statement of his disapproval. On one occasion Eve had walked in earlier than usual one morning and caught him in the act of reading the Colonist over morning coffee. He promptly snapped the paper shut and threw it on the floor. He glared, as if challenging her to state the obvious.

She would have preferred simply asking his permission to go through Prescott's papers. In that case, she could go ahead and do just that, without fear or guilt. But things had changed. Quentin had changed, and she no longer had a bearing on true North. Warner's admonition played through her head. He had advised strongly against breaking into his home. His anti-union affiliations in New York suggested a man not to be trifled with. And to top it off he'd been seen with Maddox. He'd pulled her story, written in support of the miners, and run a story on Maddox and his mines instead, casting them, against all odds, in a favorable light. Yet, the story was carefully distanced enough to support a claim of objectivity and journalistic sensitivity.

This afternoon she took her place at the hand-set type machine, as she did every Sunday, and advised him she intended to leave early. He grunted his assent, barely paying mind to what she had said. The evening wore on with very little conversation between them. When the allotted time arrived, she took her coat in hand. Quentin stared over the rim of his glasses. She reassured him of the importance of the matter and he once again relented.

She untethered Charlie and started out as though she were bound for home. She set her eyes on the edge of town, where the last of the gas streetlamps lining the street surrendered to the dark. She held Charlie, pacing him so that all appeared as it should. His pricked ears told her he knew well enough something was afoot: he felt her nerves.

When they were well-beyond sight of town, she corrected her course toward Quentin's home. Twinges of guilt and slithering fear alternated for quiet dominion in the pit of her stomach at what she had

218

to do. She struggled with herself that the situation was bigger than her own personal salvation, and that much good would come of it... For others. This was more for them, than for herself.

She was doing it for the others, for the town, for friends and her family; for the people who worked skin to bone for this town.

The realization brought a fleeting surge of joy. But now was not the time.

She dug her heels in and leaned low and seat-forward, driving Charlie faster than he was used to going.

After a time, she pulled back on the reigns and brought the horse to a trot as they approached the trail entrance. He snorted once and nodded his head in appreciation of a good and unexpected run. Eve patted his neck and promised a repeat performance; preferably by choice, and not by necessity.

Eve kept to the edge of the forest, until she located the narrow entrance to the quarry trail. She used to ride here with her friends, when she was young. It was not the fastest route, but the trail passed directly behind Quentin's home. What she would lose in time, she would make up for in stealth.

Eve ducked under a low-hanging cedar limb as she clawed a spider web from her face. She slowed the horse up and peered cautiously through the trees.

She'd almost passed it.

She slid from Charlie's back and lashed him to a tree. "I'm afraid there's no reward for excellent behaviour tonight Charlie," she said, locking his gaze. "I'll make it up to you buddy." She patted his neck, and stepped into the trees.

The wet salal immediately soaked her jeans as she stepped through to the edge of the yard. Here, the forest gave way to a vast and overgrown lawn. Quentin's home loomed in stark silhouette against the dark tree-line. The house, in all its Tudor glory, harboured questions and intrigue, like a simmer of ghosts, waiting at the windows for whomever might come inside and stir them from their restless ennui. The spectre of implication seemed to seep from every window pane. How could Quentin manage there among them? ...So many questions that needed answering.

Eve stepped from the forest and strode across the lawn as though she had every right to be there. She felt as if she were performing for some unseen audience, a prying neighbour at the very least, despite the distance between them. It was prudent to exercise perfect caution.

She was surprised to find the verandah looming above her so soon. The mischievous night was playing tricks on her mind.

She cautiously climbed the steps to the back porch.

She felt for the door knob. It was locked.

She considered the framed window to the left of the door, but found there would be no easy mark there either.

Her heart pounded alarmingly in her chest.

This must be what it feels like just before it gives in, she mused, despite circumstances.

Eve drew several deep breaths. She knew that, once inside, she had *one* chance to find what it was she was looking for. There would not be another opportunity. From the day he'd arrived, Quentin had yet to leave the office early. Whether it was to polish machinery, or look over the news copy one last time, it seemed there was always something that wouldn't wait. He was at least predictable in this regard.

She could bank on three hours at her disposal, free and clear. This week's edition was to be four pages. Two were already complete. It would be at least five AM before he was done setting the type and loading the rotary for Monday morning.

She crept back down the stairs and made her way to the side of the house. There were fewer windows here, but fruit trees, and a garden, obscured any possible sight line from the neighbours to the Eastward. She spotted a small window cut starkly into the siding. It had likely been put in sometime after the rest of the house had been built.

Locked tight.

Eve stepped from the shadows to get a clear look at the entire exterior. There were two windows accessing the second floor: clearly unreachable. Even if she had a ladder, climbing to the second floor would prove risky if she had to get out in a hurry. Or, God forbid, if something were to happen, and she were to fall, how would that look, her lying on the ground, and the ladder and the open window?

A gust of wind rose on the cooling night and buffeted against the house. For a moment she was certain she heard branches on glass – a window pane coming from somewhere nearby. Just in front of her, a desperate tangle of overgrowth - rose bushes and lavender - tucked in against a chimney and obscured a small portion of wall. She pulled her sleeves tightly around her wrists and fastened them as best she could. She studied the thorny passage a moment before choosing two branches she felt were key to the puzzle. She clutched their girth between an unforgiving gauntlet of thorns and moved them to the side. She gave one final heave and plunged her arms into the shrub. Her hands came up against a glass pane: a small window, hidden there behind the untended plants.

This was her best chance at getting in.

She placed her hands flat against the glass, to see if it would give. She gasped aloud when it slid open with relative ease. Then, just as suddenly, the window came to a jarring stop. Her heart sank. The warm air from inside the room spilled into the darkness around her. She let the window fall back and tried once more, this time with more determination. Again the window came up against something hard, but not with as much conclusion as before. She repeated her effort and heard something pop from inside the room: a small piece of wood clattered to the floor. She pushed up once more and the window slid freely open.

She was in! Her heart raced. Her fear was vindicated: the odds of coming away empty handed was now cut in two.

The bottom sill was shoulder height.

Need something to stand on, she thought to herself, now almost transcending her fear.

She considered the thick stalk of the rose bush and placed her foot against the base, where dozens of smaller stocks converged one upon the other. With her hands on the inside of the sill, she pulled herself half-way into the room. What felt like a lethal drop, she guessed was perhaps only four feet down to the floor. The rose thorns ripped at her pant legs as she squirmed to gain leverage.

Suddenly she was free and heading fast toward the floor. She managed to soften her landing with her hands and one foot. She froze there, waiting for any sound, any sign of the living in the house. She crouched beneath the window and checked her pocket for the match safe she'd brought from home.

A struck match gave instant life to shadows that fluttered and purled in the dull orange light. She found a lantern in the cloak closet. The gas lit, flickered, then slowly reached its pinnacle. She opened the draft and the flame was charged and grew to a bright orange. Eve held the lantern aloft. She checked the foyer, then the sitting room. She circled back to a large living room.

The house was immaculate, tidy, perfectly free of complication and clutter.

She briefly scrutinized the kitchen.

Peerless.

Present conditions called for extra care and attention, to leave things precisely the way she had found them.

Rooms lined either side of the hall, all of them with doors closed. Eve turned the metal doorknob closest to her. It was an immaculate ladies' bedroom billowing in perfect form: pleated ruffles, flawless duvet, spotless linens. An ivory crucifix hung to the left of the headboard: a wary, red-faced prophet casting a dour and watchful eye at the life that undoubtedly unfolded there.

Next was a bathroom.

She approached the last door on the right, near the end of the hallway. The knob was locked. And it was colder than the others. To be sure, she tried the door again. Locked tight.

Quentin must surely have the key, she thought, as she scanned the area for a logical, handy place to secret a key within reach.

A respectable ledge protruded atop the solid oak door frame. She reached up and ran her fingers slowly along the top of the frame, stirring a thick layer of dust.

Prescott dust.

She found herself impressed by the straight edge, and paid silent homage to Quentin's astute observation about the Italians and their building prowess.

A basement key was a rather innocuous thing to hide. Quentin was well organized. Obsessive. Perhaps even a touch compulsive. Everything in its place... Eve's face lit at what she felt was the obvious solution.

Every morning he'd come into the office and throw his keys into the top-middle drawer among loose pencils and pens, rubber bands, loose change. It seemed the junk drawer was the one place that fell outside Quentin's compulsions. There was a better than average chance the desk in the study, next to the foyer, had a middle drawer. The lantern jostled in her fingers as she went, all too aware that her window of opportunity was insidious and creeping to its conclusion.

Eve's hopes faded somewhat when she saw that, unlike at work, his desk here was impeccably arranged. She rolled the chair out of the way. Three drawers. She took a chance on the second. Nothing but stamps, stationary, a wax seal... She picked up the seal and admired the initials, emblazoned ornately by a skilled craftsman. But they were not Quentin's initials. The seal presented the initials J.W.P. - Jonas William Prescott. Probably an oversight while Quentin was purging Prescott's belongings.

She placed the seal back and closed the drawer, before moving methodically on to the next. There was still no tell-tale jostling of metal on wood. It came down to the final option: one drawer remained, bottom-left of the desk. She drew it quickly open and, from inside, came the unmistakable sound of keys – numerous keys by the sound of it. She moved aside a stack of envelopes and a loose piece of letterhead to reveal three key rings, each with varying numbers and all manner of keys.

She grabbed all three rings and hurried back to the hallway door she had targeted. She plunged two of the rings into her coat pocket and started in checking each key, one after the other. She paused, taking a deep breath to calm herself. There was no time for mistakes. She exhausted the entire first ring, with none of the keys fitting the barrel and turnstile.

Her body tensed as it came down to the second last key. It was a perfect fit. The lock clicked as though it had been oiled just the day before. A rickety wood stairway led down to the cellar. Cobwebs draped from the ceiling beams and the spiders gathered in corners to watch with mild interest. Alas, a room that had been neglected, perhaps suggesting that the careful sheen on the surface masked a neglected soul beneath.

Eve held the lantern above her as she steadied herself on the web-covered wall. At the bottom of the stairs the lantern struggled against the damp. Two small doorways at the far end of the basement stood next to one another other like gaping rectangular eye sockets.

She looked around the room. Against the wall, to her left, the wood crates that were taken from the press office were stacked two rows deep. She tallied what could be seen and guessed there were twenty or so boxes in total. The amount of information here could be truly insurmountable – given time and lack of manpower; she'd allowed herself to be blinded by simple optimism. Now, standing here, it seemed foolish to think she could do the job properly, to go through the mountain of information and hope to come out of it knowing she hadn't overlooked anything.

Eve thought of Quentin again, now likely wiping down each die, with deft precision - with skill afforded by years of practice, before placing them back into their respective drawer.

She strode across the room and lifted the first box within reach. popped the lid off. Prescott's papers. She set the box down and knelt on the floor. To her immense relief the documents and papers were dated. The file in her hand was dated June 1889, near the time Prescott started the Coast Miner. He went missing in Spring of 1894.

She let the folder in her hand fall closed and looked over the stack of crates. She would start from the other side, reasoning these must have been the first to come out of the office in town and the first dropped here in the basement. She was rewarded with the first box she opened, January 1892.

She needed to find boxes containing 1893 or early 1894 and spend the time she needed in combing through these files.

She opened another box: Coast Miner Proofs dated 1890. The next box was filled with documents that were dated December to March 1892.

Getting closer.

The next box she opened was heavy with ledgers. She picked up the first one and opened it. The first entry was dated August 1893.

"I'll be damned."

She pulled a box away from the others to sit on, and laid the first folder open on her lap.

Jonas' writing was fluid and readable. The first twelve pages were filled with purchase entries, supplies lists, notes for story ideas

224

and deadline dates. At first nothing jumped from the page. She cast a quick glance inside the box. Another dozen journals.

She skimmed over each page trying to catch keywords and entry titles; having to slow herself when she felt she was rushing and might miss something. She skimmed another, and began turning the page, when a spark flashed in the back of her mind. She re-read the page.

A note at the top read: *"Incorrigible? Letter to the editor, from Seamus Harker. Publish with reply."*

The notation had a letter and a number beside it.

She realized at once she'd not brought a pen or paper to make notes. Eve bent the tip of the page to mark it. She leafed through the first ledger and placed it on the floor beside her.

The three ledgers that followed referenced what were other possible hostile readers, with the same alpha-numeric notation written beside them. Some of them referenced the Copper Queen Mine at Blubber Bay, others referenced Billy Turner, owner of the sawmill at Vananda.

It seemed that Jonas Prescott was not known for his ability to make friends. With each reference to an unhappy reader, or advertiser or supplier, Eve's heart grew heavy. She was aptly reminded that nothing in practice was ever as easy as it was in principle. She foolishly thought the smoking gun would leap from the page – would spill from the many boxes, clearly an amateur assumption.

She moved the ledgers aside and pulled two more boxes from the stack. The first was filled with supplier receipts and invoices. There were hundreds if not thousands of them.

She slipped the lid from the next box: August, 1893. She half-expected to find more receipts. But instead, when she tried to lift the first folder from the box, it slipped from her hand spilling a formidable stack onto the floor. She looked at the empty folder in her hands and saw the file reference "G4" marked at the top-right corner. The next file in the box sported the designation "B7", and the others - each with their own designation, but seemingly with no discernible rhyme or reason why.

Every letter would need to be skimmed, and there was no way that was going to happen before Quentin got home at daybreak.

She made a quick decision.

She would sort out the boxes that fell into the date range she was after, and leave them hidden in the trail behind the house. She would return at the first opportunity to get them. It was evident from the thin layer of dust on the stairs and covering the rail on the way down, and upon the boxes themselves, that he hadn't been down here for some time. She would have to bank on it that he would not have cause to come down anytime soon. The question of how to get them back when she was done was another matter altogether – a bridge she would build when the opportunity presented itself.

She selected four boxes to smuggle out with her, before she stood back to survey that the two rows of boxes looked much as it had. Now she needed to carry the four boxes out to the trail. She climbed the stairs and stepped into the hall. Her breath caught when she saw that the sky had already begun to brighten. Quentin could be coming down the road at this very moment. Her spine tingled with fear. She turned the bolt on the back door and, with the box in her arms, crept outside, to the corner of the house.

The street was empty.

She went as quickly as she could across the yard and plunged into the trees, startling Charlie as she did. She crossed the trail and made her way carefully into deep brush and set the box down, where it would not be seen if anyone should happen by during the day.

The horse watched wide-eyed as Eve whisked by on her way back to the house.

Finally, with the last box in her arms, she ran out the door. She was very nearly out of danger. With the last box hidden safely in the forest she ran back toward the house. The back door stood open and waiting - a gateway offering both freedom and menace, that if she went back through she would have to close the door and lock it behind her, and for that moment risk trapping herself inside.

She ran inside and slid the bolt shut behind her. She resisted the urge to check the basement again, to see that nothing was left out. She shut the basement door and plunged her hand into her pocket.

"Damn." She had forgotten to tag the basement key. She pulled the first ring out and peeled through each one. She plunged one key into the lock then another. A wave of nausea rippled through her at the thought of having to go through all of the keys again. At that very moment the key in her hand slid into the lock like snake oil and found purchase.

She ran to the office and dropped the key rings into the drawer. Her mind screamed of the urgency to look around, to make sure nothing was left out of place that would trigger suspicion in a man who was exceptionally sensitive to his environment. Outside, she heard the sound of a carriage: wheels thirsty for oil.

Her heart hammered in her chest.

She slid the drawer closed. She could feel the hot metal on her face as she brought the lantern up to extinguish the flame. She set the lantern back into the cloak closet and was thankful for the daylight, that it would not be needed now until long after it had cooled.

She slipped from the office and hurried down the hall into the living room, where the open window offered its simple salvation. She went to the window and crouched down. She watched through the curtains as the carriage came to a stop in front of the house. The iron gate creaked open.

She reasoned that Quentin would use the access road to the west of the house. The window she had come in was on the East. If she hurried, she could time her exit well. She would slip through the window and remain hidden in the rosebush until he was inside the barn, then run the gauntlet to the forest. He'd be tired, his nerves drawn. He'd think of nothing but climbing into his bed. She might stand a chance to slip across the yard unnoticed in the dusty twilight.

The moment the carriage disappeared behind the wall, Eve scrambled through the window, making every effort to keep silent. The cold air flooded her. washed over her face, and through her clothes now damp from sweat. She swung her feet down along the wall and tried to find a foothold against the rosebush, willing herself, with every fibre of her being, to shrink into obscurity.

She slipped once and caught herself on the window ledge, a loud crack sounded through the house. She tried again for a foot hold and found it in the crux of two large stalks. The window caught as she pulled down. She jostled it and it came free and slid closed. She cringed at what to her sounded like a shipwreck, and hoped against hope she was alone in her estimation.

Eve crept to the back corner of the house, were Quentin's buggy came again into sight at the back of the house and stopped.

Quentin glanced idly at the house, hesitated a moment, then stepped down from the carriage. Through stems and leaves she watched him unharness his horse and lead it to the paddock. He went to a small shelter behind the barn for hay that he then spread on the ground beside the trough. He started in toward the house instead of bringing the carriage to the barn as she had hoped.

He paused and straightened his back, then took several long, slow steps toward the solace of home again. Eve remained perfectly still, barely breathing, until Quentin disappeared behind the house.

She could hear his keys.

She readied herself to make for the treeline.

Above her, dusk had spread across the morning sky. Somewhere to her left: the sound of keys and a back door swinging opening. There was a moment's hesitation before she heard the door slam again. She closed her eyes, in her mind's-eye, watched him hesitate at the back room, boots and coat off, then, moving on ward to points unknown. She could only hope that when she decided to run, that he was lingering in shadow and not basking in the light of an East-facing window.

She crept further alongside the house, to the extreme back corner, where she would make for the forest at the edge of the property. Her mind scrambled as she tried to remember if she'd put everything back the way she'd found it. Even the slightest variance might trigger suspicion.

Eve held her breath as she set out across the open field.

$$\Omega$$

QUENTIN ARRIVES HOME

Amor et melle et felle est
fecundissimus

Love is rich with both
honey and venom

Quentin Reynolds did not bother to get out and shut the gate straight away as he usually did, but drove his carriage directly to the open shed he'd recently built. He would feed the horses and unhook the gear and get it put out of the weather for the night.

The carriage could stay right where he'd leave it.

He snapped the reins lazily to stir the horse, whom, sensing it was near feeding time, had stooped for a tuft of grass. Just as he snapped the reins, a thud emitted from the direction of the house. Round the other side, he thought. He stopped the buggy for a moment, strained to get a look alongside the house. His eyes burned with lack of sleep. Not seeing anything alarming, he became focused again on getting things put right, so that he could trundle off to his bed for a few hours sleep.

Walking from the wagon to the house seemed a chore. His legs felt like two useless hams hanging from his hips. He put his key in the door and opened it, feeling the welcoming warm air on his face.

"Damn," He cursed, "almost forgot the bloody fence." He dropped his suitcase and started toward the service road. Just as he turned, he caught a glimpse of something moving quickly at the back property line. He squinted to get a better look. Whatever it was it had gotten in behind the shed now. Probably a deer that hadn't the good sense to make itself scarce. It was obviously what he'd heard alongside the house, he agreed with himself smugly.

Bags in hand once again, he went inside and set the suitcase down at the bottom of the stairs. He took his jacket off and hung it on the hook by the door. Then he loosened his sleeves and went to the kitchen for a drink of water.

The meeting had been a good one. Worthwhile actually. He'd not seen Charles Buckminster for several years - well before he'd made his trip here, out West, at any rate. They had planned to meet when Quentin passed through Seattle, on his way up the coast, but there was no Union Ship calling at port for several days, so the meeting was put off. Now, however, the matters at hand made it imperative.

The Holmstrom-Baker Syndicate had been successful in buying up three more independent papers on the West Coast, in what it believed would soon be key centres of commerce. But their movements had not gone undetected, and had now garnered the attention of union-oriented filibusters and the dominant news agency in the west. Quentin's own quiet bid for market share was now not so quiet. Now they had to move quickly, to make aggressive offers for papers in larger centres, and move on a handful of papers in smaller towns lying at the hinterlands of expansion. These last would be run at a loss, to be sure, but would serve to keep union interests at arms length and broaden the syndicate's bottom line until the union could be squashed altogether.

Pull the last pieces together. A simple matter.

When the offer to lead expansion efforts in the West fluttered across his desk there was but a moments hesitation. Quentin had heard about the industry boom and about the Coast Miner being put up for sale. It came on good authority there was substance to the claims of wealth and good fortune here.

The Coast Miner was the company's first paper in Canada and represented the push northward, into the Dominion. He was less than

230

enthusiastic about relocating to what he felt was yet the uncivilized, world, but he understood the importance of such a move. Vananda would serve as a key centre, if they could suppress union expansion in the Canadas, which had only just recently been infested with the termites of industry, too, gnawing their way up from the South. If the union movement caught hold here it would fortify the strongholds of ideation they had already just installed along the border – progress that would need to be stopped in its tracks.

Other industries were working hand-in-hand with the efforts of the New York conglomerate. Together they could ensure continued prosperity for the country. They had learned a hard lesson in places like Delaware and New Hampshire, in Michigan - states where the labour movement had been allowed to take hold by politicians with soft hands. Now, with some visionaries at the helm, the anti-labour movement was vast, spread across the country, bigger than even he could fathom. One simply had faith that, while he was doing what was required of him here, equally crucial matters of businss were being taken care of in other places. To be a part of something this big, this important, to the welfare of the nation, was, he supposed, reward in itself. It was nothing to imagine the powerful corporate owners holding elite meetings, planning movements and strategies to counter labour across the continent, like some vast military campaign the likes of Machiavelli, or Frederick the Great. It was all very seductive.

He would put in his time.

Quentin stood in the kitchen with the glass of water in his hand, when he once again saw a flicker of movement at the back near the back property line. He leaned into the window to see the underbrush tremble.

The tree-tops were still.

No breeze.

"Damn pests," he cursed, resolving to lay out more poison around the garden fence.

Ω

A LEGACY
AT
STAKE

Amittere legem terrae

To lose the law of the land

As Eve entered the clearing on the Tsan property, three Salish men stormed past her on horse back. A young man leading the others narrowly missed her. The two that followed split and charged past, one on either side. Charlie shook his head and snorted, his eyes wide with the excitement of his compatriots.

Heidi followed soon after on a bright black mare, and reined the horse tightly to fall in beside Eve.

"What's going on? Is everything alright?" Eve asked worriedly.

"The police have decided they do not want to wait to hold Eli's trial. They have made it sooner. They did not tell anyone."

"When is it?"

"It may have already been," she said worriedly, the horse throwing its head beneath her.

"They say he is guilty of killing my husband, and that he will be hanged in two weeks. They must first wait for a man who does such things to arrive from the mainland."

232

"What do you mean? They can't do that?"

"They do as they please. Eli is being represented by a local lawyer, who is encouraging him to say he is guilty. And he says they will show him forgiveness. But that is not their way. They will take his life. And he did not kill my husband."

A sickness washed over Eve, that the opposition against the Indian had become so strong and so fuelled by rampant bigotry. The whites had come. And though they were polite at first, they had grown weary, their shoulders slumped under the burden of moral law. The Indian was in the way, and they had no more consideration to offer. It was certain, now, that Eli's death was secondary: the intended result was planned.

The noose was tightening.

"Come with me into town," Eve said sharply, more than she'd intended. "There must be something that we can do," she softened.

"I am finished doing things by your laws. My brother is innocent and he will be a free man."

"You're planning on getting him out? How? Even if you did manage to get him out without both of you getting killed... Heidi! They're just looking for an excuse to kill him. Don't give it to them... Others may be killed," Eve reasoned.

Heidi glared at Eve. And in her eyes there was coldness and resolve.

"He is my brother. If you had a brother, and you could save him, if you could have a chance to do something for him, would you not do it? If he were here, and they tried to take him, wouldn't you do anything to try to save his life? What do we live for? What makes our lives good to live? I have already lost one man who I love. I will *not* lose another."

The black mare reeled and snorted against the reins. Heidi pulled back tight and brought the horse around again.

"Of course. Of course you are right," Eve said. "Just tell me what it is you plan to do. I will do everything I can to help."

"This is my chance. If I stay here and do nothing, I am a coward. I will spend the rest of my life filled with sorrow. All that I love would be gone from my heart forever."

"Those men that were here, will they help you?"

Quiet fell between them. Heidi tugged back hard on the reins.

"Of course," Eve said. "I'm scared as hell, but what they're doing isn't right -"

"If they execute Eli," Heidi interrupted suddenly, "there'll be no reason to find out what happened. There's a good chance no one will ever know what they are trying to hide. They *know* who killed those men. Just like they *know* who killed my husband."

"So once Eli is out of prison: what then? Where will he go? He'll never be able to show his face here again. Neither will you."

"Our tribe, our family, has agreed to help us, Eve. We are still many, and there are many places to hide. He will be kept safe as long as is needed. I will not let my brother be taken from us. The elders, my father, must understand that if we allow this to happen we will never have freedom."

"Red Sutherland will hunt you. He will try to kill you both and anyone else he thinks was involved."

"So be it."

"You have been a good friend Eve," Heidi said at last. "It would be good if you were there, at my side..." her gaze hardened. "But there is nothing you can do for us now," she said, kicking her heels into the horse.

As she watched her friend storm into the woods after the men, Eve was struck with the urge to call after her, to save her from the certain death she faced in going to her brother's aid.

The evening sky was lit silver-blue and pink, and strung across the mountains above the tree-line. Beneath her, Charlie tensed and stomped the ground at her silent torture. He looked back at her, his wide, worried eyes taking in her tears.

Staring into his eyes, she found resolution: she would go to Victoria, just as Joe Martin had said. She would do what she could from Victoria. There had to be someone she could appeal to for help, someone who aspired to justice and truth.

No sooner had this thought invaded her thoughts, than a surge of unexpected rage racked her logic, her ability to stay grounded. This was her country, yes, but before her family had come, the natives had dominion here. The Coast Salish, were a peaceful people, but they could battle with a vengeance to protect their home; to defend their

234

place in the world against unprovoked attack, or invasion.

This, what lay before them, was the threat of wholesale destruction, by an unpredictable enemy, one to which there was no hope of winning.

Ω

MEMORY DRIFTS
LIKE GHOSTS
WHERE IT
WILL

Ab inconvenienti

*From hardship,
comes a blessing*

Eve arrived at work fully expecting to be fired for what had happened at the Maddox place, and the heated argument she had with Quentin over her story being pulled. Quentin was standing by the Rotger's Press, with his sleeves rolled up and was covered in grease up to his elbows.

She stood by the door, waiting for him to light into her.

"Ah you've come to save me from myself have you?" He chuckled. "It might just be too late for that. I've put the thing back together, but there are two bolts and a spring here that are orphaned and without a hope," he smiled warmly.

Instead, he engaged her in small talk, and told her about an entertaining letter from his ex-wife, who still lived in New York. He chatted idly about news from home, as well as some of the news stories coming their way in the following week.

Eve decided to come right out with it. "...To repair broken

bridges, and bruised egos, I think he wants to apologize for pulling my story."

"The good will has come to an end has it?" Quentin mused. "It's a common thing."

"I thought for a moment, for all your talk, you were nothing more than a sycophant. I'll play along: What gives?"

"Listen, Eve. There is a Thanksgiving Day event at the hall in Gillies Bay that I'm attending this coming weekend -"

"I'm aware," Eve said cautiously, now completely thrown.

"I'd be honoured if you were to attend."

"With you?" She asked, and stopped herself sounding so incredulous. Was this an invitation, to attend as his date? She could not fathom the depths of the prospect.

"No need to coddle. My sensibilities are all in their place."

"No, Quentin. It's not that. I'm honoured. Really," Even as she spoke the words, she was shocked at hearing herself. She had come in to work this morning fully expecting to be berated and fired, both for what had happened at Christian Maddox' estate, and for her distasteful parting of ways when she'd spat at his feet. She was unquestionably out of her element.

"Why, Quentin, are you inviting me? I thought -"

"Think nothing of it," Quentin stopped her saying what she would.

"It is true that we really do not even have an inkling what the other is about..."

Eve was thrown. He was acting as though none of what had happened, mattered. He was trying too hard, in any case, but she was certain it was an act, rather than divine intervention.

On her way home that night after work, she couldn't shake the thought that she may have agreed too soon. What were his intentions? One thing was certain, the move was distinctly out of character for Quentin.

For the first time in many years she felt insecure at having gotten herself into a situation she had no right being part of.

As she walked, a warm glow began, that seemed a disembodied sensation that was sent adrift among the uncertainty and nerves. The

Goddess of logic was toying with her, for she found momentary solace in the simple notion of sharing everything that was happening with none other than Quentin himself.

She shook her head, despite that she was alone on the road.

She was being rash. Perhaps he was not living in shadow. Maybe he was telling the truth: that his motivation is simply to keep the paper in good stead, despite what the pressures of doing business might be. Then, if it were an official apology, she was obligated to find her peace with it. It was no longer about the dream. Now it was about doing what she should to help those who were being made to suffer.

Eve sat at the dressing table. Candles burned on the table, the light was soft, her skin golden as she brushed her hair. Laid out on her bed was an outfit comprising her usual attire, and beside it, a dress she had received from her birth-mother, but had only worn once. It was one of only two she owned.

No matter his intention - dress or no dress – if it came down to it, she would insist on a good working relationship over anything else that might show itself. Anything else would complicate their present arrangement, from which there was much to benefit. If it were confounded by the unpredictable complications that often come between men and women, the benefit would no longer be palatable.

She rose from the chair and stood before the tall mirror. She let her robe fall to the floor. The cool breeze swept in the window and chilled her. The way the dim candle light caught her skin, and her hair fell across her shoulders, it reminded her of when she was a girl - just out of her teens, and anxious for the uncertainty of that age to be replaced with the confidence of womanhood.

A scant knock at the door sent her scooping her dress up from the floor, just as Cathryn burst in looking her up and down with haughty derision. She was every bit the red-haired Queen, considering a servant who'd brushed too much jam on her toast. Then she lowered her eyes, and shook her head, judgement having quickly found its usual path. "Put on your clothes. Yer' supper's getting cold," she delivered her unction, true to form, and exited the room. "I've already eaten," she said as she closed the door firmly behind her.

Eve gathered her wits. "Don't you knock? Have you not a shred of common decency?" She listened for a reply, but was met with Catharyn's heavy foot-fall as she descended the stairs.

"Not a shred of womanly grace, either," Eve quietly agreed with herself.

"Fuck her," She said aloud as she pulled the gown over her head and turned to have another look in the mirror. She went to the closet and stood in front of the open door trying to make her mind up about what she would wear. Her mind went naturally to the pants. She was comfortable in pants. Her hand went to the trousers. She pulled a coat away to get a better look, but her eye drifted again to a patterned dress. She had not worn a dress since she was fifteen. The memory of it came on its own, flooding her with the weight of the unfortunate memory.

She'd gone to church by herself, was late getting chores done, and was made to walk, to and from, on her own. Afterwards, on her way home, she met Devon Hartman and his boys on the trail that afforded a short-cut from town. Devon started in teasing her and would not let up. Later, in thinking about it, it was clear they had already made up their minds what they were going to do.

And that's just what they did.

They'd come out to meet her as she cut across the Hartman's field. The three boys surrounded her. Devon stood directly in front of her, sporting his best menacing glare – a distraction, while one of the others lifted the back of her dress with a stick, to get a good look at what they might see. Ignoring the boy with the stick, she lunged for the one on her left, whose close eyes and pigeon-toed stance suggested he was an easy mark, and she'd do her best to make an impression. Even at fifteen, she was a strong girl, seasoned from several years of the hard labour Catharyn had extracted from her while her father was away at work. For her size she delivered a sledge-hammer blow to the poor boy's soft face. He collapsed instantly and lay cowering on the ground – an excellent flag bearer for what she would do to the others, were she to have the good fortune of laying hands on them.

She swung to meet the second boy, knowing Devon would opt to let his minion move in first. She could see he was nervous, but she sensed Devon moving behind her and swung wildly. He dodged in time to avoid the damaging blow.

The second boy backed off a little, then there came a voice from further down the trail. Harry Bell appeared there and sauntered up, having decided to join them.

He walked straight at her, she backed up a little and stopped, preparing to do her worst. It was then, from behind her, that Devon grabbed a handful of dress and tore it clean off, from the just above the waist. All she could do was to stand there in the field, in the middle of the group of sneering boys. She looked around desperately for help, but no help would come. Harry Bell, seeing her there exposed like that, tried to move in. She felt his hands on her backside and he tried to tear what remained of the dress but she swung again, this time hitting him square in the nose, which promptly spurted blood onto a dirt patch at the trail entrance. He stood there holding his nose, his eyes pinched with rage. In a flash, he brought the back of his hand across her cheek. She staggered, but did not fall. They would not rob her of her dignity, to fall would have been to lay down like a fawn before wolves.

She stood with her fists clenched.

Harry cursed her and brought his sleeve across his mouth, then, miracle of miracles, turned slowly and started on his way. The others caught up to him and, together, they walked through the field homeward.

The first boy stumbled after them, sobbing.

Eve stayed her ground until they disappeared, where the trail split the buck brush, which pushed in from both sides and loomed over top of the path.

It was only now that a tear escaped her, and ran down her hot cheek. She grit her teeth and choked it back, her face burning where she'd been hit.

She gathered the scraps of dress from the ground and tried to arrange them as best she could, to conceal herself, and she started the walk home. Humiliation was hers that day. And she would never let it go. Not as long as she lived.

240

When she'd returned home, she had no luck in sneaking past her stepmother, who accused her of improper behaviour, and wondered what-on-earth she'd done to bring this kind of trouble upon herself.

Eve stood before the mirror, and let go of the patterned dress and watched it fall to the floor.

Every woman would be wearing their best, outside of their Sunday finery. It would be awkward to show up in her usual. Though, at the same time, no-one had ever seen her in a dress. It was hard to say which anomaly would be the lesser of two travesties.

She was older now, twenty-four, and the boys had become young men. Some of them had moved on, others had gained a healthy respect, if not outright fear, and kept their distance.

She grabbed another dress from a hangar and pulled it over her head. She straightened her shoulders and pulled the blouse down in front. She ran her hands through her hair and pulled it back, into a tortoise-shell hair clip, and stood again in front of the mirror.

For a moment she was taken by what she saw; a beautiful young woman, with looks to snare any man. She let her hair fall, then pulled it back to reveal her face. Her blue eyes were bright in the candle light.

She walked carefully down the stairs, as though the dress might tear at the slightest provocation. From the kitchen she could see a soft glow coming from her father's room where the lamp had been left burning. She glanced at Catharyn, and went into the room. Her father's bed sheets and blankets were flawless, even swept for wrinkles and wefts. Catharyn entered daily to sweep and wipe and scrub, whether it needed it or not.

A sterling crucifix hung in perfect repose above the night table. She reached out and pushed lightly against its foot, to leave it hanging at an awkward angle. It would give Catharyn something to fret about.

She was about to exit the room, and looked at the pillows lying there in the soft light, and the book upon the night table. She could see her father, then, propped up in his bed, reading by the lamplight. He would lay the book on his lap and smile proudly.

"How could it be that the Russian princess herself is here in my very room? What have I done to earn such honour?"

"Nonsense father. I'm the furthest thing from a Russian sovereign."

"*If not, then something more, Evelyn Walker. Makes me wonder why you hide behind those clothes you wear all the time.*"

"Lord, not you too, father. It's simple. I dress the way I do, so people see me for who I am, for what I bring to the table. I want to appear capable, not incompetent and breakable. You men have a terrible habit of sizing women up by butt or bosom..."

He would wince comically at Eve's brazen candour.

"It's not very endearing, is it?"

"*A ruby is a ruby, but so much more, too, with the touch of a fine goldsmith.*"

"Yes, but was it not you who also said a diamond is still a diamond, whether in a bed of coal or on a queen's finger?"

She was pulled from her somber memory by Catharyn's acidic voice announcing that her dinner was still there, waiting, and that it would soon be destined for the trash.

"Do you have an escort?" Catharyn asked, trying her best to remain uninterested.

"I'm meeting Quentin at the hall."

"Hmmph. What kind of man is he? Leaves a young lady to fend for herself..." Catharyn scorned. No sooner had she asked the question, and she'd already drifted on to another topic of her one-sided conversation. It was her simple intellect. It could not be helped, only endured. "Take care not to get that dress dirty on your way. Hook Charlie to the wagon."

"It'll be fine," Eve said, nonplussed, as she grabbed the plate of food and went back to her room.

No long time had passed when Eve walked through the kitchen to the door and pulled on her coat. Though not a word passed between them, Eve caught her stepmother watching after her through the window as she departed.

Ω

LOST AND FOUND

---

*Etiam capillus unus
habet umbra*

Π

*Even one hair casts
a shadow*

Eve insisted on arriving at the dance on her own.

Quentin had offered earlier that day that he could pick her up, which would, of course, have been the gentlemanly thing to do. But she felt that she might somehow be putting herself at risk of too much dependence on him.

When she arrived, he was waiting on the hall steps, dressed in his best social attire, with his right hand tucked at a clever angle into his vest pocket, and the other with a cigar wedged between his fingers. He reached down and offered a hand to Eve, as she approached the verandah stairs. People standing nearby stopped in mid-conversation to watch as she accepted, though her brand of grace was distinctly lacking the demure response that was expected.

"You're enough to make even a priest think twice," he said.
She smiled politely. Though a dozen quips sailed through her mind, she managed to keep them from lighting over her tongue.

"I don't make a habit of it."

"You might consider it."

Eve flushed this time, having caught his sincerity; he'd found the small chink in her armour. She could see something in his eyes that she'd not seen before. He even stood a little straighter, shoulders back. He was grandstanding, in his own subtle way.

Inside the hall, the band started in playing a light square dance number, to set the mood for what was to come.

Quentin again offered Eve his arm.

"In all honesty, I wasn't sure you'd come," he said. "I thought it might be awkward for you, coming with an older man – your employer. I don't want to get the wrong idea across. It's just been about work for me, with getting the paper re-established. I haven't had the opportunity to mix in social circles -"

"I'm a secondary prize then? Nothing better came along? Are you always in the habit of saying too much?" Eve smirked.

"Let's just leave it at 'the dress becomes you' for now. However, I am honoured to be in your company..."

"Grovelling doesn't suit you Quentin," She smiled this time, and led the way inside, just as the fiddlers broke from a fug to a blue-grass number. In moments the sound of feet pounding the floorboards added percussion to the trilling fiddle. Someone in the crowd let out a yip; another answered.

Quentin took Eve's arm and, together, they went to the dance floor and joined in. He danced with smart proficiency: was sharp, deliberate, and struck an ease that made him stand out above most of the other men, save two or three. Eve started in slowly, but, soon after watching the other ladies for style points, stepped with a flourish across the floor, lifting her dress as she went.

Afterwards, the fiddlers broke into a two-step, and the men and women were separated to either side of the hall. Eve and Quentin were caught up in it, and so went along, taking cues from those around them. Arm-in-arm they skipped across the floor, feet falling in perfect unison, bringing to the spectacle a thunderous percussion, as if an unorthodox marching band unleashed a corps of drummers.

When the dance broke away, Quentin found Evelyn and brought her to the canteen, where they found a place to sit among others at a table. The two of them took a drink to cool off.

"Have you danced like this before?" Quentin puffed. "It looked as though you were searching a bit."

"When I was younger. But not since."

"That's a shame. It's a good time, not to mention keeps you fit," he said patting his stomach. "Why haven't you? Danced, I mean."

"Spent most of my childhood taking care of my father, keeping chores at the house and the like."

"Nervous?"

"You've unsettled me a little. I'll admit. Something of a Casanova are you?"

"Nothing of the sort. Just an admirer of all things beautiful really. Inside and out," He smiled seeming to appreciate, as he often did, his own wit.

"Nicely done," Evelyn smiled patting him on the back.

"No really," he persisted.

"I'm something of an Ariadne: you should mind yourself," She threw him a stern glance.

Quentin appeared shocked, perhaps unsettled at the turn of the tide, being used, as he was, to controlling the conversation with poise and self-assurance. A smile came slowly to his lips, and showed what she hoped might be the genesis of a healthy respect.

As they talked several men and women approached the table and greeted Quentin - business owners, women and men in positions of social influence. They acknowledged Eve as an afterthought. Rumours and speculation about Quentin had been going around since even before he'd arrived. Others, who did not have the compunction to approach the table for a word, would slow and stare as they passed, as though he were some mythical pariah, churning the great urban myth that would somehow put Vananda on the map.

"So, tell me about this unfortunate fellow – this Chinaman you found."

Eve bristled at his derogatory insult of Song Loo. But, again, she restrained herself. *It's just words, don't lose your temper,* she recited her silent mantra firmly to herself. *We want to keep the job.*

"Perhaps I was mistaken. Is this a work arrangement?" She said finally. "If I'd known this was a work arrangement, I'd have dressed the part," She managed a tense smile.

"No." Quentin insisted, laying his hand on Eve's. "Certainly we are here as friends. Don't let me ruin it. I can be a bit crass at times. I assumed, being green behind the ears, you'd be bursting to talk about your first big interview story... that "fell into your lap" as it were."

Eve thought to offer something banal, to throw him off his inquiry, a polite push-back, to stop the conversation going somewhere it ought not to go.

"After much thought, Quentin, I've decided you were right. Stirring those demons would only serve to cause trouble. I've got enough trouble on my plate at the moment." She held her breath.

"Hmmm," was all he uttered at first, then, "That's why I hired you, Evelyn. You're a fast study. We'll get on just fine, you and I. I was worried I'd lost you... And yes, I know you've probably got too much on your plate. And I truly am sorry about your father. Really is a travesty about Reverend... Mr. Millen and your mother – stepmother, my apologies."

Eve's face grew hot and red. Her vision drew razor sharp. Once again, she thought it better to bite her tongue, but spoke her mind anyway... She drew a subtle breath, to measure her words; thought about lying, then decided against it.

"What, exactly are you talking about Mr. Reynolds?"

"Mr. Reynolds now again, are we?"

Eve straightened herself, felt foolish for wearing the dress after all. *Be careful what you wish for*, she thought to herself.

At that moment, a man Eve did not recognize approached and stood adroitly behind Quentin. The man tapped him on the shoulder, presumptuously positioning himself for a warm and animated greeting, as though the sun and moon rose and set on his say-so.

Quentin turned in his chair and rose, perceiving the expectations of this adroit visitor, delivered the appropriate reaction, much to the man's liking. A few moments had passed before the man leaned in and spoke something in confidence to Quentin. Then the two bid one another an abrupt departure.

Quentin's face was set as he approached Eve again. She tensed as he took her hand. Her face was still hot from his brash comment about Catharyn. She couldn't help but think it was a deliberate

246

volley.

"I find myself again having to apologize, Evelyn. I need to attend to matters that cannot wait. I have very much enjoyed your company." He attempted to bring her hand to his lips. With as much tact and grace as she could manage, she slipped her hand from his and, instead, offered a polite shake.

"Short as it was, it was good to finally see a little of Quentin Reynold's, the man, not Quentin Reynolds the newspaper editor from New York. I'm feeling a little outdone myself. Think I'll head home."

"Thank you for being gracious about it. Would you like me to have someone take you?"

Eve declined.

Quentin gave a curt nod before exiting the hall with the stranger in tow, who had been watching from afar.

Eve sat at the table watching the people dance, smiling, laughing, sweeping across the floor. A couple were dancing so vigorously that sweat ran down the man's forehead; her cheeks were badly flushed. As she watched, she felt a hand on her shoulder. The neighbours just south of her father's property had come to say hello. They commented on her dress and shortly went arm-in-arm to the canteen for hot chocolate.

She had just gathered her wits enough to manage the trip home, when a young man approached and asked her to dance. She intended to say no straight off, but he looked at her with bright blue eyes, that were glossed over from the effects of drink. He looked harmless enough. She agreed, and in no time, was skipping over the dance floor once again. The players finished the song and started in on a slow number, to let the dancers catch their breath.

They were winding things down.

The young man caught and held her arm until finally she agreed to dance the slow number with him. Soon into the dance however, it had become abundantly clear that the man was drunk and foot-tied, having stepped upon her feet numerous times.

She finally excused herself, this time insisting, and sharply withdrawing herself, so as not to leave any uncertainty. Lifting the hem of her skirt again, she made her way to the main entrance, and out into the cool night air.

Eve stood a while on the veranda, taking in the spectacle. It was as if she were on a transept between worlds. Behind her, there was the cacophony of celebration from the hall, before her, just beyond the light, she could hear voices: couples and friends talking; their voices echoing, sometimes below the threshold, then suddenly ringing with pleasure. A laugh would pitch into the darkness and carry for some time before being swallowed by the greater noise of the celebration.

The thought of home, of Catharyn glowering, and storming from place to place, was abhorrent. She began to feel as though there may be another place for her, calling, waiting. But for now, it was home. She hadn't yet even begun to say goodbye to her father. Being assigned to the house was possibly enough. She would go out into the world in her own time.

As Eve descended the stairs, she was startled by an old woman in a long dark dress blocking her way. For a while, they stood before one another, with the lady staring at her intently with her piercing gaze. Eve smiled politely and moved to step around her once again. The lady checked her move with surprising dexterity.

"You're Evelyn Walker."

"Yes, that's right," Eve said, forcing an uneasy smile. "Can I help you with something?" The old lady only stared at her in return, squinting at her, sizing her up.

"Hey look, I'm not interested in fighting with elderly women. Seriously. Do I know you?"

"No, but I do know you," She smiled then, and at that very moment, the hall doors exploded outward, and two large men, with fists flying and bent on destruction, hurtled onto the verandah. No attention was paid to the fact there were stairs to be managed – quite a lot of them – and the tangle of men came hurtling down.

Eve thought to protect the old lady from certain injury, or worse, but there was no time to rationalize. She threw herself over the stair railing and barely landed on her feet. When she looked back, the tumble of men had already catapulted from the top step, and were followed quickly by a throng of onlookers and fans. Men from both camps were reaching into the flurry that ensued at the bottom step, in efforts to quell the explosion.

Eve searched desperately to find the old woman, but she was lost in the chaotic antics that ensued there. She walked into the fray, searching the ground among the people, for what she was certain would be the near-lifeless form of the elderly woman, but she was no-where to be found.

One by one, the men collected themselves and the crowd began to disperse, and, still, it was as if she had simply vanished.

Eve remained for a time, to ensure she was not mistaken, and berated herself that she might have imagined the whole thing.

She collected Charlie from the hall paddock and led him across the lot, to where she'd left the wagon at Bartlett's feed lot.

"I'm losing my mind old boy," she said, patting Charlie's neck as she went.

She ran through the events of the evening, shortened, as it was, by Quentin's unexpected and odd departure. Then, as she stepped from between the feedlot buildings, and the Blacksmith's shop, her world came undone. She was knocked violently off her feet and set upon by two men, who had been waiting there in the shadows.

Charlie attempted to rear up, but there was no room.

One of the men went after Charlie. The other brought his full weight to bear upon her, and he clearly intended to finish what they'd started.

She was lying flat on her back, but she let go with a blind swing and connected a solid blow with her attacker's jaw. The man grunted, then renewed his onslaught. He went for her throat. He placed a steely grip around her neck. Panic shot through her veins, and in the back of her mind, she questioned whether she'd taken a breath before he'd set about crushing her wind-pipe. Adrenaline surged through her like never before. She tried to scream, but no sound came. She could feel the pressure building in her head and in her lungs.

She would die here.

She was going to die.

She rallied her efforts, swinging again. She connected with a solid throttle to the man's temple. It hurt him. She saw his throat then just above her. She aimed and landed another solid blow to his

Adam's apple. She felt his grip loosen. And a shot of hope snaked through her mind, but it was a fleeting notion. He redoubled his efforts now, and shortly after, she felt a switch go off somewhere within her, that she might have no choice but to resign herself to her fate, here and now.

Darkness flooded the periphery. And the arm she would swing again, only fell limp to the ground.

She would surely be raped.

This must be the truth of it.

Raped and left for dead.

As her mind drifted in its dream-like torpor, she remembered smelling cigar, or was it Cologne? Perhaps linseed oil?

As if somewhere off in the distance now, she heard her dress rip, and a cold rush of air fell upon her body. Then, as if the sound of the fabric tearing, or perhaps it was the cold itself, her will to live seized upon her, pulled from her a strength that seemed impossible. And she, too, did her own part, and struggled with every fibre of strength she could summon. She felt the hand loosen for a moment and sunk her teeth into a bony wrist. Above her, the man screamed, and she broke free.

Her lungs filled with precious, cold air. Her emotions flooded... And still, there was a place in her mind where all was quiet, seemed to drift slowly, to a cadence unaffected by the actions that befell her now. The logical mind, on some level, was trying to place the voice. She searched her memory, faces came and went, but nothing that made any sense.

Somewhere nearby, the man growled, his pain turning now to rage. She saw that his face was blackened with coal or grease, and the whites of his eyes glowed starkly in the lamplight.

She managed to get to her feet, and struggled to centre her balance. Before she could defend herself, he lunged once again. This time she stood her ground, feet apart, and brought her fist hard into his nose. Blood gushed and mixed with the black grease and the sweat. She stepped back, and was about to kick him in the groin, when another pair of arms snapped like a great vice around her upper body, pinning her arms. She was pulled helplessly to the ground once again. What remained of her dress was torn away from

250

her legs.

She struggled against the brute strength of the man holding her.

She felt a hand on her thigh.

Then suddenly, inexplicably, her arms were free, and the hand was ripped away from her mouth. Almost at the same time, her legs came free, and the man there was backing away, and looking confused. She saw her opportunity and launched her foot into his head trying to connect with his jaw, but connected with a resounding wallop in its own right. His eyes glazed for a moment, and he shook his head, as if he were a dog who'd taken an unexpected plunge into a cold river. She looked back where the other had been, and saw, at first, only his feet dangling nearly a foot from the ground. A pair of much larger feet were planted firmly below them. The man who'd only moments before sought to steal her life, now had his shoulders up around his head. It was Big John who had him. Eve's heart leaped into her throat.

John had him in a massive bear hug, and his shirt was bunched up around his ears, his eyes now whiter than ever, and his face contributing a rare shade of purple beneath the black and red. John let the man go, and he remained standing, but vastly disoriented. Big John pulled his massive fist back, like an iron pendulum, and let loose, as though he were putting a spoiled farm animal out of its senses. The man fell, in a limp mess, to the dirt, while the first attacker still lay in a heap behind her.

John's man was now scrambling to his feet, and he tried to run. Eve thrust her foot between his, to keep him from gaining ground, and he crashed head-long into the wall of the Blacksmith's shop, taking the full-force of the blow.

In two steps John was upon him. He plucked his victim from the ground by his lapels, and encouraged him to his feet. He was now pathetic in his aspect, and looking like the much-abused villain in a vaudeville performance. He grimaced in pain, just as John administered another severe blow, knocking him flat onto his backside. He looked flummoxed, however, John was not finished serving justice. He picked the man up once again.

Now, however, the vanquished was like a stray dog backed

into a corner. Surprisingly, he was on his feet again. He shook the blow off with formidable constitution. He seized upon the notion of his freedom and ran for safety, stumbling once, before he disappeared in the night.

John was left holding a torn vest. He handed the vest to Eve, and, without a word, or second thought, he was after him.

"Let him go!" Eve yelled, "You're liable to kill him."

To Eve's shock, John stopped then, and walked back to her side. The sound of fleeing footsteps grew faint as the man made his get away.

Big John slipped his jacket off and draped it over Eve's shoulders. "You must keep warm, Eve. Otherwise the shock will set in."

"I'm fine, John," she insisted, seemingly unaware of her exposed condition.

"Wear the jacket."

It was not an admonition, or an outright scolding... It felt to Eve more like, in that moment, she knew what it would have been like to have an older brother. She picked up the vest. "Maybe we'll get lucky," she said, checking the pockets. "Feels heavy." The first pocket was empty. In the second she indeed felt something. Her fingers found purchase around a chain, a necklace, certainly.

Instead, she pulled out a gold pocket watch that caught the light of an approaching lantern as it dangled there between them.

Eve was quick to hide it.

Several men who'd heard the commotion back at the hall, had come to inquire.

The first attacker was collected and packaged for jail. The men fussed over Eve and made as if to lead her to the hall, where the women could tend to her injuries.

"Wait," Eve insisted. "I'd like to borrow the lantern. Big John and I will need a moment to ourselves."

The men nodded respectfully, and without question, moved off.

"What is it?" John asked.

She asked him to hold the lantern as she pulled the watch from her pocket. After a brief search, she found the clasp that would

252

open the back, where the workings were located. She knew from taking her father's timepiece to the jewellers for repair, that an entry would be engraved inside the back cover every time a repair or adjustment was made. Often the owner's name was there too.

The cover snapped as she found purchase. She asked John to bring the lamp closer. There, inside the back cover, were the initials "J.W.P., from the Guild".

She looked up at Big John. "This watch belonged to Jonas William Prescott."

She and John looked at one another, letting the reality sink in. Then she remembered how strange Quentin had acted when he left the dance early. Something big was boiling away behind the scenes, beyond the eyes of most on the Island. She was now certain that Quentin was somewhere at, or near, the root of it.

She decided, at that moment, she would turn her sharp intellect to bear upon Quentin himself. She would apply some of the rules that he had preached so often these last weeks, and bring her efforts to bear upon *him*, to see how well he stood up under his own brand of scrutiny.

Ω

A Desperate Plea

Ex Uno disce omnes

*From one person
learn all people*

Heidi loosened her hold on the reins as she wiped the sweat from her hands on the beaded deer hide dress she wore, as she neared the village. Her heart skipped as the first Clapboard houses flashed through the thinning trees. She brought the horse to a halt, to collect herself a moment, then snapped the reins again.

The leather saddle creaked beneath her, as her horse navigated a hummock in the middle of the trail. She had been granted permission to approach the Council of Elders, but the reply had been days in coming. Every day that slipped by, was another day Eli was closer to death, that is, if he wasn't already gone. But she couldn't think of that now. Her hope had to be complete in its fullness. The alternative was inconceivable.

As she broke from the trees she saw the town laid out before her, and her heart ached for that which she could not have: her husband, her brother's safety, and to be welcomed back into her home.

As she rode through the village, a young mother pulled blankets and clothing from a spray of barren tree branches, children played a rough game of tag in the street, and there were groups of young men, here and there, talking seriously and smoking tobacco.

The children stopped to watch her as she rode by, her horse pulling at the reins a bit, reminding that these opportunities sometimes

254

bore an unexpected boon, children, as they are, being partial to the spirit of giving.

As she neared the large Community House, a young girl, standing at the side of the street with her mother, broke from her arms and ran to Heidi, reaching, as she did, with a fistful of flowers, a gift for an old friend.

A group of young men sat outside a small home, all taking turns speaking over one another, talking and planning. They too halted their spirited conversation as she dismounted. Heidi could feel their eyes upon her as she walked the stairs into the lodge.

Inside the Village House, a fire snapped and sparked as it settled into itself at the centre of the room. The smoke from the main fire was drawn up and through the hole in the roof by the cold air outside. The pleasant odour of smoke from the fire mingled with the oil from the ancient carved corner posts and beams. Cedar boughs were hung and laid to dry on the beams and on the ground in places. In one corner a basket-weaving centre had been deserted, likely to make way for the revered council.

The elders - four men, including her father, and two of the elder women - were seated on one side of a large, carved cedar table. All were wise with age; most looked upon her reproachfully.

The exception was Elder Galigos, who watched her closely, perhaps more closely than the others. She nodded gently, then stared on in silence.

Heidi approached the table. She was careful not to meet her father's gaze. She could not. She was angry with him for what had happened to her brother, and for forsaking her when she needed him most... For making her choose between her husband and her people.

Elder Galigos could see that Heidi was moved to tears, but chose to clench her teeth instead. She motioned for Heidi to sit on the cedar mat laid out before them. "It is our way," she said.

Heidi knelt upon the mat, usually a thing to be honoured, but was now clearly a disgrace.

"I've come to ask for help, for my brother, Eli Tomas," She spoke as though she alone had rights to her brother's affections.

"Elder, Grace Louie, would like to speak first," Chief Tomas announced. "I will speak her words in English. She is the oldest among us, and has seen many things. She has seen when the white man first came here." He eased himself to sit again, then stood once more. He was tired. Heidi could see that. And, in that, her heart reached out to him unexpectedly.

As Elder Louie began, Heidi closed her eyes for a moment, to let the beauty of the old language – Ay-ay-ju-thum - and the old way of speaking, fill the longing in her heart. It was a lulling and gentle language, like water over rocks; it was an old song, an important song, that spoke about the old ways.

"...I was only a small child when these new people came..." Her father paused to listen again. "We would play on the beaches, and in the forests of Say-ay-in, and our only worry was to keep out of the way of the adults as they worked, and about what there might be to eat when the day was done.

"I was there on the shore when the first big boats came. There was much fear. But, then we were made to see that these strange creatures, with pale skin, and hair that was not like our own, meant us no harm, and that they had beautiful things they wanted to give us..." He paused again, listening intently. "...things that were not of this place, and must surely have much power. So we gave these people all of our furs, and we piled them there on the beach, and they wanted to give us the most powerful things in return... They traded their guns for our furs." Elder Louie paused.

There was a long silence, and the air grew close as they waited for her to continue.

"At first there was much excitement at these new people that came. The men – both young and old – would covet these guns terribly. It would make a man, who was good and well respected, want to take what was not his.

"Some thought it was the Spirits that were coming to bring us good luck. And so it was, that whenever we saw them, there was much excitement that there would be gifts, and that they would give us new things we had not seen before..." She fell silent again, while she thought deeply about what she would say next.

"It will be difficult to see with my eyes..." Then she raised her arms and swept them slowly in front of her, painting a vast skyline with her hands. "All that you see around you – all trees, all of the animals, the mountains and the water... there is..." Again she foundered. Chief Tomas waited patiently at her side. "There is freedom... to go where your feet would take you. There is freedom... to catch the fish where you have caught them since you can remember – when you were a small child, and even long before that. There is freedom... All that you see around you - that is where you can go."

Elder Louie seemed to slump in her chair now. Her body heaved as she took several deep breaths.

"...And then there were more of these people – more and more of them would come, but they would always go away again after they had gotten their furs... We watched them leave in their boats, and wondered that they must travel across the sea, to a land we could not hope to know. Then one day they came again, but this time they did not leave like before. This time they walked all over the place and kicked trees, and broke branches, and picked up rocks and stared at them. They broke the earth - there under the grass and bushes - to see what was there. They seemed happy with all that they looked at...

"Then the day had come that they stomped their feet and shot their guns, and said that all of these things," she said, sweeping her arm over the room again, "now belonged to them. And sometimes, if you did not move fast enough, you would get caught under their boot.

"Many of us became scared, and the men were scared and angry too. It was said, then, that the white men could have all of their guns back, and that it would be okay if they wanted to go back to where they had come from."

She went on, slowly now, so that all who were in the room had to listen carefully for every word.

"The white people grew angry with us, because our minds were not fast enough, like theirs were. And they made their laws, and it was then that we were without... The animals know it, too, for they were also pushed from their homes, to make room for what had come..."

Elder Louie now slumped visibly. Chief Tomas laid a gentling hand onto her shoulder.

"I will go on and speak her words for her," he said. "For I know what it is that she would say," he paused and stared hard at Heidi.

"Some of the rules that were made were not rules that were made by the ones in charge of the white man's laws. They were made up by the white people themselves, when it suited them. It is these laws that were the hardest..." Chief Tomas eased himself onto his seat. "Elder Louie, and some of the others here, they saw our people get killed for breaking a law that they had not heard of before. They did not even know what it was they were being killed for..."

He took a deep breath and looked intently at Heidi again. "Ernie had you in his heart, Heidi," he paused staring at her directly, until she could not avoid him any longer, "And you have him in your heart. I know this to be true," Her father paused, then, and his gaze fell to the floor. Heidi waited for him, and when he looked up, his face had softened. "These laws...," he drew silent again, his face a picture of long years of worry and anguish for his people, for what would become. He shook his head in frustration. "He is white, Heidi. And you are Indian. You are Tla'amin. It is true that the law says that if you follow the rules, it is possible for you to be together, but it is the white people who get angry and say that it is not."

"That is the old way," Heidi flashed. "The old way *needs* to change. Everything is changing, and we need to change too. Otherwise, we will be pushed from our lands, from all that we know, and what we believe."

"We have agreed to let the law take its course!" Chief Tomas insisted. "If Eli is innocent then we must have faith. We must believe that the right thing will be done."

"The right thing will *not* be done, father. The right thing has never been done. They will hold his trial in secret, and they will find him guilty of killing my husband. I know it. I can feel it. They will kill Eli. Like they killed my husband. And there will be no-one there to speak for him."

"How do you know this?"

"Because I go to visit him. I visit him almost every day." Heidi looked from the elders to her father. Chief Israel Tomas leaned back in his place, letting his hands slide from the table. "That is how I know he is in danger. I went to see him at the jail and he was not there anymore. None of the men there would tell me what had happened to him. It was only when I left that place that one of the police followed me, and told me that Eli was taken to trial. He did not know where this would happen, or when it would happen. This is how I know they will

258

kill him. These white men keep secrets, and it gives them power over us," Heidi stood now from the mat and implored the Council of Elders to see what she could plainly see. "The law will not protect him. It will kill him. Those men will kill him."

Chief Tomas cast his gaze to the floor once again. "We too know this to be true, Heidi."

"What?" Heidi stepped forward, a look of disbelief on her face. "What did you say?" her voice was no more than a whisper.

"It is true, Heidi. Ernie... Ernie had my blessing. I thought that it would be good for you to marry him. Then we would have a connection to their people. And we might save our selves much grief, and much pain... Much death."

Heidi remained silent, and rapt upon what he might say next. But she could not have guessed the gravity of it, and how it would affect her. From the outside, she was the practised measure of unshakeable calm, the calm of a Chief's daughter. Within her, there raged the greatest storm there ever was. It took everything in her not to run from that place, but there was no longer any place to run.

"It was not long before we could see that things had got worse for us. The very thing I would try to escape, I brought upon us...."

"What do you mean father?" Heidi said, her eyes betraying the deep confusion that was hers now, and the tears came easily. Through her tears she could see, for the first time, a shadow fall across her father's eyes; it was the shadow of understanding, and the realization that their old way of life had come to its end.

"No!" she slammed her fist onto the table. "They have a plan, and they need Eli to be blamed. You must ask of yourselves what it would do if Eli is said to be guilty of taking a life? It will not be looked upon as a man killing another man. It will be looked upon as an Indian killing a white man. There is already no trust, and it will ruin our chances for keeping our land. All of the work John West has done will be for nothing.

"What *does* John West have to say about all of this?" She asked of her father. "Surely you have been to see him?"

"John West is not here," Elder Charlie answered for him.

"We will wait until he returns," Elder Galigos said.

"He will not be here in time. It will be too late for Eli. They meant for it to happen this way. The timing is important to them. They know it will ruin us."

"In my heart I know there is more to it than just this, my daughter" Chief Tomas said, finally.

"Of course there is more to it. That is what I am saying father. They have timed it this way."

"Still, one cannot be too sure," Elder Galigos said again.

"This is maddening," Heidi yelled, prompting Elder Charlie, who, until now, had remained silent, rise in his seat to challenge her. Chief Tomas raised his hand. "You must stop yelling at one another. I ask for respect for our ancestors. Let us not forget this is a sacred place. We must believe the ways of the past will lead us to the future. But we must choose our course wisely. There are questions that first must be answered, before we can act on the wisdom you bring to us."

"What questions father?" she said, exasperated to no measure.

"Are you certain he did not kill Ernie Tsan?" Elder Charlie asked.

Heidi's hands fell again to her sides. She stared at her father, her mouth agape with disbelief, at the devastating outcome that now seemed assured.

"It is true that your brother was humiliated and ashamed by your decision to marry Ernie Tsan. He did not keep secret about it."

Heidi's eyes narrowed. "Has that ever happened before father? Are we to trust that the court will be fair for my brother, for *your* son?"

"Tish. You must be respectful," Elder Charlie said again, in his stern way, like a grandfather who loves his grandchildren, but who is not very good with kids.

Her father remained silent.

"No. It has not happened before," Heidi answered for him. "If what you say about Eli is true, than I am the last one that should speak in his favour! I do so because he told me he did not do it father. He is *innocent*! And I believe him."

Her father stared at her for a long while. "Heidi. You may come home, come here, back to the village" her father spoke slowly, deliberately, "but we must leave things as they are. It is for the safety of our people, of the village, and to give hope to our children, and our children's children some day."

260

"No, father!" Heidi shouted now, losing herself in her desperation. "We need to send our people, as many as we can, women, children, the elders, as soon as possible to the jailhouse. We will set up a camp there, with fires and bedrolls and blankets, and they will stay there for three days. The newspaper will write about it, and we will ask help from the King."

"For what purpose?" Chief Tomas bristled. "I have never known anything like this to work. We must live by their rules, or we will pay for it in some way. We have already lost too much."

Heidi stared at their faces and saw they were resolute and hardened to the truth. And behind them, there were fear and uncertainty: a fear to act with resolve.

"You have come with a big heart," her father began again, "full of love for your brother, full of love for your husband. But I am reminded by some here in the village that he is no longer your brother. It is an easy thing for me to forget, too, for my own heart sometimes aches for the way it once was. And I must remind my heart that this is the way of our people, and it cannot be changed, even though so much around us has changed."

Heidi's intense grief boiled and threatening to overcome her. With tears once again streaming down her face, she turned toward the door, then stopped. "You are afraid," she blasted now, turning to face them again. "You are afraid to do what is right. But to do *nothing* is much worse! You will see the truth of it soon enough, but then it will be too late."

"Heidi," her father called after her.

She turned on him with a whip-tongue, "We are facing the enemy and you would all be content to sit there and let us be washed away," She raged at them through a blur of tears. "Eli is my brother! *My* brother, and nothing you say - nothing any of our ancestors would say - can change that. The white man will finish us. The old ways will not work against them. And we must change if we expect to live and be free."

She stopped herself leaving a moment longer, "Never mind, father. You hang on to the dead. I will save the living myself."

Heidi stormed from her father, her tearful eyes locking upon the Nenqam carved into the door posts, as if they alone might save her having to turn back.

Heidi stood a moment outside the Village House. The massive Cedars and the Firs at the edge of Si-yat-sen, had turned dark against the cold. Smoke curled in narrow ribbons from houses nearby. She lifted her face to the rising wind. It signalled a coming turn, and in her heart there was also a stirring – a restless shift, but she lacked the strength to call it courage.

As she climbed onto her horse, Elder Louie's words echoed in her mind, that what they had once known to be their freedom, was to be no more. Though every urge in her body told her to ride as fast as she could away from the village, as far as her horse would take her, instead she forced herself to ride slowly among the houses and the children. She did not notice, through her tear-stained eyes, that the groups of young men she had passed by when she had arrived, were nowhere to be seen.

By the time she reached the edge of the forest, the urge to fly had left her. Instead she let the horse plod lazily down the middle of the path, and let her sorrow flow freely from her. She tried to hold her thoughts, but could not. There was nothing left to hold. She did know, however, that her brother needed her, and *she* would not forsake him. She would give her life for him, to repay the debt what he had lost due to her own selfish desire to marry Ernie Tsan.

As she rode, her mind fluttered back and forth between guilt for what had happened to Eli, and concern for herself - a selfish concern that would see her hanging from the end of the rope she had tied when Eve first found her there in the barn. She would feed the animals, plenty of food – enough for several days, and then re-tie the noose. It seemed the simplest solution to her unbearable grief.

It was dark in the trail when she heard hooves approaching quickly from behind her. For a moment an inexplicable fear struck through her, but her emotions were frayed and her deep sorrow flashed quickly to rage. Suddenly she pulled back hard on the reins, and wheeled her horse around to face whoever had come.

At once, in a rush of wind and leaves, three young Salish men brought their charging horses to a halt next to her. She peered through the dim light to see their faces, but could not.

"I heard what you would do for Eli."

At once she recognized the voice of Eli's friend, Tomey Humma.

"Do not take what they say. There are some of us who want to help. Our numbers are not many, we have only twenty or thirty of us here, but we will do what we can to help your brother."

Heidi closed her eyes at the flood of emotion that once again threatened to overtake her sense. "I cannot... I will not risk another life, Tomey."

"Our brothers and sisters have heard about what has happened here," he continued on, ignoring her plea.

Heidi met his eyes now, and still, despite everything, she felt a spark of hope.

"...And they say that our voices would carry much further if there were more of us."

Heidi drew a shuddering breath again, trying her best to ride out the emotion that threatened to sink her.

"They are coming to help us."

"Tomey, who is coming? You must tell me."

"They are all coming. The Salish brothers and sisters: the Klahoose and Homalco from the north, and the Shishalh from the south..."

Heidi closed her eyes nodding slowly, partly in thanks, partly in prayer.

"All of our brothers and sisters are coming, Heidi."

Heidi sobbed now and unleashed the flood she could hold not a moment longer.

She stood nodding, and she wept for her brother, and her father. She wept for her own people... And her entire race.

Ω

JUDGMENT DAY

---

*Cessante ratione legis
cessat ipsa iex*

*When the reason
for law ceases, the law itself
ceases*

- -

Eli Tomas opened his eyes and stared directly into the lit flame of a gas lamp.

"Get up Tomas."

Eli lay motionless. He could sense at least two men in the room, and see the silhouette of a third outside the cell.

"I said get up Goddamit," a heavy boot came down hard into his side. With teeth clenched he sat up on the wooden bench. The light from the lamp was in his eyes making it hard to see what the men where up to, or where in the cell they had positioned themselves.

"Whoa now," he heard the men shuffle. "Don't go doin' anything foolish. You're liable to get yourself killed here and now. Come to think of it, probably better that-a-way. That way Judge Noble needn't bother wasting his time."

Eli's eyes adjusted to the room. He caught the glint of a rifle barrel near his face, but that was pointed at his heart.

"Stand up now and put your shirt on."

"Where are you taking me?"

"You'll see soon enough," One of the men snapped.

"Truth be knowed, you'll be rat food sooner 'n later," said another.

In the spirit in which the former information was given, he was further encouraged with a solid boot to the side of his knee.

Eli slipped from the bench, and was on his knees on the floor, fighting to stay conscious. The man standing just inside the cell door threw a shirt at him. Slowly, Eli picked up the shirt and pulled it on over his head. He tried to let instinct take over, sensing where each man stood. Their movements told him they expected a fight; that they would indeed kill him if he tried anything. He was sure to move deliberately, and slowly, as if he were hunting, so as not to startle his prey.

"Put your hands behind your back," the man with the gun said. Another came forward with a length of rope and cinched his wrists tight.

"I demand to know where I'm being taken?"

"He speaks good for a wild man don't he?" The man behind him jammed his boot into the back of the same knee that had just suffered an insult. Eli tried to catch himself, but with his hands tied behind his back he lost his footing and fell to his knees again. Another boot to his lower back sent him face-first to the cold dirt floor. He winced in pain. But mixed with the pain, there was a certainty that, in fact, it was true what some of the elders had warned: the whites cannot be trusted. They are here to take, with an appetite that is never satisfied.

His mind seethed with anger. The worst enemy, and one capable of doing the most damage, is the enemy one does not know is there.

A pair of police-issue black leather boots appeared in front of his face. His temper threatened to blow as he got a close look at the medium of his pain.

In an instant he was back on his feet. The men scrambled backward. A rifle cocked behind him.

"Another move and your're one dead Indian."

He set his jaw against the pain in his chest and in his knees. But that pain was little in comparison to the breaking he felt in his heart, and sinking in his soul. It was not his own life he feared for; it was the fear of what would come after – for his family, and all that families that would come.

For now all he could do was resolve to show his enemy none of his pain.

The rope tied to his wrists was strung down between his legs. One of the men lunged for the rope and tugged him violently toward the cell door. He was pushed from behind, out into the narrow aisle that ran between the cells and the length of the prison basement. He was led up the stairs and out into the brightly lit office, where he stood squinted at the rush of bright light for a moment, while the main doors were unlocked.

Outside the House of Law, the cold air felt good, and he breathed deeply through his nostrils. He was escorted into a closed wagon waiting at the bottom of the jail-house steps. He sat on the badly worn wood bench that lined the wall. The doors thudded shut and the iron bolts clacked loudly as the gate slammed home.

Moments later the wagon was in motion, the packed road riding rough under the iron wheels.

Eli could hear muffled voices of the men up front. They were talking and laughing, as though his fate did not matter; as though his life, and what happened to him, was meaningless to them.

As it was.

They rode on for some time - how long it was impossible to tell. Then the men grew quiet and, soon after, the wagon lurched to a stop. The doors were unlatched and flung wide.

There were different men here. The three from the jail in Vananda were now acting differently than they had before. They were quiet, and stood with their shoulders back, and their chins up: a deep respect for something, or someone, it seemed. Eli wondered what it was that would command such respect.

There was a man on either side of the doors. Each took hold firmly under an elbow and he was led outside, where he stood before a large white building with many windows.

His arms were untied and he was again compelled to move forward, this time with much less force than he had come to expect.

Though he had been at a court case before, when his uncle had been accused of killing another man, he had managed his entire life to avoid the cell, and the law. He was the son of Chief Israel Tomas, and

266

he knew it was important to carry his name with honour.

Two wide doors opened into a vast foyer, where portraits of bearded white men lined the walls on either side of a great hall. At the far end of the hall two officers stood, straight legged, and in majestic uniform, their hands folded neatly in front of them. They stood at either side of another set of large double doors. He was led through them, and into yet another vast room, with high ceilings, and many solid wood benches arranged in rows, with a narrow path leading between them. It was much like the church in Vananda. And here were two more uniformed officers standing at the front of the room, on either side of a large pedestal. In one of them he recognized the man who shot and killed his two friends.

Red Sutherland stood at the front of the courtroom, leaning against the pedestal, talking casually with the man sitting there, and with much less formality and concern than the others.

Eli was brought to stand before the judge. Red Sutherland walked to a table situated nearby and sat down.

One of the officers took a few steps into the centre of the room: "The Honourable Everett Noble presiding," he said, and stepped smartly away from the esteemed man.

Judge Noble's eyes were cold, but Eli was no less proud, and did not look away. He watched the judges gaze fall upon his knees, which, until now, he had not realized were bleeding. Blood had stained through his pants, and ran down onto his feet. "Someone get the prisoner a rag, so that he can tend to his injuries."

The courtroom was silent while one of the attending officers disappeared through a side door. He returned moments later carrying a rag.

Eli did not want to wipe his knees. His pain was real. His blood was real. The blood was part of the story, part of the reality in this moment. To wipe it away would be to pretend it did not happen.

The officer held the rag out to Eli but Eli refused to take it. Instead he continued to meet the judges icy stare.

The blood was truth, and the truth should speak for itself.

The outer doors swung open and in walked a man in a suit and clean leather boots. He let the doors slam shut behind him. "Apologies for my tardiness your honour. My mule ate my time piece." he said dropping his carrying case loudly onto the table beside Eli.

Judge Noble chuckled.

The man sat in one of the chairs and threw his feet up on the table. He stared at Eli for a bit. "This my charge?"

"This is Eli Tomas, the man whom you will represent," the judge explained, smiling tersely. "And if it pleases you to respect my courtroom, remove your filthy boots from my table at once, or I'll have you standing up here beside Mr. Tomas pleading for mercy yourself, instead of pleading his case for him."

The man slid his boots from the side of the table and let them fall heavily to the ground.

Something was wrong. This was not how he'd remembered his uncle's trial. There were rules. And there were more men in long robes, and suits; and as many of his family members as could fit into the courtroom. Still others waited outside. Where was his family? Where was John West, the Government Indian Agent? John West was not here!

Eli's heart thumped in his chest. None of these men cared for blood, nor truth. And the man that had killed his friends sat quietly a short distance away glaring at him, as though it didn't matter if he were alive or dead.

Eli Tomas was summarily found to be guilty of the charges laid against him, a conclusion which sat comfortably with his keepers.

However, it was not this that shook him.

"Load the prisoner for transport to the Gaol, in Victoria, where he will be held until the sentence can be carried out," the judge slammed his gavel heavily onto the heavy oak bench that splayed before him.

Though his face did not betray him, Eli was, for the first time since being arrested, scared for his life...

Ω

Book II Coming Soon

Author Biography

Dean Unger was born in Powell River, BC, and grew up with the vast wilderness surrounding the town as the unmarked playground he and his friends were privileged to enjoy. During his 25-year career in the media and publishing arts, Dean was editor for numerous successful publications, including BC Musician; Gonzo Music, Film and Culture; Snowbirds RV Traveler, Bodysport, Guide to Dining Out in the Okanagan, among others.

While living in Kelowna, he was media writing and professional development instructor at Centre for Arts and Technology, and, in addition to the magazines, wrote for several newspapers both there, and in Vancouver. He's had short stories published in The Malahat Review, and Wild Life Magazine.

Through his career, he has interviewed and written, on and with, many high profile personalities and musicians, crafted public relations campaigns for numerous companies and non-profit organizations, and served on the board of directors for Central Okanagan Brain Injury Society, Lifestyle Equity Society, BC Special Olympics, and Kelowna Friends of the Library.

As an avid reader in many genres, and despite bleak thinking to the contrary, Dean is of the firm notion there is immense potential for a long, well-thought, responsible and vital livelihood in both conventional and emerging publishing mediums.

Ω